NEVER BEEN TO MARS

LARRY GENT

Shannon
Thanks for not having a hidden 'Q' in your name :)
Welcome to Ben's world

ALSO BY LARRY GENT

The Benedict Forecasts
Be All That You Envy (2018)
Never Been To Mars
To Money And A TV
Bedroom Walls That Save Us (2018)

The TOP SECRET Mac Files
She Who Trains Under Death

Avalon Lost
Lightyears To Go Before I Sleep

Vörissa's Catalyst Online
Patch 1.01:   New Game+
Patch 1.02:   Escort Mission
Patch 1.03:   Corpse Run
Patch 1.04:   In Another Castle
Patch 1.05:   Silent Protagonist

LARRY GENT

Published in Canada by Midnight Reading Publishing, Ottawa

Gent, Larry, 1983-, Author.
        Never Been to Mars / Larry Gent
ISBN: 978-0-9959515-7-0
Ebook ISBN: 978-0-9959515-8-7
Copyright © 2018 Larry Gent

This is a work of fiction. All characters and situations are either the product of the author's imagination or are used fictitiously. Any resemblence to actual persons, living or dead, events, locals or businesses is coincidental. No part of this book may be reproduce or transmitted in any form or by any means, electronic or mechanical, including photocopying and recording, or by any information storage or retrievial system without writen permission from the author, except for brief passages quoted in a review.

Cover Design: Valérie Gent

Midnight Reading Publishing
511 Brittany Drive
Ottawa, Ontario
K1K 0S1

This book is dedicated to the man who once said:

"If I were to drive past a crane with my three children, my daughter would be drawing it, my youngest son would be figuring out how it works and my oldest son would be imagining himself running up it to save a damsel in distress."

Years later and my sister is a photographer, my brother is a carpenter and I am an author.

This book is dedicated to my Day. We love and miss you.

The Benedict Playlist

Music has always been a big part of my life. I use it for everything. I use music to sleep, I use music to play video games, I use it to read, to exercise (as if), play Magic and above all else I use music to write.

When I want to write a certain character I need to get into his mindset, I need to feel what he's feeling. I do that by music. A happy song has the power to energise me, a sad one to turn my mood foul and a raunchy song will.....well you see where I am going with this.

Sex. I was talking about sex.

So below is what I am calling The Benedict Playlist (because I can't call this I Stole This from Carrie Vaughn PS I love your work Carrie). These are the songs that I listened to over and over in the writing process of Never Been to Mars. They are the songs that, while not always being lyrically appropriate, had verses in them that related to what Ben is doing now.

I don't own any of these songs, sadly paying $0.99 on iTunes doesn't count as owning them; they belong to the talented people who wrote them. So to them I give as many thanks as I would anybody else who helped me out. For without your lyrical skills I wouldn't be where I am today.

Here to the Cowboy and his music.

Songs

- Is Anybody Home? – Our Lady Peace
- Here's to Us – Halestorm
- Where My Heart Will Take Me – Russell Watson
- Blind Mary – Gnarls Barkley
- Frank's 2000" TV – Weird Al Yankovic
- Hammerhead – The Offspring
- The World can Use a Cowboy - Adam Gregory
- You Can't Always Get What You Want – The Rolling Stones

Chapter 01
It's About Time I Get You All Sweaty

It all started with a ring. From 1892 until today, major events all across the world started in an identical fashion: a ring. The tones have changed, from the simple chime of a bell to the synthesized monstrosities that pass for music, but thousands of lives across the globe have changed with the sound of a ringing phone. Six months ago my phone never rang; the only sounds it made were from my music or those silly little games I play involving irate aves, but recently it seemed like the thing just wouldn't shut up. I couldn't complain about it too much, aside from the fact nobody listens, because these calls meant work and work meant money.

That morning my phone rang again, blaring the theme from Rocky, and pulled me from my sleep. The voice on the other end was a man begging for my help, he needed me today and he was willing to pay good money for it. In truth they were never asking for me directly, they were asking for the services of SRG Security, but SRG was operated solely by me. I'd never known exactly where the company came from but I had a guess. One day I got a large brown envelope couriered to me, with no return address and no sender. The envelope was like Christmas, filled with little toys and gifts for a good little boy, so when I ripped it open tons of paperwork came pouring out. Contained within my mysterious package were all the paperwork, documents and licenses needed for a private security company; in less time than it took for me to finish a can of Coke I had become a PI; a gumshoe; a detective and I even had a list of contacts. Two days later the phone started ringing. Somehow people knew SRG existed and they wanted to hire me, best of all they were high-end clients like big businesses and Fortune 500 corporations. When my phone started ringing it never seemed to stop.

God I hated it.

Six months ago all I wanted to do was sit in front of my flatscreen TV and watch my stories. I didn't want a job and I didn't want to go solving people's problems. I tried to disregard the calls at first. I hit ignore until there was a finger-sized dent in my screen, but they kept coming. Turned out the only reprieve I got was from answering the damn thing and coming to the rescue.

I am Benedict Thompson and this is my life, the life of a superhero.

I'm not a great superhero. I'm not super strong, I can't fly or climb walls – hell I can barely walk without the assistance of a cane, so I'm not likely to be fighting crime anytime soon but what I can do is read items.

The technical term is psychometry. According to Wikipedia it's the ability to relate details about the past or future condition of an object or location, usually by being in close contact with it. Isn't Wikipedia great? In the normal tongue of everyday people if I touch an object I see a moment from its past. It doesn't work on anything that lives or breathes and it is always a moment from the past, never the future. Well, almost never.

After an early morning phone call, a quick shit, shower and shave, and a ride in a waiting car and I found myself standing in the offices of Starmoore Entertainment. I was greeted by Jacob Wilis, the man from the phone, and was quickly given a non-disclosure agreement to sign. I handed him back the contract and followed him into his office. He was like every middle management stooge you'd expect; a suit and tie, an effective short hair-cut, and sweat pouring from every hole that would allow it and a few that wouldn't. Deducing that he was nervous and worried seemed like a waste of my PI license.

"Are you sure you're the best SRG has to offer?" he stammered, glancing back at me as we walked. "I know my lawyer, Iris Scott, told me to call you but you sure don't look like corporate security."

I couldn't fault him for his doubts. I didn't really look like I belonged here. Most investigators were tall men who wore slick suits, had stern faces, and were the statuesque examples of toughness. I, on the other hand, was wearing jeans, a pair of leather gloves, a collared shirt, a brown leather jacket, and a cowboy hat. I also hobbled along using a cane to walk. My cane was a wooden walking stick with derby handle made from a blend of silver plate and faux ivory. The handle had a mustang horse carved in basso-rilievo.

"I'm the best agent SRG has, Mr. Willis," I assured him. I was the *only* agent SRG had. "So how about you just tell me what you need me for and we'll go from there."

Jacob gave me another hesitant look before ushering me into his office. I peeled off my right glove and gently dragged my fingers across the cold metallic door. A familiar shiver shot up my back and my eyes began to twitch. The office and all the people in it instantly froze as if somebody holding the ultimate universal DVD remote decided to hit pause. Then, following the cosmic press of rewind, everybody started to move backwards. They walked backwards, talked backwards, and even laughed backwards, slowly at first but quickly gaining speed until their movements were nothing but an indecipherable blur. They eventually slowed down and returned to normal reverse speed then froze once again, but only for a second, before they moved forward at regular speed.

Jacob Willis stood behind his desk as his boss, Alex Ludlum, yelled at him. "It came from your computer, Willis. They're going to fire you and then they'll sue your ass."

"Jesus, Alex! I didn't do it. I'd never do this," Jacob pleaded. "Let me prove it."

Alex ran his hand through his hair and shook his head. "I can stall the board for a day, tops. That's all I can give you," Alex said as he walked out the door. "After that you're screwed."

In a blink the vision faded and I was back in present time with not a second having passed. My visions always work the same way. I get shoved into a scene and watch it play out before me like an omnipotent voyeur. Sometimes I get details or information tidbits but normally it's like changing the channel to a movie at the halfway point. I'm stuck there studying the people and the places trying to figure out what the hell I'm watching. This time the universe decided to rewind time to show me what I missed.

Be kind, rewind.

Is that phrase even relevant anymore?

I pulled my hand from the door, slipped it back into my glove and sat down on the other side of his desk. Jacob looked at his desk but is too nervous and scared to sit down. He grabbed a small folder and handed it to me. I opened it up and started to read it over as he explained.

"Starmoore Entertainment is a film company." He was nervous and beginning with the obvious. SE films have made some of the most beloved animated children's film and family live-action films of all time. I should've interrupted him but instead I let him rant. He seemed like one of those people who calmed down by talking. "They also own Dynamic Action Comics. Recently they have been making a great deal of money off of the film adaptations of DA Comics."

I nodded. Superhero movies weren't bad, I'd seen my fair share, but I much preferred a solid action film to a cape flick any day. Spider-Man was cool but he was no Rambo.

"This year at San-Diego Comic-Con we were going to announce our next big film franchise, *Quantum Crusaders*." I recognized the name. My nephew Robby loved comics and he loved that title. It was about five random space superheroes who came together after a space-catastrophe to fight space-villains; in space. Did I mention it was a sci-fi?

"This was going to be our show stopper, our big announcement. But when I came into work today I found out that somebody had leaked it to a major comic website. It's everywhere now."

"The blame is falling square on your lap," I finished. "Doesn't SE have internal security that could investigate this for you?"

Jacob shook his head. "They tracked the leak to me, to my computer. In their eyes they did their job, they found who was guilty: me. But I didn't do this, Mr. Thompson. I love this company, I love this franchise. I am the comic book geek that got his dream job. I get to turn the books I loved as a kid, and still love today, into awesome movies. I wouldn't risk that for the world."

Crap. I believed him.

My SRG calls normally dealt with internal security. Something had gone missing and I needed to find it. Sometimes the case involved theft, somebody took something now find out who. When I've dealt with theft I'd normally been hired by the innocent victim but occasionally I get hired by the bad-guy. The thief would hire me to find out who stole the object in question to see if he got away with it. I hated working those cases. But as I looked at Jacob, and watched him plead, I can tell he's innocent. I can tell he's truly worried about not only his job but this project as well. Jacob was, in every definition of the word, a true believer.

If comics were a terrorist cell then Jacob had been radicalized years ago.

"Okay, I'll see what I can do." I flipped through the file and started to read over the briefings. "It says here the leak was the movie's announcement and the list of possible lead actors and that it was sent from your computer here."

"Yeah but I wasn't here and the worst part is there are no cameras in the offices."

"Okay. I'll need access to your computer, phone, and office." I had to stop the poor man; he was starting to repeat himself. "And some time to work. Do you want to get a drink or anything?"

He nodded meekly as he walked out. I pulled off my gloves and dropped them onto the desk. I looked at the bureau with envy, it was far nicer then the kitchen table I used. The executive desk had steel legs and had a glass top. I dropped my fingers onto the desk and watched as the world around me dissolved with a shiver and a twitch. My vision kept me in the office only this time there was a sexy brunette with her skirt hiked up past her waist and her blouse tossed across the room. She bent over the glass desk as Jacob, his pants by his ankles, thrust into her from behind.

"Harder," she screamed euphorically. "You're so much bigger then my husband."

Reality snapped back as I jerked my hand away. I didn't need to see that, I didn't regret it, that woman was a looker, but now I had to face Willis. My visions were closely tied to emotions. The stronger someone felt when they interacted with an object, the more pungent the memory was. Sometimes it led to me seeing the most hateful and horrifying acts imaginable and other times I got to see a live sex show.

Sex; in this universe there are few things more emotional then sex. Be it love making with your soul mate, knocking boots with a hotty or tapping that ass while your spouse it at work, sex is just dripping with emotion. Love, guilt, lust, hate, envy, regret, ecstasy and pure loathing; I'd seen them all involving sex. You'd be amazed how often I see sex. Sometimes it's beautiful and romantic. Other times it's not.

I plopped down it to Willis's chair, carefully put my cowboy hat down on the desk, and reached into my jacket for my phone. Thumbing down the iphone screen I pulled up my SRG contacts. When I got my mysterious package, the one that effectively made me a superhero detective, it came with a list of SRG subcontractors. They were people who worked independently but came to my aid whenever I called. I tapped the name Hotwire and waited. I could operate a computer on par with most people, with an extra trick or two added in for good measure, but Hotwire wasn't most people. In order to dig deep into a corporate leak and digital frame job you needed a high level of skill with a computer, a decent hardware setup and a very loose set of morals about hacking into personal information. Luckily for me Hotwire completed the triangle of necessary skills.

The phone clicked and a young voice came across the line. "This is Jimmy."

"Hey, it's Ben."

"Hey, Cowboy, you have another job for me?" Hotwire, or as the real world knew him Jimmy Wilcox, was the most helpful of all the contacts I had. He always answered, anytime of the day, and was constantly willing to go the extra mile to help me.

"Yep, we're going to save a man's career." I quickly explained the situation and our objective. Jimmy listened eagerly, injecting his tidbits of information as I spoke, before eagerly chuckling. "What are our options?"

"I just brought up list of their employees," Jimmy explained. "I'm going to go start digging through their finances. If you get a name or even narrow it down to a possible few, let me know. It'll speed up my job."

I hung up and frowned. I was going to have to dig deep with my powers. When my powers first manifested themselves I was in constant pain. Every vision, even the smallest ones, resulted in me curled up in a corner crying like a child. The more I used my powers the less they hurt. I had even learned how to navigate the visions, albeit to a very minor effect. Yet despite my experience, if I over used my powers I still suffered the ill effects. It's not a *crying-in-a-corner* headache but more *honey-I'm-not-in-the-mood headache*.

Okay I have to back up a second. When I said I was crying in a corner. I wasn't really crying. I mean I was but I was crying man tears. Tears made of meat that hurt when they come out and make you cry more. It's a vicious cycle.

If I was going to figure out who was setting Jacob up then I would have to start by touching each major item in the office and comparing my visions. I ran my bare hands across the chair's armrest. With a shiver climbing up my back and a twitch in my eyes I watched as the history of this chair unfolded before me. I could see images of the assembly line and the overseas manufacturers who assembled it. I watched as image after image of every person in the chair appeared before me, like a police lineup of the usual suspects and I had to choose one.

The images of five people resonated stronger than the rest. Jacob Willis, for the obvious I'm-going-to-loose-my-job reasons, a redhead secretary named Michelle Almeida, a blonde VP names Kim Raines, a balding man named Graeme Heller and a fellow producer named Tony Dessler. I pictured them lined up in a police line with Keyser Söze rounding out the end.

I moved to the phone next, a black landline with a thousand and one buttons, and got a similar vision with comparable mirages of the phone's past users. Once again specific faces resonated stronger than others, only this time it was only Jacob Willis, Kim Raines, and Tony Dessler.

With nothing important left to touch I reached for the computer. I saved the more complicated device for last because it was also the most difficult. When you, and by you I mean me, deal with multifaceted objects like a computer you have to deal with literally thousands of components, each wanting to be heard and none of them having the decency to wait in line. When the visions assault me they all come at once. It's my job to weave through them, to act like the nurse who keeps order in the emergency room. I deal with certain memories and tell others, in a saucy Latino-nurse accent, to sit down and wait their turn.

The computer tower, stored beneath the glass on the floor, screamed out at my touch as thousands of visions bombarded my mind. I saw everything. From the assembly line to tech support updating the software I saw it all. I tried to focus; pushing visions aside as I look for the most recent strands. I saw Willis at his computer, tirelessly working, I saw Kim Raines uploading files from a thumb stick, and I saw Tony

Dessler sitting alongside Jacob, both debating over the casting decisions. But try as I did, focusing with all my strength, I couldn't find any memories from last night.

I withdrew my hand and looked around the room. I was running out of significant things to touch. Without anything to touch I would be left with no leads and that would make me feel sad. I need to touch random things to feel good.

Oh god, that sounded different in my head.

I grabbed his phone and quickly redialed Hotwire. He picked up after only one ring. "You get a name?"

"I have two. Tony Dessler, and Kim Raines." I looked up at the door and made sure Jacob wasn't on his way back in. "Also give Jacob Willis a check, just in case I'm getting played."

"Will do. In the meantime you should start checking his computer for outgoing data,"

I pulled a small USB drive from my pocket and plugged it into the tower. My fingers rapidly tapped the keyboard as I started to explore the computer. Using the skills I learned in the military, combined with the programs installed on the USB drive given to me by Hotwire, I started to investigate the computer. I traced all outgoing data, from email programs, internet browsers, and other online programs, backtracked them to their source and dated them. Yet as the minute hand ticked away and the hours passed, I still hadn't found a workable lead. Aside from a file sharing torrent he had running through the night for a couple of naughty movies in the *Sexy Secretaries* series, I found nothing. Seeing how he was an office guy, I understood the appeal but it didn't help the investigation. However this leak happened, it didn't come from this computer.

I leaned back in the chair and ran my hands through my scraggly blonde hair. I glanced over at Jacob. He looked back at me, worried and scared. I needed to bounce ideas off of someone and while he wasn't my first choice he was the closest person. If I was going to continue this SRG gig I was going to need a Dr. Watson. Truth be told I was going to need a Holmes, I was probably closer to Watson, but until one could be found I was going to have to do my best impression.

"Okay, nothing came from this computer," I explained slowly, partially to for him but mainly so I had time to think. "So this means he sent it from a phone." No. That didn't make sense. "But a smartphone wouldn't register as coming from this office. It couldn't even be tracked by SE's system, unless the phone was on a wireless network. There is a wireless in the office building right?"

Jacob shook his head. "There is one but the wireless wouldn't read it as my office. It would read it as a moving signal."

"What is it that makes a signal register that it's from your office?" As the words came through my lips the answer shot through my brain. I dropped to the floor and climbed under the desk. A computer, especially a laptop, could be brought anywhere in the world. It could move from office to office with ease. The only thing that tied it down was the Cat 5 cable. The Cat 5 is that wire, normally blue, that plugs into the Ethernet card in the back of your computer and hooks it up to the network. It works like a wireless but it's normally faster and with less interruptions.

I grabbed the modular connector, the plastic plug thingy, and pulled it out. My body reacted and I felt the familiar shiver climbing up my back combined with a twitch in my eye. I watched as Tony Dessler pulled the cable free of the tower and plugged it into his laptop. He mumbled to himself as he frantically typed on the portable computer, spouting words like *revenge* and *cheating bitch*.

In a blink the vision was over. I had my suspect, I just needed a motive. I grabbed the phone and dial Hotwire. He answered in one ring. "Yeah?"

"Tony Dessler. He's our guy." Jacob climbed from the couch and cried out in protest. To him it wasn't possible. "Can you send me his file?"

Hotwire agreed and we both hung up. Second later the phone beeped with a file containing everything I needed and a small text message.

Hotwire: Searching T.D. bank info. Give me 5.

"You're out of your mind," Jacob defended. "Tony and I have been friends for years. Why the hell would he set me up like that?"

With a few flips of my thumb I had my answer. Tony was married to an Erin Dessler, nee Hamm. She had been working for a small independent film company five years ago when Starmoore Entertainment bought out the company and integrated it into their own. I shook my head as I stared at her picture.

"He's mad because he found out you were sleeping with his wife." She was the woman from my vision, the one Jacob had bent over his desk; a desk I suddenly hoped he'd washed since then. The face, which I'll admit of all the parts of her body I admired in the vision got the least amount of attention, was unmistakable. "You screwed her and now he's screwing you."

I wasn't proud of that last remark. I'm not the rude crass detective guy who hated the world and drank too much. I'm the nice guy. I'm the Wal-Mart greeter of detectives. On second thought scratch that. I don't know where I fit. All I know is that I'm less Christopher Walken and a little more Anthony Michael Hall with a pinch of cowboy.

Psychometry is not always the blessing that it seems, in fact it rarely is. Actually I question anyone who claims it's a gift at all. I spend my day learning the past about objects I could care less about or truths about people that I don't want to know. On my way back home from SE offices, leaving a relieved Jacob Willis with the proof needed to clear his name, all it took was a touch of the car door for me to see the fight the driver had with his wife the night before. I stopped for coffee and took a sip and I saw all the financial woes the barista is going through. If my visions were more like they were back in the office, witnessing a buxom brunette in the throes of passion, I'd enjoy my powers but more times than not they were closer to *The More You Know* section of Yahoo's front page.

Did you know that Janie and Phil Jordan's marriage is on the rocks?

Did you know that the Taxi-cab driver had a meatball sub for dinner?

Did you know that while Peter Engle was polishing the brass door handle he was cursing out his boss?

According to my nephew Robby I share this power with Marvel's Adrienne Frost, DC's Jack Hawksmoor and some cartoon guy called Tuxedo Mask. I take the kid's word on it. The only thing I know about comic books is that recently they've allowed Hollywood to basically print their own money. Robby is also the one who told me my cowboy hat was actually a Stetson and that Stetsons are cool.

I'm single, chances are I'll be so for awhile, so when it comes to the kid department I'm happily lacking. So when it came to the *spoiling-a-kid* aspect of my life I turned to my nephew Robby. The kid's eleven years old and was basically the walking encyclopedia for all things geeky. If there's a superhero film he'd seen it, if there's a monster in Lord of the Rings he could name it and if there's a race in a Star Wars film he could write you an essay on their history and culture – except he hates school work. The kid's awesome. He looks up to me. I'm the cool uncle.

Robby belongs to my older sister Annie. When she was twenty years old she met a man, fell in love and got pregnant. Six months later the man panicked, packed his stuff and ghosted like Swayze. We haven't seen him since and to be honest we're all better off. At twenty-one years of age Annie gave birth and named me the godfather. Ever since then I've done my best to be part of this child's life. He grew up with an army uncle and, after I introduced Annie to an army buddy of mine, an army dad so the kid was used to the drill. His dad would go away for months at a time but he would always come back. Then I would go away and I would always come back. But when an IED detonated my Humvee and pumped a fist full of shrapnel into my leg he took it the hardest. Months later Annie told me Robby thought I was never coming back, that I was gone for good. But I came back, a little more reliant on my mustang-cane then when I left, a little more broken in the mind then before, but back in one piece because I promised I would.

The day I first saw my nephew, leaning over his crib staring down at his newborn body, I made him a promise that no matter what happened I would be there for him and his mother. It's the type of promise that every family member makes as they stare down at a newborn child. It's the type of promise that comes to your lips easily and is rarely tested. But when all hell broke loose and I lay on the ground bleeding, under fire and waiting for back-up I found strength in that promise. It kept me going when all else seemed hopeless.

So that's me and my lifelong promise. It sounds fanatical and depressing and just a little theatrical but the truth is it's not that hard of a promise to keep. He's eleven; he doesn't really get himself in that much trouble. The most I do is slip him that new video game his mom would never buy him and come to the rescue with a cheat code or two.

So there I was, back home, changed and just about to plop down into my favourite chair when my doorbell rang. Now I'm psychic, this is a fact, but I didn't need to dig deep into my mystical bags of tricks to know who ringing my doorbell. Climbing from my chair I hobbled over to the door to see the stunning beauty that was Elaine Moeller, my physiotherapist. She's a brunette with curly hair that hung by her shoulders, a round face and an adorably infectious smile that seemed to spread like a disease.

"Hey, Cowboy," she laughed. "I think it's about time I get you all sweaty." Why do those words never mean what I want them to?

The problem with an injury like mine is that I'm forced to use a cane, albeit a kick-ass mustang-cane. I'm not going to bore you with medical mumbo-jumbo, mainly because I don't understand the half of it, but with a cane my leg doesn't get the proper amount of exercise it should. So unless I do my physio my leg would shrivel up like Mr. Burns. I could have gotten a stereotypical German woman who yelled at me and ripped my limbs off and beat me with them but instead I'm laying on my back, with Elaine pressed up against me pushing my leg high up into the air, thinking about how much I'd lucked out.

"So what's new and exciting in the world of Ben Thompson, PI?" she said with a laugh. "Have you found your cleverly-planned sidekick yet?"

"I was thinking like an alcoholic racecar driver or a doctor that can't use his hands for surgery anymore. You know something low-key." Talking to Elaine is like talking to that female friend from high school. She's cute, easy to talk to and before you realize it you have a massive crush on her but she's dating that guy who is like totally wrong for her. "Actually I just got back from a case earlier this morning."

"Oh really? Was it murder and mayhem or did you just uncover a stolen car ring run by school teachers?"

"You do know there are other mystery shows then those on the Disney channel right? I mean HBO and Showcase have a couple gritty shows. Even AMC is pretty decent." It often surprises me how easy it is to talk to her. I hate to sound like a love sick child but she gets me.

"Oh sure, if you want to get gritty or dark, but I like the wholesome mysteries, where no one get hurt and the criminal gives up without a fight," she explained. Her voice changed as she slipped into a bad imitation of a TV villain. "Well done, Columbo. How did you figure it out?"

NEVER BEEN TO MARS

"There was the monkey's paw-print on your amulet," I played along, trying my hand at an admittedly bad Peter Falk impression. "Oh... one more thing."

Laughter; it comes so easily around her. She is exciting, she is friendly, and she is so far out of my league it's not funny. "Actually my case involved the show business." I chose my words carefully. The last thing I needed was a lawsuit for breaking an NDA. "Somebody was framed for tanking a movie and I had to swoop in and rescue him."

"Well aren't you Captain Heroic?" Elaine lowered my leg and, much to my regret, peeled her body off of mine. "You are getting better, Ben. You keep this up and one of these days you may not even need the cane."

"You mean I'll be a real boy again?" The uplifting music of *Rocky* pulls me from my flirtatious endeavour and forced me to hobble to my phone. A quick look and I see Robby's smiling mug light up on my screen, his toothy smile with the appropriate gaps for a ten year old boy. I give the screen a tap and quickly answer.

" Hello?"

"Ben, it is Annie." She was crying on the other end. Annie doesn't cry. "Robby's missing."

Chapter 02
I Swear My Brain Has No Sense of Continuity

A quick shower and a generously offered ride from Elaine and I was standing at the doorway of my sister's house. My best-friend-brother-in-law, Staff Sergeant David Belledin, met me at the door with a concerned look and a hearty hug. He looked like soldier's solider; six foot one, two hundred and ten pounds, dark hair maintained in a crew cut and a look of strength about him. I met Dave years ago when we were both in the infantry. We were stationed together stateside until I got posted to a different division. It didn't take long before I introduced him to Annie. The two had hit it off and before long he had married into the family. He was perfect for her. Who wouldn't want their best friend as part of the family?

"Dave." One word is all it took. He was scared and he was hurting. He ushered Elaine and I in, and I see the drama unfold.

My sister is on the couch, scared and crying. She saw me and rushed over, embracing me in a powerful hug. Annie and I look alike, dark black hair, strong piercing eyes, and sturdy shoulders. The only differences, aside from the obvious *she's-a-woman-and-I-am-not*, are the long curls that reside in her dark mop, the foot I've got on her, and the large belly that carries child number two.

"Benny," she sobbed. "Thanks for coming."
I gave her a squeeze and try to comfort her. Stress and worry

were the last things she needed. We Thompsons are tough people. We don't scare easily and we aren't big on talking it out. We're independent folk but when one of us needs aid, we converge.

"Excuse me." The sudden voice startled me. I looked over at the two suited FBI agents standing in the room, one male and one female. How the hell had I missed them? I'm a really sad private investigator sometimes. It's a good thing I have powers. The male suit approached. "You are the uncle right?"

I nodded.

"I have a couple questions." He looked down at his notepad. "Is your name really Benedict?"

I nodded.

Benedict Butler Thompson; I get this question a lot.

Amongst all of our similarities the Thompson clan also shares one other trait, a love of westerns. Our fondness of the genre was passed from my Grandfather to my Mom and down to me and my sister. My mom's love of the cowboy way was so big she named all her kids after famous cowboys. It's like those parents who are so obsessed with *Twilight* and *Final Fantasy* that they named their kids Bella or Cloud. The only difference is cowboys are by far much cooler then vampires or androgynous super soldiers.

I was named after the famous Ben Thompson. Mom always said he was a gambler and gentleman, a man who'd only fight to protect others and even though he walked with a cane he never let it keep him down. Sadly Mom didn't know how prophetic that name would become.

Annie Belledin, nee Thompson, was named after Annie Oakley, the legendary cowgirl who was a famous sharpshooter and exhibition shooter. The obsession didn't stop there. Annie ended up naming her firstborn son Robby, after the cowboy photographer Robert E. Cunningham.

"Have you seen the child today?" I shake my head. I hadn't seen Robby in two days. "When was the last time you saw Greg Hazeltine?"

That question threw me for a loop. Greg was Robby's biological parent. I hated to use the word father or dad when referring to him because he was neither. "I...um...I haven't seen him in like....two years."

Annie's head snaps over at me, a look of surprise taking hold on her face. "You've seen him? Why didn't you tell me?"

I just shook my head. "I saw him shortly after my return, after my accident. He approached me, asked about the accident, bought me a drink and asked about Robby." I explained. "It was like an hour tops."

"You didn't punch him out did you, Benny?" God, I hated that name. The short form of Benedict should never be Benny. But hey, try telling Annie that.

"I could barely walk let alone start a fight," I explained. "So no, his nose went unbroken." I looked at both the suit and Annie. I needed more answers, not creepy out-of-date questions.

"Why are you asking me about him?" The suit just shook ignored me and scribbled in his notes. I looked back at Annie. "What happened?"

"We got a call from his teacher," she sobbed. "He went out with the class for recess and he never came back. They called us, searched the area and called the cops. They don't know what happened."

"Is anybody out looking?" I asked as I escorted Annie to the couch.

"Yeah, family friends are driving around for us."

Annie looked at Elaine and sniffled. "Did you bring a date here?"

I smirked. Humour; whenever things got hard, humour was there. "No, she's my physiotherapist. She gave me a ride."

Annie snickered slightly at the word *ride*. "Is she the one you've been talking about?"

I gently elbowed her. "Hush." I tried to focus on the older-sister routine Annie was performing, but I was finding it hard to focus on anything but the woman in the suit. She held her phone to her ear and quietly talked into the receiver. This lady wasn't telling me everything. I hate not knowing everything. I hate being lied to. I walked over to Elaine.

"How are you holding up?" she whispered.

"I don't know," I stammered. "I'm here to be a supportive uncle and brother..." My voice trailed off. I kept looking at the suit.

"What is it?"

"They're FBI or something," I explained. "But neither of them is telling us anything."

"Is there anything I can do to help you find out?" I couldn't think of a single thing she could do to help me, but the truth was, I could help myself. I was, after all, a superhero. This brings up the elephant in the room.

Do I use my powers to learn more?

I began the mental debate between reason and curiosity. A sane mind would debate this with a list of pros and cons. I, on the other hand, am a Thompson, and my kind is far from sane. My debate takes place on a wooden dock deep on the edge of a coastal city. The white capped waves rise from the ocean only to crash back in, each current pushing a large wooden ship further inland. The ship, the S.S. Curiosity, is captained by a swaggering pirate. He steps off the ship with a clap and stumbles inland past the burning torches, a bottle of rum clutched tightly in his grasp. The pirate stops, looks around, and draws his cutlass as a dark clothed ninja leaps from the shadows, his sword slashing downwards. The ninja, a trusted member from the Reason Clan, is out for blood. The two steel blades clashed as I debated the facts.

I don't like being lied to. I never have.

The pirate struck fast, his swaggering step allowing him to move quicker, slash faster, and strike swifter.

The FBI was taking care of this. They were trained to deal with missing children; they were trained to find them.

Suddenly the ninja ducked, the cutlass missing its mark by a mile, and his ninja sword slashing across the pirate's torso.

Statistically a missing child case proved to be nothing, some kid walking away and forgetting to tell an adult where he was going.

The ninja slammed his foot into the pirate's knee and watched the leg buckle. He lined up his blade to the sailor's neck and readied his blade to strike.

But what if it wasn't a normal case? What if this was a kidnapping. They asked about Greg. I've watched a lot of TV, and I mean a lot, and kidnapping stories all say the same thing: That child kidnapping cases were normally done by parents and they normally only had forty-eight hours until the child became a body. I was on a clock.

The pirate swung his bottle upwards, catching the blade and shattering the bottle, sending booze flying everywhere. The pirate caught the ninja with a lucky uppercut and scrambled back to his feet, his blade making wide cuts as he forced the ninja back.

This was Robby. I'd go to hell and back for him; I made him that very promise many years ago.

The pirate yanks a burning torch from its stand and tosses it at the ninja. The flickering tongues make contact with the alcohol soaked clothes and sent them erupting in flames. With a smirk and a woman on his arm, the pirate swaggered off content in his victory.

Once again Curiosity reigns supreme. Reason doesn't have a very solid track record with me. Wait a moment, where did the woman come from? She wasn't there when he stepped off the ship. Damn it. I swear my brain has no sense of continuity. I really need to work on that or else the narrative becomes a mess.

I subtly pulled off my gloves and hobbled closer. Lady Suit eyed me as I approached. "Excuse me, agent," I began, my hand rising up to scratch the side of my head. "Can you give us any updates?"

The agent moved to speak, most likely to give me some government excuse, and I used that moment to reach for

NEVER BEEN TO MARS

her jacket. A single touch is all it would have taken for me to read the past but the agent didn't give it to me. She deliberately jerked back, leaving my hand to only touch air.

"Oh no," she asserted, shuffling back a couple steps. "I have a serious no touching rule when it comes to psychics."

Wait; did he just say the P word? What the *actual* hell?

"Don't look surprised," she said. "Your file has the magic P word written all over it. Personally I think it is all hoo-hah, just a bunch of crap made up by some young Fox wanna-be agent. But on the off chance you're too legit to quit, I have my own secrets I'd rather not get out."

I wanted to make some wiseass remark but all I ended up doing was stammering like a damned fool. "Why does the FBI have a file on me?"

"How about this, Houdini," the agent offered, ignoring my previous question. "You put that magical hand back in your glove, follow me into the kitchen and we talk like God intended us to, face to face with words and lies."

You ever notice how you always come up with the best response to a situation days later. You'll be walking down the street, or hobbling in my case, and suddenly you're like *Right, I should have said that!* This agent caught me so off guard that even two days later the best response I could come up with was *Screw You.*

Left with no other option I slid my hand back into my glove and followed her. "Okay then. Let's talk."

"I'm Senior Special Agent Puzo." Lady Suit looked tough. She wore a blue collar shirt, a black suit, had long blonde hair tied into a ponytail and had diamond studs in each of her ears. She didn't look like the beautiful actress, flawless in every way, who played FBI agents on TV. Instead she looked like a good ol' girl; smooth skin with a tear or two, a well worn hand, and a thin scar that ran the length of her neck. Lady Suit looked like the type of girl who could have a beer, toss a bale of hay and kick your ass all in the run of a day. "And you are the magical uncle."

"Magic... is kinda pushing it," I stammered. Why couldn't I get my act together around this woman?

"Normally I would make you an offer. I keep you in the loop and you stay out of our way. However your file says you're a licensed private investigator," Puzo read, as she placed both her phone and her notepad down on the kitchen table. "This means the rules change. You private dicks are just that; dicks. It's like the entire profession is made up of guys who have watched way too many movies."

She got me in one.

"So instead I tell you nothing and warn you that if you hinder our investigation in any way I let my partner there arrest you; deal?"

I'll be honest; it wasn't a very fair deal at all but her partner, Special Agent Ryman, looked like the silent thug type. I wanted to say something, puff out my chest and put a chip on my shoulder but Elaine came to intervene. She grabbed me by the shoulder and ushered me out, Puzo giving me a cocky victory look as she pocketed her notepad.

"Come on, Cowboy," Elaine suggested. "Let's step outside for a moment."

She's always the voice of reason. I let her guide me out. I'll admit it, I was worried, I was anxious and I was letting my emotions get the better of me. I wanted to help my family and find Robby but somehow I doubted getting into a fight with Agent Thug and getting my ass thrown in jail would help anyone.

I stopped at the door and look back at Agent Puzo. "How long have the FBI had a file on me?"

Puzo just smiled. "For about six months."

Chapter 03
His Real Gun Not His Double Entendre

Six months ago. Throughout the entire span of my existence, my life has gone through numerous changes. The first of which was birth. You'd be surprised to find out how influential to my career birth was. Other major events were my enlistment into the US Army, my acceptance into Ranger school and that fateful overseas accident. After I came home, my leg a broken facsimile of what it once was, I thought my life had reached its apex. Nothing ever really changes for a war vet who's given up. Six months ago that changed again. Six months ago I met the man with a thousand names. Six months ago I met Agent Joseph Price.

Back in the day, I used to do nothing but eat, go to physio, and watch my TV. I watched way too much TV. It was unhealthy. I didn't see my family much; I even cut down the amount of time I hung around with Robby. Seeing the kid like this, correction, having him seeing me like this was too much for me. Instead I locked myself indoors and did my best impression of a city-bound hermit.

Imagine my surprise when two men in black showed up at my door. They said my government needed my help, that I needed to go with them but they were unable to tell me what until they got there. The whole thing was freaky. I half expected Will Smith to start rapping in the background while Tommy Lee Jones wiped my memory with a flashy pen thing you order out of a sky mall catalogue.

Now I'll admit I'm a cheap date. You mention the words *civic duty* or *serve your country* and I'll basically jump into bed spread eagle while muttering something about how I'm not that type of girl. So when two secret service agents declare they needed my unique set of skills to examine an artefact I said yes. Like that head cheerleader at prom night, I say yes and let the well dressed man escort me to somewhere special so he can show me his secret.

Yes. I am aware of how dirty that sounds.

I am a highly trained soldier. I have complete trust in my government. I go where they tell me and do what they ask, most times with bells on. (Disclaimer: I actually did not wear bells. They mess with our stealth.) When I got injured the government looked after me and they still do. In all my years I have never distrusted the government, hell I'm Uncle Sam's favorite nephew but what happened that Sunday afternoon was basically page by page from the *Super Spy Playbook*, or as it's known by its other name *How to Freak Ben out by Appearing Like Every Bad Spy Movie He Has Ever Seen*. I think the first name was the more popular one.

They piled me into a black Lincoln Towncar, drove me miles out of town to a secret military base, the type that could be torn down in a matter of hours, and ignored me the entire ride there. When I arrived at the base that never-was I saw dozens of suits, MIB and army folk. Every government agency from the FBI to NSA and the Collation of Meter Maids: Union 501 was there taking notes. I learned I was one of nearly a dozen men and women scooped up to serve their country. Apparently each of us had special skills and I doubt it was doing the tango. They stuck us each into a separate room and made us wait.

I'm not a paranoid guy but I am impatient and I am curious to a fault. So when men in black and army soldier boys put me in a room and make me wait I start touching things. Turns out the government frowns on it when you use superpowers to spy on them. I don't get why they were mad though. I mean honestly, remember me, Benedict Thompson, the guy who can touch things and read their past? You invited me here and shoved me in a room. Of course I was going to touch stuff. I'll touch whatever I can get my hands on.

Yes. I am aware of how dirty that sounds.

There are many problems with my powers, how you see things you don't want, how it can leave you in awkward positions, and how if you touch the wrong thing during sex, like the headboard, you see the girl you just picked up getting friendly with half the men of an army platoon, damn army bunnies. But one of the worst elements of psychometry is that whatever cosmic force decides what I see it has no sense of storytelling structure. It gives me half images, like changing channel on the TV to a show already in progress, reveals awkward spoilers, like scrolling down too far in Wikipedia when you are looking up an actor, and forces me to put it all back together.

This brings me to the man with a thousand names.

When I first met him he was Special Agent Ryan Cook; a Secret Service agent in a black suit with a Jason Borne build and a conservative pair of glasses sitting on his nose. When I touched the car I learned that that was a lie. He wasn't Secret Service, he wasn't Ryan Cook and I highly doubted, despite his build, that he was Jason Borne. When I touched his gun, his real gun not his double entendre, I saw a vision of him kicking down an apartment door and riddling everybody inside, including one woman, with bullet holes. In that vision he looked a little more James Bond, carried a bigger gun, and was known as Mr. Wind.

This made me very suspicious of him.

Things got worse when the government agents revealed the artefact. It was a bomb. No, not a bo-. A bomb. A big bad, I'm not cleaning up afterwards, bomb. Turns out the bomb had been smuggled into the US and they needed to know how. They had exhausted all other non-super-hero methods and were left with only psychics. They sent their MIB to grab anybody who was a psychic yet to be proven a fraud and see what they could divine. I don't know what the other psychics told them but when I touched the bomb and started spitting out information, like where it was made and how it got past security, they all seemed to sit up and take notice.

It turns out that the bomb landed in the states and used a Portuguese ambassador's diplomatic immunity. This meant that somebody betrayed both governments and that there was a traitor in their midst. Now I only had the facts my visions had given me, jumbled facts and very heavily out of order, so when they said traitor I immediately suspected Agent Cook/Wind. It seemed obvious. He lied about his name; he'd broken into apartments and he'd killed people. It all seemed to fit.

Spoiler Alert: It wasn't him.

When I touched his glasses I learned that Agent Cook/Wind fought on the side of angels. In fact he was the one who found the bomb planted beneath a financial center in Broadway and stopped it from detonating. He was a hero. On a side note, he had a different name for that mission too. That time he was called Red Five.

Six months ago I met the man with a thousand names. A couple days later my brown envelope showed up and I became a detective. I think he had something to do with it.

That was my first foray into government based psychic work. I went with them when they asked, I read a bomb with my powers, I accused the wrong man for a crime he didn't commit and then I cleared his name. And when all was said and done I ended up in the FBI database, and god knows who else's, with a big PSYCHIC stamped across the front. I'm not sure how I feel about that. It probably doesn't even come with a tax credit.

I just realized something. I signed a government non-disclosure agreement form before I left. I don't think I'm supposed to talk about what happened that day. Do me a favor and disregard everything I just told you.

Chapter 04
Candy and Lollipops Version of Jail

I hate nothing more than being angry and outside. It always feels like I lost an argument and was kicked out of the house. I grumbled as I hobbled around the front lawn, fuming at the FBI agent. Why do the sexy ones always end up annoying the crap out of me? Why can't they be like Elaine? Cute, funny, pleasant to be around and still won't sleep with me. On second thought that's no better either.

"Alright there, PI, it's time to do your thing," Elaine beamed. "If they won't keep you in the loop then you'll have to investigate."

I wanted to give her a dirty look while I stated the obvious. How can I investigate when I have nothing to go on? But as I turned to face her my eyes caught two things that simultaneously surprised and scared me. The first was the wicked grin plastered all over Elaine's face and the second was the Senior Special Agent Puzo's smart phone resting in her hand. She had swiped the phone. This girl was crafty. In fact she was *License to Ill* track 3 crafty and that was pretty damn crafty.

"You didn't tell me how I could help," she boasted. "I came up with a plan on my own. Great distraction B-T-W."

I hated the out loud net speak but damn I was impressed. I pulled out my phone and quickly scrolled down the contact list. I tapped on Hotwire's name and impatiently waited for him to pick up.

"Calling me so soon," he teased. "Did you miss me already? Is it my smooth voice? I've been told I should be on radio."

"Hey, I need your help. I'm on a case."

I hear the clack of keys on the other end. "I haven't received any updates of new cases."

"This one is personal. I'll pay you from my pocket for this one." I hear him grunt in approval. "I have a smart phone. What is the quickest way to copy everything she has so I know what she knows?"

I put my phone on speaker as Elaine and I switched devices. Hotwire guided me through copying Agent Puzo's data. He spoke in short words and gave me simple instructions that were perfect for a grunt like me. You could have replaced his flawless American dialect with a Middle Eastern accent and he would have been the perfect for a stereotypical, and probably slightly racist, tech support call center employee. My fingers danced to his words, jumping to the web browser and pulling up the city library's webpage.

"What the hell am I doing here?"

He scolded me for interrupting, and mocked me while doing so. Apparently I had the attention span of a nine year-old girl in a sparkly ponies and unicorn sticker store. Hidden deep beneath the library's page I found a link, carefully hidden. I gave it a click, and then three more just like it, and ended up staring at a small hidden program. With a double click the program had installed and ran, carefully concealed in the background of the phone's system.

"Okay, everything on the phone is being sent to me, and I in turn will send it back to you. The owner will be none the wiser. Now just give the phone back to...." His voice trails off. "Senior Special Agent Puzo of the FBI? Are you freaking nuts? You're going to get us thrown in jail. Not fun time jail, with candy and lollipops. I'm talking real-time jail, with knives, terrorists, torture and rape."

I was curious about his candy and lollipops version

of jail but I figured it was better not to ask about it. "Look I didn't have a choice. Read the missing person case file. It's my nephew, he's missing."

Silence.

"Okay, I get it. Let's just limit the amount of obstruction and treason we commit today. You're not Jack Bauer; you won't get away with it."

Elaine smirked. "You use a cane, Ben. You can't outrun them either."

I heard coughing and snorting on the other end. Hotwire was trying his best not to laugh. I hung up before he got the chance. I handed the stolen phone back to Elaine and nodded toward the front door. Our hidden link into Puzo's phone would be useless if she reported it stolen and had it disconnected. We needed to get it back to her. My phone sang a jaunty tune to signify a pair of incoming texts. I gave it a look as we re-entered my sister's house.

> **Hotwire:** I'm sifting through all the data I can find. The police report says he vanished from the school yard.
> **Hotwire:** FBI acting like it's a kidnapping. Start with the school. See what you can find. I'll keep digging.

Elaine moved to casually drop the phone back on the table and I went to sit beside Annie. My sister was worried, what mother wouldn't be, and we had no right to tell her not to be but she was pregnant. The last thing we needed was for her worry and stress to trigger her second baby a month early. Dave poured two pills from a bottle labelled Ephemiphan and handed them to Annie. She downed them with some water.

"I want to be where I can do the most good," I explained. "But I don't know if it's here."

Annie looked up at me in disbelief. I had tried explaining the SRG Security thing to her in the past but it was hard to describe it when I had to leave out everything that happened six months ago. I had tried numerous times, but in the end it always ended up boiling down to four little words. "I'm a detective now."

She hadn't believed me any time before, but that day, as her look of disbelief had faded into a grim veil of hope, her eyes had told me to go, to do whatever is was I did, and to find Robby. I stood up and made for the kitchen. Elaine stood there, nervously tapping her foot, as she waited for me.

"Well?"

"I need a ride."

"Let's go." She handed me my hat and moved for the door. "But I'm warning you this is a onetime thing. I'm no sidekick."

A physiotherapist helping her psychic patient solve mysteries; sounds like a TV show to me.

Elaine drove like a woman possessed, tearing through traffic in a fashion that would make cabbies fearful, and all the while I was trying to bite back the greatest woman-driver joke ever conceived. I wondered, as we drove, if she had heard Senior Special Agent Puzo use the dreaded P-word. I'd never mentioned my powers to Elaine nor had I ever planned to. I kind of liked this girl, and I mean like liked her, but somehow I doubted that her thinking I'm crazy for believing I have powers, or weird for actually possessing them, helped my chances at a relationship. Yet she was quiet, relatively, as we drove and she never mentioned it. So I let it be. When we eventually got there, in one piece and ticket free, I hobbled out of the car.

That woman driver joke would have been amazing.

The schoolyard is much different than the one I grew up in. Annie and I had grown up in a rural area, our school had massive yards with plenty of space in which to play and do kid stuff. This schoolyard, built deep in the city, was as different as day is to night, as fire is to ice and as Coke is to Pepsi. Trust me on that last one. This schoolyard lacked the endless green fields and towering trees. This schoolyard was a concrete playground with a steel gate built along the parameter, to protect the kids from the speeding cars that ran along the nearby street and to protect the cars from the kids.

I pointed to the northern corner. "The report says that Robby was last seen there. Partway through recess the yard monitor, a Ms. Briery, says she had to tell Robby to get off the fence. Apparently he likes climbing up it."

Elaine stood by the car listening. She didn't say much, playing the silent Watson to my monologing Holmes. I moved to the fence and peeled off my glove.

"We need to find clues of some sort," I postulated. "Something to give us a lead."

I touched the fence. The metal chains were cold and harsh to the touch, and I felt the familiar shiver up my back and the twitch in my eyes start to take place. The cars on the street and the few pedestrians walking by melted away as children began to appear on the playground, popping into existence like a light bulb being turned on. The cries of laughter and fun fill the air, from the foolish dares of little boys to the incessant teasing of young girls while a blue Mustang sat parked across the street. There, on the fence, was Robby, a mop of blonde curls on his head and had a smile three miles wide.

"I'm Spider-Man!" Robby declared as he climbed upwards.

"You are not," a friend challenged.

"Yeah I am. I have an Uncle Ben." Robby was talking about me. It was his favorite joke. I was Uncle Ben so obviously he was Spider-Man. I couldn't fault the kid's logic. I mean, I went through high school believing that since God created women, and then created me, that I must be God's gift to women.

"Yeah but Spider-Man's Uncle Ben died. Did yours die?" the kid taunted.

"He almost did. He went to be an army man and almost didn't come back." Ouch. I knew he took it hard, but I guess I never really knew how hard. I watched for a couple minutes more until the vision faded away. More taunts, more dares, and more childish insults, of which Robby is fairly poor at. I should really teach him a couple zingers when his mom's not around. The vision ended with Ms. Briery yelling at Robby to get down off the fence.

I kept looking at my phone as I walked along the fence. The report gave me all that it could but Elaine didn't know that. I pretended to study the report when in truth I was just scanning items for visions. I disliked lying to her but it was needed. I mean sure, Anthony Michael Hall didn't need to lie to John L. Adams in *The Dead Zone* show but he wasn't trying to sleep with his physical therapist. You know, that show would have been very different if he had been. I used to really like that show before I gained my powers, but now it just seemed too real. I mean you don't see doctors watching *Scrubs* or *ER* (series finales aside). We watch TV to escape our lives, not relive them.

I reached the fence door and give it a touch. A shiver ran up my spine and my eyes twitched as the world around me altered for my latest vision. Robby and his friend were hanging around the door chatting.

"Is your uncle really a soldier?"

"He used to be until he took a bomb to the knee," Robby explained, "Now he can't fight anymore."

"So what does he does he do now?"

Robby just shrugged. "I don't know. He says he helps people who need him but he really doesn't have a job."

He seemed so excited about me when I was an army guy, a little green plastic soldier marching endlessly into battle, but now that I was a gimp cripple he didn't know how to react to me.

I tried to push my nephew's words out of my head. I needed to focus on finding him. I looked around the surrounding area, trying to notice anything in this vision that could help. I saw it on the street, the blue Mustang, parked with a man behind the wheel.

I let go of the door and hobbled across the street. The

Mustang was there in both visions. There wasn't a vast time span difference between the two visions which meant that it could be just a mundane car parked nearby but it was there in both visions, clear as day. In six months I have discovered that my visions have changed slightly. In the beginning I got my apparitions all willy-nilly. It was random crapshoot of images. They could be anything, relevant or not, but often when I'm on a case and I saw something it was usually important. I don't know why my powers have changed, or if it is I that had changed instead. Maybe fate, God, or whatever controlling source that grants me my powers has decided to be nicer to me or, and more likely, through my increasing use I have learned to navigate my visions to an nth degree. Either way that Mustang had appeared twice in my visions which is normally enough to make me pay attention, normally.

"What are you doing?" Elaine asked as I knelt at the since vacated parking space.

"The FBI is acting like this is a kidnapping," I explained. "So if somebody took Robby from the school yard then they would have had to park out here to watch the yard."

"Oh, you mean casing the joint?" And people think I watch too much TV.

I gave her a nod and touched the street. The shiver up my back was intensified and the twitch in my eyes caused me physical pain. I was assaulted by thousands of images, each crashing against me like a bucket of paint tossed out onto a white wall. The visions splashed against me until each blended together. My visions are based around emotions. The stronger the sentiment, be it anger, joy, guilt, worry or any other hanging around in the bag of wonders, the stronger the vision. There are a few places in the world that are emotionally charged. Churches rate high on the list, as do graveyards and funeral homes, and so do airports, train stations and bus depots. Surprisingly, the parking space outside a school proved to be stronger than I expected. I got images of worried parents dropping kids off for the first time, scared children not wanting to leave their mommies, students nervous about a test, boys crushing about that cute girl, girls nervous about that same boy and the joy at the end of the day when parent and child were reunited. The visions were endless and overwhelming.

I tried to focus, to narrow my supernatural sight on only the car, but it was difficult. Each echo of history cried out begging to be heard and seen. The cries resonated in my head, bringing with them pain for each vision that went ignored, but I pushed them aside and tried to delve closer. After much effort, and an unexpected amount of pain, the unwanted visions faded away leaving only the blue Mustang. I know very little about cars, it was never my thing, but this vision came with data. It was a 2005 Ford Mustang painted Pepsi-can blue. I walked around in my vision as I studied the car and the people within it. I see the New York Licence plate, DCH 7659, and the small OnStar logo on the dashboard. Then I looked at the driver. He was an older man dressed in a suit and a tie.

I pulled back my hand and snapped back into reality. I was at a loss. I now had new information, most of which made no sense. The problem was that there was no logical way I could have learned that information, at least not in a way I could think to tell Elaine about. I could have faked an email from Hotwire saying he gave me a lead, but I didn't want to dip into that well too often. If I did that it could become unbelievable or worse, Hotwire would get all the credit.

"What the hell are you doing in front of my lawn? Just because you're not in your blue car anymore doesn't mean I won't call the cops on you." A stay-at-home mother bellowed at me from her front door. My solution sang to me like a choir of angels. "You freaking pervert, if I see you here again I will call the cops and watch as they beat you down with their nightsticks."

That is one bitchy choir of angels.

I removed my hat and moved to the front door. "Excuse me, ma'am, but did you say you saw a car here earlier?"

"Yeah, what is it to you?" she back stepped slightly, fearful of me for whatever reason.

"I'm a detective," I explained. As I hand her one of my SRG Security business cards. "I'm working a case involving a student that went missing here earlier today. Could you tell me about the car?"

"The missing boy? The one the cops were all here about earlier?" I nodded at her. "Oh dear, that is a tragedy." It's amazing how quickly some people can change their attitude. "What can you tell us about the car?"

"It was blue, like the Mets, and had one of them damn horses on the front." She explained. "I had a boyfriend in high school that had a car with those damn horses on it. Cheating bastard chose a skank cheerleader over me for prom." And she was back to being a bitch.

"You mean a Mustang!" Elaine beamed. "A blue Mustang, we can find that."

I asked the lady a couple more questions and got nothing but bitch-a-tude in return. Eventually we gave up and left. I grabbed my phone and quickly typed Hotwire an email. I gave him the license plate number, the make and model of the car, and the fact that I saw an OnStar logo on the dashboard. Within minutes I got a reply. "You up for another ride?"

Elaine nodded eagerly. She seemed to be enjoying herself. The girl liked solving mysteries on dates. I would have to remember that. In his email Hotwire detailed how he used the plate number to track the OnStar account, and then used the GPS locator to find its whereabouts. I'm paraphrasing his email because I re-read it three times and still only understood half of the techno-babble. I gave Elaine the address and we were off.

It took almost thirty minutes to get to the address Hotwire provided us, an upscale private practice doctor's office. The blue Mustang sat parked in the corner. According to Hotwire the car belonged to Dr. Marcus Caine, an obstetrician. Elaine followed me as we entered the building. From signs in the lobby we quickly learned that the private practice held the offices of dozens of doctors, many of which were fellow obstetricians, gynecologist, pediatrician and other family doctors. The practice was owned by a woman named Doctor Melisa Proce.

Behind the lobby desk was a young blonde woman dressed in formal clothing. She was a perky woman who, while always smiling, always had a stern look on her face. Elaine gave her a smile of her own as I subtly touched the phone desk with my ungloved hand. Shivers up my spine and a twitch in my eye and I was diving through a pool of apparitions to find a helpful vision. I eventually found myself at that exact desk just three days earlier. I saw the same secretary answering a ringing phone.

"Proce Medical. How may I help you?" My visions aren't like a phone call scene in *24*, with split screens where we can hear both ends of the conversation; a lot of times you're left hearing only one end of the chat and having to guess the rest. "Hello, Mr. Banks, sure I can re-schedule that for you. Just give me a moment here; excellent. Your appointment is set for next Thursday at 3pm."

The vision faded away and I glanced at my phone. It was indeed Thursday but it was only 2:30. "Hi there; I'm Mr. Banks. I'm here for my 3 o'clock appointment."

The secretary looked down at her book and smiled. "Oh yes, here you are. You are scheduled for a prostate exam."

Well - Crap. That backfired.

"Head up to the fifth floor and Dr. Milano will be right with you."

I gave her thanks and Elaine and I headed to the elevator. Once we were out of earshot Elaine looked over at me. "How did you know to use the name Mr. Banks?"

I smirked. "Lucky guess."

The metal doors closed behind us and the shaft began to move upwards. "We're heading to the sixth floor, room 712. That's Dr. Caine's office."

I just nodded. I didn't know what Caine had to do with Robby, but if he was the man parked outside his playground then hopefully he could tell me where to find him. The doors opened on the seventh floor and I hobbled off. This floor was quiet, with only a few offices and a couple small labs. As we headed down the hall the door at the end opened up; my eyes bulged as I saw a familiar face exiting the room; the slick grey hairs, the cold eyes and the unmistakeable mustache and the hint of beard. The man passing us in the hall was Burt Reynolds; Burt Freaking Reynolds.

Yeah, that didn't make sense.

It wasn't even recent Burt Reynolds as seen in *Burn Notice* or *Reel Love* but instead it was 1997 Burt Reynolds: *I-played-Jack-Horner-in-Boogie-Nights* Burt Reynolds. Everything from the hair style to the short-sleeved blue shirt and the ascot screamed Jack Horner. Somebody was messing with me and, to be honest, I didn't like it one bit.

I eyed the legend of film and screen as he passed, not sure how to react. Do I get his autograph? Do I stop him for some reason? Do I start quoting his movie line? In the end I just let him pass. It was Burt Reynolds after all.

Elaine reached office 712 first, opened the door and looked in. Then she screamed. The room, an elegant high-class medical office, looked how you would expect it would. There was high-end computer equipment on the desks, medical tomes lining the bookcase, and the wall decorated with diplomas, all with the natural light pouring in through the massive glass windows. What you wouldn't expect was the bullet hole in the massive TV that hung from the wall, the electronic bits scattered across the office and the dead guy on the floor with two bullet holes in his chest and one in his forehead.

Well - crap.

Elaine was shaken in fear, her back pressed up against the wooden door. Up until that point, playing detective with me had just been an ABC show, but the moment she was confronted with a dead body she switched networks. This had become a Showcase special, filled with blood and gore. In short, shit had just gotten real.

"Elaine," I whispered. She stood there unmoving, frozen in fear and shock. I fished her phone from her purse and gently pushed it into her hands. "I need you to listen to me. I need a big favour. I need you to take your phone and call the cops."

Elaine nodded slightly as she slowly dialed. The dead man was an older guy dressed in a suit and tie with a lab coat to cover the ensemble. The deceased was the same old man from my vision. I leaned in and read the name tag: Dr. Marcus Caine.

Well - double crap.

My only lead was dead and the only person I saw nearby was Burt Freaking Reynolds. Yeah, nobody was going to believe me.

My obsessive love of television has taught me numerous times not to touch a crime scene. It was rule one of crime TV, but this was Robby. I pulled off my glove and gently touched the bloodstained lab coat. The world faded away with the usual side effects, a shiver up my spine and a twitch in my eye, and my vision took hold. I was in the very same office, not a half hour earlier. Dr. Caine was pacing back and forward before a large television, a web camera desperately trying to track his motions. On the screen two faces looked back at him, one a woman and the other a male. I recognized the female face from the lobby below, Doctor Melisa Proce: owner and founder of Proce Medical.

"The child was taken," Caine exclaimed, his voice heavy with panic. "He was nabbed off the street but it wasn't by one of us; this was somebody different."

Dr. Proce interrupted her panicking colleague. "Are you certain?" Caine nodded. "Then this is a problem. The last thing we want is to draw attention to ourselves."

The unknown male spoke up. "Could it be our opposition? We're supposed to have security measures in place."

"We do, sir," Proce explained. "This, however, was unexpected."

"Do we need to call in Upper Management?"

Proce shook her head. "That's the last thing we want. Let's keep it within Croxallé for now. We don't know if this actually involves us or if it's a coincidence. In the meantime

NEVER BEEN TO MARS

we activate any security we have available to us and start a widespread investigation. We also need eyes on our other endeavours. Sir, I'll need your go ahead to activate our agents." The mysterious man held up his phone and tapped onto the screen, "Authorization has been sent. Our head of security will be on route immediately. We need to deal with this now. I don't have to remind you that shit rolls downhill. If I take the heat from this, you do too. And this little practice I fund, well, losing it will be the least of your worries."

"You don't need to resort to threats, sir. We are handling this."

The webcam suddenly exploded and bounced off the desk. The TV suddenly sparked and shattered leaving only a bullet hole in its screen. Caine spun around. Burt Reynolds stood in the doorway, a silenced pistol held tightly in his hand. Caine opened his mouth in awe, partly at the gun but most likely due to the fact that Burt Reynolds was holding it. Burt leveled the pistol at Caine and quickly squeezed off three rounds, two into Caine's chest and one into his head.

"Two in the heart and one in the head, it's the only way to make sure they're dead." Burt rhymed in the final moment of my vision, marching towards computer as the vision faded away.

Jack Horner has just freaking shot someone. This was unreal. This was beyond unreal. At that exact moment I was only 63% sure I hadn't snapped and gone bonkers.

I needed more information on this Proce Medical, on Croxallé, on Burt and on, well, damn near everything. I hobbled across the room. I had to find out what this Burt wanted from the computer and I was guessing that I didn't have time to do it the mundane way. I pressed my fingers down onto the spacebar and fell head first into another vision, mere seconds after the last one ended.

With the usual shiver and twitch, or shivitch as I think I'm calling it now, I see Burt placing his gun on the table and quickly typing away on the keyboard. He's moving through the computer's operating system faster then I move through the 100+ channels on my TV. Screens popped up and vanish in mere seconds until he found the files he was looking for. It was a medical database filled with data on a drug trial being run by Croxallé. They were testing a fertility drug called Tenasine. Burt slid a USB drive into the side of the screen and started copying the database. When the files finished Burt removed one USB drive and replaced it with another. From the second drive he opened a computer virus and installed it across the entire system.

As reality returned I glanced at the computer screen and saw nothing but an error screen. Burt wiped the computer to cover his tracks. I moved away and I looked over the room. I wanted to take in more of this crime scene; to read every minute detail like the detectives of legend but I wasn't that good. I cheat at the best of times, seeing facts from the past that nobody is supposed to know, and then I stumble around making false accusations until I trip over the truth.

So there I stood standing in a crime scene with more question then answers. Why was there a Faux-Burt Reynolds? Where was the real Burt Reynolds? What would it take to get an autograph from the real Burt Reynolds? Could I pass off an autograph from Faux-Burt as one from the real Burt? And more importantly what the hell did Faux-Burt want with Robby?

The ding of the elevator and the stomping of boots were all the hints I needed to guess that the police had arrived. They stormed the room and see me standing over a dead body with an absent minded look on my face, Elaine huddled by the door crying, and neither of us with an explanation worth telling.

Well – crap.

Chapter 05
Rich People LIve Very Interesting Lives

One of the reasons I love cop shows is because life is simple and so are the cases. If they arrest somebody with fifteen minutes left to go, chances are they have the wrong guy. It's probably best that real police don't work like that.

"You're under arrest Mr. Criminal but I still have fifteen minutes left on my shift so I'm letting you go. Chances are you're the wrong guy anyways."

But one thing I do hate about cop shows is that they always have that bad episode where the main character gets framed. It's the same for every show. Your tough female cop and her quirky male civilian sidekick have been flirting around for four seasons until in the epic finale where they finally get together and do nasty stuff. Then season five hits and our male lead get framed for a horrifying murder. We know he didn't do it, he's the male lead and it's not even an anything-goes season finale, its episode five. We're still in October. But as much as we hate it we sit there and watch the interrogation. We watch sassy female cop grill quirky male sidekick for ten minutes as they try to drag out the tension. That scene right there is why I hate those episodes.

"Oh my god how could my quirky sidekick be a psychotic murderer? It's so unlike anything he's ever done, ever." He didn't do it. You've known him for four years.

However, today I learned that police interrogations

are much scarier then TV. Police were scary people. Add Senior Special Agent Puzo in the mix and things got worse. My interrogation room wasn't all bright and colourful like on *Castle* and it wasn't all high-tech like in *24*. No, my interrogation room was grey and bland. There was a table, handcuffs, a couple chairs and a two-way mirror.

I don't understand why they still use those things. Thanks to TV everybody knows how they work. They take the person you least want to hear you speak, shove them behind the glass, and then grill you till you spill your guts.

The police grilled me about the crime scene asking me all the standard questions. Why was I there? What was my connection to Dr. Caine? Did I see the murderer? My favourite question was after I mentioned Burt Reynolds; do you think I'm an idiot? But that all changed when Senior Special Agent Puzo showed up.

She stormed into the room pissed off and with Ryman in tow. With a thundering clap, she slammed her hand down upon the steel table. Her eyes were wide and her chin stern, her lips pressed so tightly against each other that if I'd placed a piece of coal between them she'd be spitting diamonds and I'd probably have enough to make bail if I was getting charged.

"One thing, I told you one thing and you ignored me. Let's see if you remember that one thing. Can you tell me what that one thing was?"

"Let you handle this?" Despite knowing the answer my response sounds like a question. Damn, I must really fear this woman when she's mad.

"Let me handle this, exactly." Puzo tossed a beige file folder onto the table. "Right now I have trespassing, I have interference in a police investigation and I have you on suspicion of murder. Somehow I doubt that any of that equals letting me handle it."

I wanted to say something to defend myself, but it didn't take a psychic to figure out now was not the time to defend myself. Instead I just watched her move back and forth, her blonde hair held tightly in a bun save for the strands that fell in her eyes. I watched as the light glimmered off her diamond studs and as her suit hugged her body like a second skin.

"I've been debating with Ryman about you. I think there is no possible way that there is an excuse for what you did, Ryman thinks there is. I am really curious which of us is correct. So why don't you enlighten us and tell me just what the hell you were doing by a dead body."

This was my moment in the sun, my moment to wow them both with my investigating skills and my abilities of deduction. This was my sole moment to show off my capable skills as an investigator but all I was able to get out was the ability to sheepishly say one word. "Investigating?"

Her eye twitched as she loomed over me. I expected a scene where the cop flips the table, grabs the perp, and then slams him against the wall in a threatening manner. The cop would scream at them until they succumbed to fear or the Captain pulled them off. But it didn't happen. Puzo's eye twitched, her neck tensed and she looked about two seconds away from drawing a pistol and blowing my head off.

"Investigating?" she said between clenched teeth. "I'm going to need more than that,"

"First tell me where Elaine is." I was worried about her. She just seemed to shut down when she saw the corpse, lifeless as she just lay on the floor.

"We released her. She's gone home. Now spill."

"I went to the school to investigate and met a woman. She told me about a blue Mustang that had been parked outside the school the last couple of days. This led me to Doctor Caine, the deceased. I snuck into his office to interrogate him and he was dead. We passed a guy on the way in."

"Who happens to look just like Burt Reynolds; yeah I read that part." Puzo shook her head. "And I'm supposed to believe Burt Reynolds, who is in LA shooting a movie and has no motive, kills a man."

"Burt's working again? Awesome." My brain has the

worst priorities. "Wait, I don't have motive either."

"Your sister's doctor is spotted stalking your nephew. Robert goes missing, you blame him, you confront him, a fight breaks out and you shoot him. Sounds like motive to me."

Doctor Caine was Annie's doctor? This was news to me. Doctor Marcus Caine was an obstetrician. This meant that he probably dealt with Robby back in the day but why would a birth doctor stalk a child years later? I stammered again, not knowing what to say. I still wasn't sure if Robby's disappearance was connected to all of this but something was going on with my nephew.

"My motive is thin," Puzo explained; her demeanour calming with each passing second. "Paper thin; I know this and you know this, hell the DA knows this. I also don't think you killed him. Now I've also gone over your statement, the one in the official mundane report, but I need more than that. Your FBI file has the magic P-Word all over it, remember? So what happens if I ask what you saw?"

She emphasized the last word with a wavy hand gesture from her left and two finger of her right pressed against her temple. See this is why I don't tell people I'm a psychic. They make fun of me.

"I'm more than happy to cooperate but not from this room and not with that two way mirror. I don't know whose back there." Great now I sounded crazy and paranoid. Puzo looked back at Ryman. Neither spoke, they just seemed to lock gazes, tilt their heads and raise their eyebrows, but somehow they knew what the other was speaking.

I missed that.

Nothing you do in the army is done alone; it's always done with a fire team partner. When you're in the field you do everything with this person. You look after each other, you check each other's gear, you sleep next to each other, you eat with him, you even shit, shower and shave with him. As long as you're in the field you have a living shadow. Because of all the time you spent together you learned to think like each

NEVER BEEN TO MARS

other, talk like each other and communicate without making a sound. Ever since I was medically discharged I no longer had that.

"Okay deal. Let's go, magic boy." Puzo escorted me to an empty desk and returned my stuff. I grabbed my phone and quickly checked my messages; nothing from my sister and nothing from Hotwire. I eagerly fired him off a text.

> **Me**: My lead just turned up dead. Do you have anything?
> **Hotwire**: FBI lady is working on finding the Bio-Dad.
> **Me**: I need you to do a search on her and her partner. Shit's getting weird here.
> **Hotwire**: On it.
> **Me**: One more things can you find the home address for Dr. Marcus Caine?

"Okay, Nancy Drew," Puzo mocked. "You can text your BFF after class. In the meantime talk to me."

So I spoke. I explained about the mysterious three-way phone call, the panic in their voices about Robby's kidnapping and about Burt Reynolds. I told them how Jack Horner popped the guy with three rounds, copied files from the computer and then wiped the thing. To her credit Puzo just listened, she didn't interrupt; she just silently took notes and listened. When story reached the obvious finale, me being arrested by the po-po, she put down the pencil.

"I don't know if I believe in all this psychic mumbo jumbo," Puzo began quietly. "I tend to trust what I can see and touch but then I look at your file. You served in the army, you were a ranger and that's not an easy task. Your file says that in 2003, when you were in Iraq, your unit faced off against the elite Republican Guard."

She was listing facts of my past with such ease. For those of us who were there, who engaged the elite guard in firefights, it wasn't an easy memory to recall. There was a reason the troops were called elite.

"Your file lists your military service, which is respectable, and then we get to the bottom, the magic P-Word section." Her face scrounged as she tried to find the right words to use. To be honest I found it kind of cute. "This section of the file was created fairly high up. According to the file you and almost a dozen others fell under the notice of the FBI and various three letter agencies. They call you the *Sahara Forecasters*."

Three letter agencies. That was slang for the big boys; FBI, CIA, DND, MLB, NSA, NHL, DHS, and the long list of others, including the most feared: NFL. These were the who's who of the government world and somehow I appeared on their list with the cute name.

"This all happened six months ago? You want to tell me about that?"

One of the major criticisms of the American medium is the overuse of certain plots and phrase. In the internet world they called these tropes; devices and conventions that a writer can reasonably rely on as being present in the audience members' minds and expectations. Things like 'I could tell you but I'd have to kill you' and 'It's on a need to know basis' are prime examples. It's the classic movie and TV lines. So when I got the opportunity to use one myself I leapt at the chance.

"That's confidential." I was grinning from ear to ear. I may have derived more pleasure from that then I should have. My smile faded, completely by choice and not by the stern glower she was giving me, and I returned to sincere talk. "I really cannot speak about six months ago. I signed so many forms saying I wouldn't and received a great many threats about bottomless holes and lightless prisons that I'm not even risking it."

Luckily that worked. Puzo rolled her eyes, shrugged, and carried on. She'd been expecting that answer from me but had had to ask anyways. "Alright; so six months ago the FBI higher-ups decide to make a file on you, and when I say higher-up I mean nose bleed section. This means I have to take what you say, somewhat, seriously. I don't know how to deal with a murderous Burt Reynolds but we can draw some

NEVER BEEN TO MARS

information from your... episode."

She made me sound senile.

Puzo turned to Ryman. "Call the unit. We upgrade this to a full kidnapping. A place like Proce Medical has off-site back-ups, they cannot afford not to. We need access to them to find out what Not-Burt..."

"I'm calling him Faux-Burt," I interrupted.

"What Not-Burt stole," Puzo continued, ignoring my interruption. "But how do we link the murder, which isn't our case, to Robby's?"

Ryman adjusted his tie before pointing at my latest police file. "We use him. His official report links Caine to the scene of the kidnapping, then the doctor shows up dead."

"It's thin," Puzo replied.

"Paper thin," I added. They both glared at me. I needed to stop injecting word-things.

"Worse comes to worse we string him up for a while and run with that. He was at the murder and it is his nephew." Puzo nodded in approval. Ryman cleared his throat, a signal he had something else to say. "Are we really going on the word of a psychic vision? Shouldn't we be focusing our attention on the bio-father?"

"You've seen the file. You saw the origin's designation. Psychic or not we really need to take him seriously. Don't pull men from the bio-dad search, who knows when that may pay out, but we can't just spin our wheels until we find him. We have other leads now." Puzo looked back at me. "Croxallé is a medical giant that funds Proce Medical, so we are going to ask for their files. Croxallé are going to be assholes and say no. So we'll get a court order for them. Spoiler Alert: They'll fight it. We have a missing child on our side, we will win. This brings us to you. It's obvious you won't let us handle this alone and I can't legally arrest you, yet, so now I get to make you an offer magic boy. We keep you in the loop and you keep us in the loop. Okay?"

I nodded quickly, my head bobbing like a twelve year old boy who was just asked if he wanted ice cream or a nineteen year old boy who was just asked by his first college hook-up if he wanted her to take off her shirt. Either way my head nodded very, very quickly and very, very eagerly.

"There is just one rule to this, no more breaking laws. Can you promise me that?"

"I promise not to break anymore laws." I lied.

An hour later I was at the home address of the now deceased Doctor Marcus Caine. Hotwire, using his techno powers that had nothing to do with music, found Marcus' wife, Meredith Caine, and tracked her phone's movements to the police station. She'd be there for a while which gave me at least an hour to search his place. With my Bluetooth earpiece firmly in place, and the soothing sounds of Hotwire's voice in my ear, I entered the elevator. In buildings like these the elevator was normally key-locked. The Rangers taught me how to pick a lock, it was part of room clearing classes, but I was grossly out of practice. For the first time in years fate seemed to be on my side. Instead of a key lock there was an electronic lock that required a key code.

A key code required a key pad, which was an inanimate object that people had to press over and over again. Lucky me.

I touched the electronic pad with my bare skin and waited for the shivitch to escort me to my vision like an usher at a wedding. The sky turned black and snow covered the ground as I was whisked away to an unknown time. A young blonde girl, who just turned eighteen a month ago, stood in the metal elevator. She was the babysitter, my vision was kind enough to inform me, but she was dressed nothing like the babysitters I had growing up. This young girl was dressed in tight black jeans that she wore to make her ass look good and a lacy red shirt that hugged her chest magnificently. She quickly looked herself over in the reflection, pursing her seductively red lips, pushing up her breasts for more cleavage and adjusting her low riding jeans so they teased just the right amount.

"I didn't get a no before my eighteenth birthday," she

teased. "I'm not getting one now."

She pressed 5, 9, 4 and 7 on the keypad, the light flashing green and the elevator roaring to life. My vision faded.

Marcus Caine was a dick. He was stalking children and sleeping with the babysitter. I'll admit, she was one hot babysitter, but if her soliloquy was any hint, he had been doing it while she was minor.

I punched in the numbers. The door clicked in approval and the elevator roared to life. I rode the steel carriage upwards, expecting another door to bypass once I got off on their floor, but as the elevator slowed to a halt I stared in wonder as the door opened into the apartment. The home was magnificent, a five-thousand squared foot loft with hardwood floors, three bedrooms, an office, and classic columns to hold up its insanely high ceilings. There was a spectacular landmark view from a 50-foot wide expanse of mahogany-framed glass doors that open onto a magnificent 19th century wrought-iron balcony. I came to a realization there; I might be watching too much TV shows about rich homes if I can pull that from memory.

I headed to the kitchen first and raided the fridge. I grabbed and apple and took a bite out of it. I've learned a lot from television, tricks with elevators and call centers, how to create a make-shift silencer and how to patch a tire but some of my shows get a little craftier in their lessons. One of my favorite shows, *Burn Notice*, used narration to give lessons on how to be a spy.

Michael Weston's Spy Lessons! Class One: When breaking into a home don't look like your trying to break in. This means no black clothing and no ski-masks. It's hard to defend your actions when you are wearing a ski mask in the summer while indoors. Instead look like you belong. Grab a bite to eat from the fridge, maybe a drink, that way if you are caught, you just act confused.

So with an apple in my hand I was ready. "Okay, I'm in."

"Good work, Cowboy," Hotwire clapped. "Now start

with the phone and look for calls." I hobbled across the floor and grabbed the cordless phone. I shivered and twitched and dove into another vision. Meredith Caine, a woman in her early forties, was crying into the phone. Having just heard about her husband's murder she grabbed her keys and darted for the door. Reality returned and I felt sorry for her. Her husband was a child-stalking-babysitter-boinking-dick (allegedly) but she didn't have to suffer through the loss. Nobody did. I returned my attention to the handheld and flipped through its functions. I read off every name and number to Hotwire, he put them into his magic computer and did a compile or search or some such nonsense and check each one for relevance. Sorry if I get too technical.

I returned the phone to its place and moved through the apartment. I touched random objects as I traveled. I was hoping for another mysterious phone call or perhaps a monologue from Caine explaining every detail I needed to his wife but instead got visions of family time and mundane life. I was treated to a slight surprise when I touched the black leather couch in the family room. With the usual shivitch I fell into the past. Meredith Caine, with her long brunette hair that fell past her shoulders, was dressed in a grey skirt, a very flattering red shirt and matching shoes. She sat on the couch, her head back as she moaned in pleasure. As my vision panned around, like a TV camera, I saw the source of her orgasmic bliss. Kneeling between her thighs, and her hiked up skirt, was a blonde mop of hair attached to a lacy red shirt and an extremely tight pair of black jeans.

Marcus Caine wasn't sleeping with the babysitter, Meredith Caine was.

Rich people live very interesting lives.

My hand lingered on the couch longer then was necessary as I watched the vision until its completion seconds later. I am fully aware how I seem, peering into the past like a time traveling voyeur, but it's been a while for me, a long while. It's still no excuse, at least not a good one, but it's the truth. Being a hop-along-Cassidy war vet with no job is not

NEVER BEEN TO MARS

the greatest way to pick up chicks. I've had success, if you could call it that, with military bars. Army bunnies love to throw an injured solider a bone from time to time, doing what they call their civic duty for those who served, but truth was pity sex had its limits.

With the vision ended and the lovemaking, if the scene inspired from an internet fantasy could be called that, fading back into the past I moved out of the living room and into the office. The office in his home looked very similar to that of his work. A sturdy desk with a computer upon it, a wall full of books and a massive TV hanging on the wall connected to a webcam. The layout was different and so was the look but essentially the rooms were the same.

A laptop, sitting on the sturdy desk with its screen glowing brightly, caught my gaze. "I got a laptop." I touched the mouse and the screen saver vanished, leaving only a password query in its wake. I described it to Hotwire.

"Oh, he has a secure set up on this, beyond simple password protection. Nab the laptop and bring it to me. I can hack it. Search the room for USB drives, external HDs, CDs, DVD or hell even a disk. Scoop them up and bring them as well."

I did as I was told, for once, and slipped the laptop into a nearby leather briefcase. I quickly searched the room and grabbed any discs and drives I could find. I pried open a wooden drawer and smirked at its contents; an external hard drive, hidden beneath a locked drawer. This had to be important. I slid that into the briefcase as well and hobbled for the front door. It was time to go see Hotwire.

Chapter 06
Kickass Stroganoff Meatballs in the Fridge

My cab came to a screeching halt outside a nightclub. I tossed a few bills at the driver and awkwardly climbed out of the car. The club, called Torri's, was Hotwire's base of operations. Jimmy Wilcox, the hacker's real life alias, owned the night time hotspot; he bought it a couple years back after his illegal activities started paying off. I hobbled inside.

Hobble. I say that word a lot, and I mean a lot, but in my in depth search of the English language (in depth search = watch TV) I have yet to find a word that better describes what I do. I don't walk, that requires two good legs, motivation and a night with nothing on TV. I don't run, you have to walk before you can run and I think I just covered the walking scenario. I definitely don't limp, because limping has that weird step and looks of pity associated with it. No, what I do is hobble. Even the word describes it perfectly. Saying the word out loud sounds wobbly when the Bs kick in and even the spelling is all wonky. It starts with an H, the hand-me downs of letters, ends with and E, the letter that's basically the experimental college girl willing to try everything and go anywhere, and has two Bs in the middle. Who puts two Bs together? Putting two Bs side by side is like taking that bro-friend of yours, the one who never backs down and even leapt off the roof of a house on a dare, and setting him up on a blind date with the girl who once stabbed herself in the leg to win a bet. B needs to be

NEVER BEEN TO MARS

hooked up with Q. You match lower case Q and B together and they look like two cops fighting back-to-back. I may have too much time on my hands

So there I was, the hobbliest hobble from Hobble Town, New Jersey, standing outside Hotwire's home. The three-floor club was a high-end spot, with four dance floors, seven bars, and thousands of volts of neon lights. It looked like any other club, but had an aura of class about it. I hobbled across the well-lit floor and headed to the back stairs. Clubs vary greatly in their lighting, and in Hotwire's you could see everyone and everything. Good visibility was the enemy of drunken decisions. The first three floors of the building belonged to the club. The fourth, and top floor, belonged to Hotwire. The entire floor was his home. He lived there, he slept there, and his hardware setup was there. As I passed through the world of booze and entered the world of tech I saw Hotwire in his kitchen making a sandwich.

In the last six months, I'd talked to Hotwire more times than I could count. Out of the list of contacts I had received, none had proven as helpful as he had. This being said, in all that time I had only met the man once. This time was number two. Hotwire wasn't the man you'd expect. TV stereotypes make you picture him as tall, lanky, thick rim glasses and living in the basement of his mother's home. None of this is true. Jimmy Wilcox looked more like a playboy dynasty then a techno-geek. He had slicked hair, a goatee and Italian suit and tie.

"You're indoors, Cowboy," he smirked between bites of bread, meat and cheese. "Hat off."

"Every time I talk to you I get a picture in my head," I explained as I removed my Stetson and placed it on a hook.

"And I never live up to it; yeah I get that a lot," Hotwire laughed as he returned to his desk. "What do you got for me?"

Hotwire's desk was thing of beauty. It was shaped like a C with a wall of six monitors, three towers and a massive cooling unit. His computer was a testimony to the art of technology. I hobbled over and handed him my briefcase of stolen gear. He withdrew each item one by one, examining each before plugging the laptops and the external drives into the towers and slipping discs into drives.

"I wrote a scanning program to help sort through all of this," the hacker explained. With each addition another screen lit up. "This will probably take a while, so grab a bite to eat if you'd like and help yourself to the fridge."

In the heat of the investigation, the worry and trepidation of Robby's disappearance, I was sure I had missed details or forgotten something vital, but until he mentioned it and brought it to my attention I hadn't realized how hungry I was. Hunger and I had a very strict relationship. I kept my stomach full and he left me alone, if I failed my end of the bargain then he became loud and grumpy and took it out on me. Yet oddly, despite not eating since before I arrived at Starmoore Entertainment, hunger had been silent. Like a child waiting for the right moment to yell, for the moment he knows he'll be heard the most – like a Walmart -, hunger suddenly started to scream at me. My stomach rumbled and clenched in pain. How had I forgotten to eat? It went against everything I had been taught as a Ranger, as a soldier and as an unemployed layabout. I thanked Hotwire and awkwardly scurried to the kitchen.

"There are some kickass stroganoff meatballs in the fridge," he called from his desk. "Trust me. Take those. Plates are above the sink and to the right."

I grabbed a white plate with blue flowers and placed it on the counter. The fridge was a rich person's fridge with ice maker functions and water dispensers. Mine was an old, crappy one that required me to punch the side for the light to come on. His was also filled with food, beer and Red Bull energy drinks. Mine was not. His fridge and mine were vastly different. I withdrew the meatballs, and a Red Bull, shoveled the food onto the plate. I slid my leftovers into the microwave and set the time for two minutes. With a hum, a dose of radiation, the microwave came alive.

"Okay program's running. It shouldn't take very

long," Hotwire updated as he entered the kitchen. "By the way I have your data on FBI lady and her thug."

He had my attention. After the beep of completion I withdrew my leftovers, grabbed a fork, and started to eat. "So spill. What do you got?" I asked between mouthfuls.

"Okay, Senior Special Agent Rachael Puzo. Age: 32. She joined the bureau straight out of college. About five years ago she made it into the FBI's *Crimes Against Children* program and quickly joined a *Child Abduction Rapid Deployment* team. After a series of successes she quickly ran up the ranks until she gained leadership of her own CARD team. She's good; she has an amazing track record."

"So she's got talent. That's good to hear."

"There is something odd about her caseload though."

"Odd how?" I cracked open the Red Bull. I was running on fumes and needed to keep my energy up. I normally don't drink energy drinks but I was sure I wouldn't make it through the day without its caffeinated assistance. Granted I could get the same effect from say cocaine. Both were very similar when you examined them. They were both expensive and a stimulant. The only major difference between the two was one was far more damaging on the body then the other. I should have stuck with the safer of the two but where was I going to find cocaine at this hour and without a time machine to bring me back to the eighties?

"Well, she and her partner often gets cases handed to them that they shouldn't. Cases that would be either better suited for other agents and cases that belonged to other agents. Stuff like that."

"That kind of thing happens though, right?"

"Yeah, but it happens to them a lot more than it should."

"Why doesn't this get noticed?" I asked.

"Because she has a near perfect record for successfully closing those transferred cases." The news was weird, not unsettling weird, but weird like Clint Eastwood could have been James Bond weird. "I also hacked into her email and texts. Turns out Miss FBI lady broke up with her bf three months ago and is now single, lonely, on Tinder and looking for love."

I nearly choked on my Red Bull. "How the hell does that help me on the case?"

"Finding Robby, probably not at all, but after we all save him you know she'll be up for victory sex."

I wanted to shake my head in disgust but in reality I couldn't argue that the idea wasn't appealing. Puzo, who I was having a hard time thinking of as Rachael, was a looker. Back in my *I'm-totally-healthy* days I would've pulled out my *I'm-overly-cocky* attitude and thrown every move I had at her in attempt to spend one night between her thighs. But then again you put any strong woman in a nice suit or a uniform and give her a gun and I fall head over heels in lust. It happened in Afghanistan, it happened in Iraq and it was happening here. I couldn't deny it; I had a type.

"What about her partner, what can you tell me about Agent Thug?"

"Special Agent Kyle Ryman. Age 26. He's been with the agency for five years now; was paired with Puzo almost immediately; was promoted to special agent last year. If he keeps up his success record with Puzo he'll be slated for a CARD team of his own soon."

"So they're good."

"Why do you ask? Are you getting a psychic vibe from them?"

When my mysterious package showed up I got a list of contacts to call upon when I needed them. I got an accountant to handle SRG's bills, a forensic person to call on for icky blood and forensic stuff, Hotwire and a couple others. I never knew how much Hotwire, or the others, were told. This however seemed to prove he knew. "How did you know?"

"When I scanned Puzo's phone she had your file. It had the word--"

"The magic P-Word?"

"Yeah, that one." Hotwire grabbed a Bull of his own

NEVER BEEN TO MARS

from the fridge and cracked it open. "When I was given you as a client I was warned you were..." he paused as he looked for the right word, "Peculiar."

I had to laugh at that.

"Is it true? Are you Psychic?" he asked. He seemed hesitant to ask me that; it was odd. I had never seen, or heard, him be hesitant about anything before. "What am I thinking right now?"

I smirked. Somehow it seemed easier that he knew. "That's not how it works. I touch and object and I see the past." He raised an eyebrow in disbelief. I hobble to the front door and give it a touch. "I touch an object with my bare skin and three things happen. I get a shiver in my spine and twitch in my eye, I provisionally calling it a shivitch, and then I'm thrown into the past."

My vision took hold and I was thrust into the past. From reality I could hear Hotwire talking, asking me questions. "What do you see?" It was peculiar. I've never had someone talk to me during a vision, there has been chatter in the background like conversations or a nattering paranoid war-vet in the back seat beside me, but it was little more than noise in the background. Having someone talking to me directly was different. It was like the narrator of a film; like hearing Morgan Freeman talk while we watch penguins walk. It somehow made everything more personal; more intimate.

"I'm in your apartment," I dictated. "The lights are off and the room is quiet. If it weren't for the hum and glow of your computer this room would be pitch black and deathly silent."

"A black room is all you get?"

"I hear two people climbing the stairs. Your door opens and the apartment lights up. You have the apartment built with smart technology."

"Who is there?"

"You are entering the apartment with another man, a young guy. He's blonde, has a British accent and looks kind of, but not really, like Daniel Craig. You two are chatting, he shoves you playfully and then you...." I cut myself off. I didn't expect to see what I just did. "You and the British man just kissed."

"Okay, that's enough. Please."

"When I release the object," I explained. "The vision fades away and reality returns."

I hobbled back to the kitchen and those magnificent stroganoff meatballs. "I'm sorry about that. I didn't mean to pry into your personal life. I have control issues with what I see."

Hotwire just shrugged. It's wasn't an apathetic shrug but one that simply didn't assign blame. "It wasn't intentional."

"I didn't know."

"I'm not really out, family reason," Hotwire explained, his shoulders making their best imitation of a devil may care shrug. Silence fell between us as neither of us knew what to say next. Thankfully the tenor vocals of Russell Watson singing *Faith of the Heart* cut through the hush. "My search program is done."

> *It's been a long road, getting from there to here*
> *It's been a long time, but my time is finally near*
> *And I will see my dreams come alive at last,*
> *I will touch the sky*
> *And they're not gonna hold me down no more,*
> *No there not gonna change my mind.*

The song was immediately stuck in my head. Damn you, Rod Stewart. Damn you to hell. Oh, who am I kidding? I can't stay mad at you. Isn't Rod Stewart just the best?

Hotwire, Bull in hand, sauntered to the computer. "Be Tee Dub: Don't call it shivitch. That's just silly. Come up with something better." He had a point.

Hotwire plopped down in his chair as his eyes darted from screen to screen, quickly taking in the large amount of data that was there. He returned with a tablet in hand. "Okay we have a lot to read through," he declared as he handed me the tablet. "I've split the material. You take half and I'll tackle the other."

I made my way through the files, started with reports filled with medical jargon I barely understood and kept going until I reached the journals. Dr. Caine had filled these files with his thoughts, his musing and inspirations, both medical and personal, of the last two decades. Everything from his ethical dilemmas to his latest worries about patients, past and present, was recorded. I started with the most recent files and tried to work back.

I feel time has become my enemy. I have been attached to Project: Canaan for many years now, from its earliest development back at the farm to the more recent project at Croxallé. I feel more confident that out procedures have less damaging effects to our patients and their families, but still I often have to think back to the earlier days and the ticking time bombs that still exist in the world.

Ten years ago we stimulated the Lycotta gene in dozens of children as part of our 3rd Triad experiments. The subjects were classified in the Choirs. Most of the subjects, 3rd Choir, have yielded no results, The 2nd Choir have had surprising revelations, but the one that really matter, the ones I fear, are the 1st Choir. These are the subjects we expect great success from. That's our problem.

The very nature of the Lycotta gene means that we have no clue as what properties the emergence will possess. Some of them will be deforming, some of them will be powerful and many of them will be dangerous. This is what keeps me up at night. Our mandate is exploit the Lycotta gene for whatever gain possible so long as we keep our parent company hidden. If children start becoming dangerous because of us, our secret will be out. The world will change.

> Luckily there are only four of the 1st Choir children. Four souls we have to watch but all it takes is one. I have two in my area, one home schooled and another attending public school: Child #10248. I pass his school throughout the day. I know I'm supposed to ignore them, allow security to maintain a presence but I can't help it. I helped bring this child into the world, I help stimulate his gene. I feel connected. So I stop and watch him, quietly seated in my Mustang, waiting for the day his power emerges.

What. The. Fuck. I reread the entry twice, desperately trying to make sense of this. Emergence? Lycotta Gene? Powers? Caine was watching Robby because he was going to have powers? Robby has powers?

"What do we have on Project: Canaan or the Lycotta gene?" I called out, suddenly not caring if I was being rude or not.

"I've got some files here." I moved over to Hotwire and looked at the screen.

Visegar File: #38759846
Project: Canaan
Mission Statement: To stimulate the Lycotta gene found in certain humans for the benefit of achieving enhanced-human attributes.

I read the file, the words making littler sense the more time I spent staring at it. From what I could decipher from the medical jargon there was a gene in Robby called Lycotta. It could be used to spark super-powers.

"Is this real or did we stumble onto his fledgling sci-fi writing career?" My tech guy said exactly what I was thinking. This was unreal. "This file has your sister's name on it. It says Robby is an experiment."

"That's insane."

Was it though? Was it really? A couple years ago I

would have said psychic visions would have been impossible but here I was touching objects and reading the past. I'm a super-powered human and I wasn't the only one. Six months ago I met Agent Price and he could shoot beams from his eyes. He had a look that could kill. In a world with laser eyes and psychics were superhero children and evil medical science really that out of place? It was driving me mad, all of it, and worst of all it was getting me no closer to finding my nephew.

"So have you ever heard of Visegar Company?" Hotwire asked. I shook my head. "Basic searches are turning up blank and my internet-bred spiderbots are being bounced back."

"Spiderbots?"

"It's my own personal search program. It sends spiders out across the web." His voice trailed off as my look of confusion grew. "All you need to know is my typey-typey isn't working."

Hotwire shook his head as I rubbed the bridge of my nose with both hands. "This is just so much information here and none of its getting us anywhere."

I looked at Hotwire and listened. If he had an idea, that would be great because my detective skills were once again proving to be the least useful thing in the world. "We might be digging too deep here," he began. "Let's pull back and look at what we know. Croxallé is keeping an eye on Robby. They didn't take him."

"It's actually the opposite," I interjected. "They want to keep him safe."

"Exactly. Now somebody else wants him; somebody who was willing to nab him and cover up his tracks with a murder."

"Burt Reynolds!"
"What?"
"Nothing. Keep going."

Hotwire stared at me for a few moments, unsure of what I just said. He slowly started up again, quickly regaining his cadence. "Croxallé had what somebody else wanted: the kids."

"They got the data they needed from the files; something about a drug trial." I racked my brain to try and remember the name. It was long and medically and began with a D or a B. "The Tenasine trial." Okay, I was way off there.

"Okay good." His fingers dashed across his keys. "I got something here. According to the FDA it's a pre-natal drug used to strengthen pregnant woman. It's also shown signs of lowering the chance of at-risk disabilities or diseases."

"And what does it say in Dr. Caine's file of truthy truth?"

Hotwire clacked away on the keyboard, the crisp snapping of the keys the only sound in his silent apartment. "I have no clue. The drug name is popping up in way too many files. I'll have to go through some of this more thoroughly but I do have this."

A large file splashed across his wall of screen. It was a medical document that documented the trials. A long list of names, each with a corresponding number, filled the list, each an access point to databases of information.

"This is about the Tenasine trial," Hotwire explained. "This file has hundreds of names, but what I did gather is that there are two medical centers doing the trial, both owned by Croxallé. We have Proce Medical and the Delahon Clinic."

"Whoever went after Proce Medical might go after the second clinic?"

"I think that's a safe bet."

"I should call Puzo." I grabbed my iphone and fished in my jacket for the Puzo's card.

"Um...Cowboy." Hotwire pointed at the screen. "You need to see this name."

Annie Belledin. The two words sat there on the screen, staring at me, taunting me. I tried to ignore it, to push it into the back of my mind until I could deal with this mess, and dialed my cell. "We need to find out what this drug does." I mumbled.

NEVER BEEN TO MARS

The phone picked up with Puzo business like demeanor. "This is Puzo."

"It's Ben. I'm keeping up my end of the bargain." Well, the keeping her informed part. "I need you to keep an eye out on a place called Delahon Clinic. Whoever killed Dr. Caine might hit there too."

"You really are psychic aren't you?" Puzo replied. "I'm already at Delahon Clinic. There's been another murder."

Chapter 07
Burt-on-Burt Action

Another cab ride put me at Delahon Clinic. Between the police lights and the sirens the place was lit up more than Hotwire's night club. It wasn't until I stepped out of Torri's, and heard the loud thumping dance music, that I realized how late it had gotten. It was way passed my bed time and I didn't see my night ending anytime soon. I tossed more bills at another faceless cab driver and climbed out. I had been to a crime scene before, as early as this afternoon, but arriving at one after the cops have is a different event. There is the media circus, the massive number of looky-loos and that's before you cross the police tape. Once you cross that threshold you get uniformed beat cops, detectives, ambulance workers and CSI and, if you're a good boy and very lucky, you get the FBI.

The clinic wasn't what I expected. Delahon Clinic and Proce Medical, despite being funded by the same company, had two different looks. Proce was a higher-end medical facility. Delahon was a clinic, reserved for those without insurance or means. Ryman was waiting for me at the tape. He held up the plastic barrier, urged me to duck underneath, and escorted me to Puzo.

"Who was killed?" I asked, unsure how I was allowed to act around Ryman.

"You're psychic. Don't you already know?" His reply carried a hint of a growl.

NEVER BEEN TO MARS

He didn't like me. Maybe I should try harder to win him over or maybe, and this is just because he's got a gun and knows how to us it, I should listen to reason and let it be.

"Hey, come on. I'm only trying to help." Reason doesn't have a great track record.

"Really? And every other asshole psychic who wasted a cop's time said the exact same thing." I wanted to defend myself but he didn't give me the chance. "Oh, but you're different. Your powers are real."

His mocking continued as he pushed his palm against his forehead and feigned a surprised look. "You can see a place far, far away. It's red, everywhere, and cold. I sense lots of cold and death. There is no life here. I must be viewing Mars."

I knew what he's talking about. When my powers manifested I started looking up psychics on the net. Some of the most famous, or infamous, cases involved men and women claiming to see in their mind worlds far beyond our sight. Mars was a common example. No one could ever disprove their claim because they've never been to mars, no one has.

"The only reason you're allowed past that line is because my boss lady seems to think you're useful. So why don't we both play nice until this is all over."

Yeah, I should've listened to reason.

He brought me through the Clinic to the upper floors, up the stairs and into a hallway. For the second time in half as many days I saw a dead doctor lying on the ground. Except this time there were two more bodies scattered around. The walls were littered with bullet holes, the halls filled with blood splatters, exit wounds from bullets, and the floor was scattered with broken furniture and discarded equipment. Puzo eyed me from across the hallway and I'll be damned if she didn't smile.

"Mr. Thompson," she said as she approached. "You couldn't time your vision any better could you? Give me a little notice next time."

"I... it doesn't work like that," I stammered. "And please call me Ben."

"Of course it doesn't. Okay so what happened here is..."

I cut her off with a frantic wave of my hand. "Please, don't. I need to see this for myself."

I pulled off my glove and looked around. I was almost scared to see what had happened there; three dead and a hospital clinic that looked like Iraq. My upcoming migraine aside, this was not going to be pleasant to witness. I looked over the place with my mundane vision first, wanting to deduce what I could with my normal two eyes before using my third.

One doctor, female, lay dead on the ground. Just like Caine she was in nice clothing, sturdy shoes, and a white doctor's lab coat to cover it all. She'd been scared; you could see it on her face, and not just for the moment of death. A look of terror stays with you; it haunts you even past your demise. She lay on her chest, two bullet holes in her back and one in the back of her skull.

The two men were clearly security: black pants, black jacket, navy blue shirt and a holster attached to a gun belt. Each had cuts, stabs and gun wounds in legs and arms. There was firefight and these men lost.

"Were did it start?" I asked.

"The doctor lady came up the elevator; the shooter came up the stairs."

I nodded at her and moved to the elevator. With a deep breath I touched the elevator doors. This was going to be messy.

With the usual shiver and twitch my vision began. I was inside the elevator watching as the female medical professional, Doctor Janice Anthony, panicked as the steel carriage rises. She grabbed the elevator phone and slammed her fist into a panic button. "We're under attack. He's coming up the stairs. Third Floor; third floor."

The metal doors opened to the two armed security men there to greet her. One grabbed her by the shoulder and pulled her out while the other ushered innocent people into the safety of offices and rooms.

One vision faded and as I touched the door to the stairwell a second one started, the new vision picking up mere seconds from where the last one ended. As the two security guards ushered people to safety as the stairwell door handle rattled as it turned. The guards quickly drew their firearms and leveled them at the stairwell. It was like watching the police station scene from *Terminator*. The still moment before Arnie burst through the door and starts to shoot up the place. The hallway was still and quiet, the only sound from the rattle of the firearms quivering from nerves. I stared at the door, wondering what was about to emerge that had frightened the doctor so much. I was expecting an Arnie or a Stallone, maybe even a Keanu Reeves dressed in black with guns strapped to every available inch of his body. With a startling crash the door smashed open, the horror emerged. He was a young man with a fresh wide-eyed face, brown curly hair, jeans and a blue shirt with rainbow shoulders.

This was Mark Wahlberg, not just any Marky Mark but Dirk Diggler from *Boogie Nights* Mark Wahlberg.

Dirk Diggler stormed into the hallway with a pistol of his own, the barrel firing round after round down the hall as he stormed onto the third floor. The bullets caused the security to scatter, diving to the side or ducking behind a medical cart. Dirk's gun seemed to fire nonstop, covering the makeshift battlefield with gunfire. As the pistol made the inevitable click, the one a firearm makes when there is no more round to fire, Dirk's hand was on a doorknob, cranked it opened. He ducked into an office and quickly reloaded the gun.

The two securities scrambled to recover, climbing to their feet and firing down the hall as they tried to retreat. Dirk was patient, using the office as cover he stood out of harm's way and waited for a lull. When the gunfire paused Dirk emerged. The more I watched the more it became clear of the large difference of skill between Faux-Mark and the two security guards. The rent-a-cops were trained to shoot but their skills rested in crowd control. They were keeping everybody back but when they fired on their attacker their hands quivered, their barrel shook and their aim faltered. Faux-Mark was different. He was trained to kill. He moved without hesitation, never vacillating in his shots, and never letting the heat of battle unnerve him.

Dirk spun out of the office and fired. His first shot ripped through a guard's arm and sent him spinning back to the floor. His arm shifted as he fired on the second guard. The bullets pierced his knee and forced his legs out from underneath him. The kneeless guard bellowed in pain as he crumpled and collapsed on the floor like his partner.

Dr. Anthony turned and ran, her screams echoing down the hallway. Dirk leveled his gun at her back. His gun fired twice. The two bullets ripped through her back. Dirk marched over to the body and lowered the barrel. He aimed the gun at the back of her head and squeezed off another round into her skull.

"Two in the heart and one in the head, it's the only way to make sure they're dead," Dirk rhymed. He repeated the process with the guards, firing two into each of their hearts and one into their heads. Like the signature in an email the rhyming words followed each kill.

My visions expanded the fight as my hands crossed the third floor, touching anything it could. I saw how, before he died, the injured guard fought back, smashing a steel tray into the side of Dirk's head, how the guard swung again and again trying to put the actor's doppelganger down but the clone was better than that, better then the guard. I watched as the guard's next swing hit only air as Faux-Mark ducked beneath it, I watched as Faux-Mark grabbed a discarded scalpel from the fallen gear and struck back with it, the surgical tool slicing through skin as easy as butter. Dirk moved with great speed, slicing at the guard's arm and legs until the poor rent-a-cop could barely move. Dirk retrieved his gun, and just like the two others before, finished the last guard with a trinity of bullets and a simple rhyme.

I had seen some violent visions before but most of

them involved my own past. I'd touch a watch or my dog tags, something I had in my days of service, and I'd be instantly brought back to before. Being one of the Rangers, marching into Afghanistan in 2001 and then into Iraq in 2003. That was war, this was murder. This was a whole new level of brutality. I hobbled into Dr. Anthony's office and tapped on her keyboard. A shiver and a twitch escorted me back into my visions. Just like Burt did at Proce, Mark walked straight to the computer, copied the Tenasine trial files and then wiped the hard drive. My vision faded.

"Mr. Thompson," Puzo asked, "what did you see?"

I started to describe what I saw, feeling a little like William Dafoe in that movie about murderous brothers as I re-enact with fingers for guns. As my little display ended I turned back to the FBI and pointed at Ryman. "I'll start the ass kissing with you."

You know that guy who uses movie quotes in regular life regardless of who will actually get the reference, I'm that guy. I couldn't help myself. Ryman wasn't impressed and if Puzo found it funny she was doing her damndest not to show it. In fact her not-funny face was so well practiced that I actually believed it was real.

"You done, funny man?" I sheepishly nodded. "Okay you've confirmed what we knew and something that we didn't."

"This makes two attacks in one day on small medical buildings, each of which was owned by Croxallé," I interjected. "So what do we do from here?"

Ryman frowned at the word we. Puzo eyed her partner before she looked back at me. "We started searching files and police reports. We came across a small lead. Apparently the Delahon Clinic filed numerous complaints against a small construction company called Hinsworth Construction."

She paused to see my reaction; there wasn't one. I stood there waiting for the other shoe to drop. "It employs a man named Greg Hazeltine."

Damn it. There it was. I hadn't seen or heard from

Greg in nearly two years and now he's back in my life. The FBI wants him and now it seems he might be connected to Robby's kidnapping. "Jesus. So you're going to smack him up? Bust him? Slap him around until he talks?"

I didn't expect Ryman's frown to possibly get any bigger but somehow he found a way. "We don't beat suspects in the FBI," he scowled. "We don't slap them around."

"Can I then?"

Puzo cut us off. "We've just got one problem. We can't find him."

"Yeah, we've had that same problem for years." After he knocked up Annie he vanished. We used everything we had at our disposal but he just vanished. We couldn't find him. "He's evading the FBI. How does that work?"

"Well we have a three state APB out on him, if anybody sees him he's ours but until then we keep searching using every angle we have."

Ryman and Puzo turn back to their team and starts getting updates. They had an entire team at their disposal working to find Robby and I was just standing there spinning my wheels. It was infuriating. The deeper I dug the further away I found myself. "This is getting us nowhere." I muttered.

I leaned against a wall and slumped to the floor. What good were my gifts, my powers, if I couldn't even save my nephew? Puzo gave me an eye and plopped down beside me. "You know your contaminating the crime scene right? Any fibers from your coat or jacket may pop up in the crime report."

I tried to get up but she stopped with a hand on my shoulder. "It's too late now. Look, you've been helpful here. You know that, right?"

I stared at the wall across from me, at the bullet holes. "See those holes, a TV detective would have used super CSI tech to analyse it, found a serial number and traced it to the seedy gun shop owner who sold the bullets."

Puzo shook her head. "Ever think you watch too much TV?"

"Oh, I know I do." There was no sense denying what she already knew. "So what will your tech guys get from these bullet holes?"

"We'll get bullet size, which will help narrow down the gun. Then we do what we can to track the bullet to the gun and the gun to..." She paused for a heartbeat, wrinkling her nose before completing he sentence. "And the gun to Burt Reynolds or Mark Wahlberg. That's how mundane police work goes. You gather evidence, mostly small pieces, and you carefully examine each. Then you build a case. One thing leads you to another, then another and so on until you find the culprit, save the child or arrest the murderer."

The words ran through my head. You gather evidence and you carefully examine it. One thing leads you to another, then another and so on. That's what I'd been doing all day, running from one clue to another and another. I was chipping away at a mystery involving Robby and Annie but I wasn't sure it was the right one. All of the advice she gave me was for mundane investigation; did it really apply to me? I mean what I did wasn't that much different then what they did, as long as we didn't bring skill into the equation. I use my visions to gather evidence and build a case. I mean her people examined the bodies and the crime scene, so did I. Her people tracked the battle and everybody's movements, same here, and her people examined each bullet and...

Oh hell! I jolted up from the wall. That's what I'd missed. I, awkwardly, climbed to my feet. How could I have been so stupid? Did I really suck this much at being a detective? My hand trembled in excitement. "I need to see the bullets."

"The bullets? Why?"

"I missed a crucial part of investigating. I'm not looking at all the evidence. Think about it. I walked through the crime scene, I placed everybody and tracked their movements and then I stopped. I didn't follow through. It's like hitting a golf ball."

"I haven't golfed in years, Thompson," Puzo explained.

"That's okay, neither have I; blame the bum-ass leg." Using my cane as a 2 Wood facsimile I preformed a mock swing. "In golf you need to follow through with your swing, you can't just stop when you make contact or else the ball slices to the left or right."

"What does this have to do with anything?"

"I'm the club; when I hit the ball I'm not following through, so instead of flying straight I veer to the right. Wait, am I the ball instead? Am I the club and the ball? Okay my metaphor is falling apart on me. I haven't been fully investigating; I've been making contact with my visions and running off half-cocked."

"First of all, in that metaphor you're probably the golfer." Puzo was already on her feet moving for the CSI men. "Secondly, if I understand, you want to touch the bullets and get a vision."

"Exactly," I dramatically declared. "I want to visionize the bullets."

"That's not a word," she yelled back. Puzo returned with a tray of small plastic bags. "Each of these contains a bullet fired in this hallway or a discarded casing."

I smiled. I tried to clap Puzo on the shoulder, friendly thanks of sorts, but she pulled away again. "I said no touching, psychic boy."

"Oh right, your secrets." I'd never met anyone who actively tried to avoid my touch, aside from the men and woman who are ashamed of my injury and try to avoid me because of it, and I wasn't sure I liked it, especially when my lonely self would have broken a great many laws just to get my hands on Puzo's body; Puzo's consenting body. I had to correct myself. That last part sounded creepier then I intended.

"A girl's allowed to have her secrets, boyo." She pointed to the bullets with a gloved covered finger. "So we have to do this one at a time. Each bullet needs to go back into the bag we got it from."

NEVER BEEN TO MARS

We went through the bullet one at a time. Puzo would throw them out and I would carefully take it into my hand. I'd shiver and twitch and dive into the past. The first wave were bullets from the security guards, the casing and crumpled rounds escorting me to a vision of security officers in preparation. Some rounds showed a guard filling empty magazines, others showed defense procedures and one showed an intercompany memo warning of the attack.

Then I touched the bullets fired from the assassin.

The first bullet of his I touched took me out of the clinic and into an unknown room. The room was your stereotypical hotel room; a dirty bed not far from the door, a small desk, and glowing neon sign out the window that flashed the words Joe's Dinner over and over, the electrical hum an annoyance akin to the buzz of an absurdly large insect. Faux-Burt sat the desk; his Glock pistol lay on the table to the right, near the room phone and a hotel pad of paper, and his cell to the left, both out of the way but not out of reach. Before him were numerous empty magazines and a box of 9mm ammunition. One by one he thumbed another round into the mag while he watched the floor bolted television. The screen danced with familiar images of the real Dirk Diggler and Jack Horner.

Jack looked at the camera and said: "You know this is the film I want them to remember me by." With each word the real Burt spoke, the line forever captured on film for the annals of time, Faux-Burt mimicked. The doppelganger knew each word like he'd seen the film countless times. The cell phone rang. Faux-Burt muted his film self and answered the cellular device.

"Lieutenant Chapman."

"We have need of your skills. We are texting the location to you. When you're done report back to Major Heins."

The line went dead, seconds later the phone vibrated. The promised message had arrived. Faux-Burt tapped on his screen and intently read his next mission. He climbed up from his chair and reached into his green duffle bag that lay on the bed. He withdrew a round suppressor and screwed it onto the pistol's barrel. I returned back to reality.

I tried the same with the other bullets, carefully touching them and searching for a vision but I got nothing new. With each round I got a glimpse of the horrifying gun battle or another look of the eerie mirror effect of Burt watching Burt. With a splitting headache I dropped the last bullet back into its plastic bag. "So I have a lead, I just don't have any way to give you an official police connection."

"Tell me what you got and I'll worry about linking it to the investigation."

I explained to her the seedy motel room, the unsettling ammunition loading and the creepy Burt-on-Burt action. She just listened, nodded and raised an eyebrow when I mentioned the words Burt-on-Burt action. In her defense I probably could have used a better description.

"What was the name of the motel?"

I closed my eyes and tried to remember, focusing back into the room. I could visualize the dark room and seedy atmosphere but I couldn't figure out the name. I thought back to the paper by the room phone, the words on the pad of paper slowly forming in my mind. "The Traveler's Motel."

"Ryman, you're with me and magic boy." She pointed to her other agents and barked orders, telling them to finish up here and report back to her when they got results. I slipped back on my glove and followed her down the stairs. God, I hate stairs.

Chapter 08
Homeless Orphans and Sick Puppies

Ryman steered the car through the street. Puzo sat in the passenger seat looking at her phone. I sat in the back staring out the window at the nearly empty streets. A city never sleeps; it just beats to a different drum at night. I remember in my younger days I thrived at night, existing everywhere in the shadow of darkness. I would be at a club picking up women or at a bar causing trouble. Nowadays I was like a troll, rarely emerging from my cave.

Puzo and Ryman talked between themselves, coordinating how they'd approach the motel and how they'd deal with the attendant. I tried to listen in, I wanted to compare it to the TV dialogue, but between a headache from overexertion of mental powers and the unending thought of Puzo's jacket I couldn't stay focused. Puzo's jacket was within my reach. If I was careful I could touch her suit, get a vision, and figure out what she was hiding from me. The question wasn't *could I*? That would be obvious, I was a superhero (name and theme song pending), and of course I could. The question was *should I*?

Reason told me not to but curiosity demanded to know. Like always, the debate wasn't a civilized event, it was a seeming endless stretch of overpass highway, a dangerous looking stretch where only the most skilled survived, filled with the everyday traffic of cars, vans, trucks and even the occasional 18-wheelers.

Speeding along the stretch, going faster than anyone should, was a highly modified black 1986 step-side GMC Sierra Grande with 4x4 drive. The driver, Reason, tore through traffic with a roar, swerving through traffic with an unmatched level of precision.

She was hiding something from me. In my head, I couldn't help but wonder if she was involved in Robby's disappearance.

The black pick-up jolted as it was rammed from behind by a 1969 black Dodge Charger. With a roar of glee the muscle car and its driver, the undefeated Curiosity, veered away only to ram the truck again.

Puzo agreed to work with us and she had been keeping us in the loop. She could cut off those privileges if we broke her trust.

Sparks flew as the Sierra Grande grinded against the Charger, the power behind the truck forcing the muscle car into oncoming traffic. Curiosity's hands moved rapidly as he steered the car to the left, missing an oncoming Kia by mere inches. He slammed his foot down on the accelerator as the Charger roared forward, gaining speed as he barreled headfirst towards the oncoming traffic. Curiosity tried to get back into the proper lane but the Sierra Grande was blocking the way. Reason wouldn't let him pass.

What if she had been keeping something crucial from me? What if it was a government thing?

With a hard pull right, the Charger crossed back across the divide and slammed hard into the truck's side. He had seconds before the van barreling at him collided head first, seconds to force the truckzilla back.

She admitted she had a secret she didn't want to tell me. She had even been avoiding my touch. Only guilty people did that.

Again and again he slammed the side of his car into the truck, each blow causing the truck further back. With a final slam the Sierra Grande gave way, pulling away from the

Charger, and allowing it to enter its proper lane, just as the van zoomed by; another mere miss tacked onto the Charger's history.

She could turn on me just for doing it.

The truck slammed slowed for a bit, letting the Charger pass by, then picked up speed. Curiosity slammed the nose of the truck into the back wheels of the muscle car. Reason felt his world spin beneath him as the car spun 90 degrees.

This history with Croxallé and Visegar seemed to go deep. She could have been a double agent and turned on me anyways.

Reversal! Reason's hands quickly pulled on the wheel, his right foot pumping the break as his left slammed on the clutch, the car spinning the last 90 degrees until he now faced completely the opposite direction. He grabbed the shifter, slammed the car into reverse and slammed on the gas. The Charger roared to life and peeled backwards as all the traffic he'd left in his dust came barreling down him. Curiosity sneered as the Charger sped past him, in reverse a-la-Nic-Cage, down the highway. Reason sped by in the black muscle car and couldn't help but laugh as he flipped the bird to the truck's driver.

You don't want to get on the bad side of the FBI. They can make your life a living hell.

Reason slammed on the gas, calling on the dozens of illegal modifications for power and causing the Sierra Grande to pick up an unheard of amount of speed. Like a bullet it shot forward, flying right at the Charger for the kill.

I nearly missed one piece of evidence by being a bad detective, I wasn't about to miss another.

Curiosity had less than a second to time this. If he swerved to early then the truck could simply alter its direction and still slam into him, if he altered too late he'd be road rash. Praying he was choosing the right time, Curiosity pulled hard on the wheel yet again, the Charger pulling a backwards turn to the right, the truck's left, as the Sierra Grande blew past it. Curiosity pulled the e-brake, turned the wheel, and shifted into first as he did a dramatic 180 turn in the middle of the highway. Once again facing the right way, he slammed on the gas. The car roared with power, the front wheels lifting off the ground, and fired forward after the escaping truck.

This is Robby. I had to know she wasn't involved.

The Charger slammed into the truck, forcing the pickup to the right. The steel side of the truck pushing a mini-van full of homeless orphans and sick puppies through the guardrail and off the overpass. A ball of fire erupted from below as the van crashed into the ground and exploded.

If she was involved, it would be easier to get the drop on her if I knew ahead of time.

The Charger pulled away, driving to the furthest safest point available, only to steer back into the truck. The two vehicles slammed together. The Sierra Grande was bigger and stronger but try as it might it couldn't hold up to the sheer power that curiosity had brought with it. The Truck spun ninety degrees and the vehicle, unable to keep upright, flipped onto its side and rolled down the highway like a tossed set of dice. It bounced across the concrete, each spring smashing another piece of glass and breaking another piece of steel. The truck finally came to a halt, upright on the road, and Reason sighed in relief, an emotion that lasted only until he heard the air horn of an 18 wheeler. The Sierra Grande was big but an 18 wheeler was bigger. The tractor trailer tore through the Sierra Grande like a hot knife through butter, or some other cooking simile, and scattered the pieces across the menacing stretch of road. With a laugh normally reserved for the subjects of Spy vs Spy, Curiosity, the victor and reigning champion, sped away into the distance.

Had my debate just killed a mini-van full of homeless orphans and sick puppies? My inner mind was beginning to worry me. I mean, that had to be a sign of something bad, right? People don't just imagine accidently running orphans and puppies off the road do they? I really needed to talk to someone and soon. But first I had to worry about this vision. I pulled off my gloves and carefully reached forward, my fingers gently caressing the jacket material. The familiar shiver shot up my back and my eyes began to twitch as I fell into my vision.

Puzo and I were in her office in an FBI building, and she slammed me against the wall. Her lips met mine and we kissed. It wasn't a peck on the cheek or a soft, gentle kiss. It was a passion filled kiss that bordered on violent. I hungrily kissed her back, moving my way down her neck, teasing her already excited nerves with the tip of my tongue. She pulled away, just enough to be out of reach, and ripped open my shirt, a move that sent buttons flying everywhere. Her fingers teased my ripped chest. I scooped her up by her legs and carried her to the bed. We both fell to the mattress and continued our powerful convention of lips. She squealed with glee as I pinned her arms above her head with one of my hands and unbuttoned her blouse with my other.

I pulled my hand back from her suit a little too quickly, as Puzo turned and gave me a quizzical look. She looked at my bare hand and frowned. She might have guessed I just touched her. She had told me not to touch her and I couldn't help it; I touched her. Okay, that sounded dirtier then I intended.

I should have been planning damage control but I couldn't rip my mind from what I had just seen. None of what I had just watched play out in my mind had ever happened. Had that been the future? My powers don't normally work like that; they always show the past. Always, that is, except once.

Six months ago, after I humbly saved the day, Price drove me home. He had given me a business card and told me to call him if I ever needed a serious favour. The moment I had touched the card, I dove into a vision. This one had come with a shiver up my left leg and a twitch in my right hand and, for the first time ever, a look at the future.

There I had stood, holding the card and dialling the number in my iPhone. The line had rang three times before whoever I had been calling picked up. I heard Price's voice on the other end. "Thompson, what's wrong?"

"I'm calling in that favour. I'm in trouble."

That was the only time I'd ever seen the future until today. But the more I thought about it, the more it didn't make sense. My spine shivered, not my leg, and my eye twitched instead of my hand. The signs pointed to a regular vision; an everyday regular mundane supernatural otherworldly vision. It's amazing how quickly your definition of regular can shift.

The shiver and twitch weren't the only anomalies. Certain facts in the vision didn't make sense. The first, and most flattering, was my bare chest. Puzo ripped open my shirt and revealed to the world a perfect, well formed, bare chest. It was the peak of physical appearance. I wasn't. Even in my prime I wasn't that good. Then there was how I carried her to the bed. As hot as that was, it was almost impossible that I would ever be able to do that. Elaine said that if I keep up my exercise I should be able to forgo the cane one day, but I will never be that strong. And speaking of the bed, where the hell had it come from? What FBI office has a queen size bed in it?

This vision made no sense; a version of me that really wasn't that me and beds that magically appeared like the wenches for my pirate in my internal debate. Oh, bite me on the ass! This wasn't what happened. This is what she wanted to happen. I just saw her fantasy.

Wait, what? Did Rachael Puzo have the hots for me? Sexy FBI lady with a gun wanted to jump my bones? Nice. Nice.

See, now what was I supposed to do with that? Should I have made a move? Should I have become a forward acting man and tried to get with her? For all I knew she was attracted to me because of the way I was; for being the guy that wouldn't be that forward. Maybe she didn't like forward men and if I tried to make a move I would have turned her off. Maybe I should have done the complete opposite and just ignored the situation, let her make the first move. But what if she didn't and I had missed this golden opportunity because she thought I didn't like her? What I had seen was a drop of water in an ocean of time. Maybe that was her reaction when she first saw me, maybe she didn't feel that way anymore. It's like when you're at bar or at a party and you see that cute blonde girl in the corner. She's smoking hot, has everything in the right place and is giving the world that I'm good to go vibe. You saunter over, talk to her and within minutes you realize what type of person she's like, and suddenly you're thinking there is no way I am sticking anything of mine into her. What if it had been like that?

I had just found out from a vision that the girl I touched liked or had liked me, and I didn't know how to respond: First World Psychic Problems. Super-touchy psychic powers, or psychometry to the rest of the world, are a curse. Still, all worrying aside, she thought I was hot, or used to. I could deal with that. And as long as I survived the inevitable murderous attempts of Faux-Burt and Faux-Mark I might even be able to do something about it.

Celebrities causing murder and mayhem, that would be just what TMZ would have wanted to get on film. That had brought up the question of how their appearance was important though. I knew that they were killing for the Tenasine trial files, something in there was important, but why were they killing as Dirk Duggler and Jack Horner? Why Mark Wahlberg and Burt Reynolds and why that movie? I saw the Faux-Burt watching the Boogie Nights movie on TV. Was he practising the voice? And why were there multiple assassins as multiple roles? Did that mean that there was a secret cabal of assassins obsessed with Paul Thomas Anderson movies? Was it like ordering a Ninja Turtle for a kid's party?

"Hi, I'd like somebody killed with style. Could you have Burt Reynolds come kill a guy for me?"

"I'm sorry; Burt is unavailable at the moment. We do have Daniel Day-Lewis from There Will be Blood or Adam Sandler from Punch-Drunk Love." Somehow I didn't fear the Adam Sandler assassin.

The black FBI car came to a halt outside the Traveler's Motel. I gently put my brown cowboy hat on my head as

I climbed out of the car, my legs using my trusty cane for support. I looked around and instantly cringed. This motel looked disgusting. It wasn't that it was dirty or that trash was laying everywhere. It was the colour of the walls, the chipped paint on the door and the neon light that just made the place look off putting; sketchy even. I pocketed my gloves as we hobbled into the main office. By we, I obviously mean me because those two FBI agents didn't need to hobble with their ever so perfect legs. Snooty show offs.

I looked around the parking lot as I approached, seeing if I could spot Burt or Mark anywhere but sadly detective work is never that easy. Think how weird of a show *24* would have been if it was.

"Okay CTU. A terrorist has a nuke. We need to find him before he blows up the President during his tour of the Fox Network headquarters."

"Um....Jack. He's right there, across the street."

"Oh. Sweet. Now we can spend more time on Terri's amnesia and Kim fighting a cougar." God I love *24*. Seriously, I legit love *24*.

There were more people out on the street at that late of an hour then I expected. There were a couple guys making what was obviously an illegal deal in the shadows and the most pathetic looking hooker standing beside two blue SUVs. I always suspected that hookers were supposed to look hot while not looking obvious that they were hookers. This woman looked like she was from a bad porno. The tube top and jean jacket, dolphin shorts and knee high tube socks, and the wavy blonde to top it all off. She was something from the seventies. It was almost laughable.

I ignored them and headed inwards. I touched the glass door and dived into a vision. A young red-headed girl entered the motel's office and looked around. She wore simple clothes, blue jean, a white shirt and black jacket, and didn't really stand out save for the jeweled butterfly necklace she wore. She reached the empty counter and looked around for assistance.

NEVER BEEN TO MARS

I let go of the door and returned to reality. I was hoping for a vision of Faux-Burt or Faux-Mark but all I was getting was this girl. That was the problem with super-touchy psychic powers. I didn't always get what I wanted. It's the same lesson the Rolling Stones had been teaching us since July of 1969.

No, you can't always get what you want
But if you try sometime, you just might find
You get what you need

Puzo and Ryman both threw up glares at the attendant, asking for information on his clients and permission to go into the rooms. The attendant, a grey haired man with thick black rimmed glasses and a shirt with a 70's style V-neck, said no. He threw up a glare of his own and started quoting laws and his rights. I ignore both sides as I touched the counter. My shiver and twitch brought me back to the red-headed girl.

She stood by this very counter, her hands drumming the top. "Hello?" she called out. "Is anybody here? Um...the ice machine is broken. Can you help me?"

She tapped the silver bell twice, the ring echoing throughout the room, and continued to look around. She stepped around the counter and started to walk into the back room "Anybody here?"

Reality returned. Why did fate, Spongebob or whatever it was that decided what visions I got, keep wanting me to see this girl? What was I missing? I looked around, my attention temporally drawn away from the case at hand. I looked the entrance as the door opened. The obvious hooker was stepping into the office. Our eyes locked as I saw her face for the first time. She had wide eyes, a fresh face and kind of looked like Heather Graham.

Heather Graham isn't one of those actresses whose careers I eagerly follow, she's no Rosario Dawson, but on the flip side I don't hate her either. I mean she's cute and a decent actress so I'll watch a movie if she's in it. I liked her in *Austin*

Powers 2, she was wonderful in *The Hangover* and apparently she was nominated for her role in *Boogie Nights...*
>*Boogie Nights?*
>*Boogie Nights!*
>Oh shit. That was Heather Graham.

Chapter 09
Heather Graham has a Gun

Heather's eyes narrowed as she seemed to recognize me. As her hand darted inside her jacket I grabbed Puzo and dove behind the counter. "Gun!"

Ryman didn't even question me, he just reacted. He dove to the side as Heather, who I assumed it was safe to refer to as Faux-Heather, drew a gun and opened fire. The motel attendant, seeing the gun, dropped to the floor and started to crawl into the back. I'm ashamed to say that my reaction time to the gun fight was nowhere near Ranger standard but in my defense I'm out of practice. Puzo wasn't. Her gun was in her hand, safety thumbed off and rhyming off rounds as she returned fire. She needed to either drop Faux-Heather now or at least push her back. Ryman was defenceless in the open. I peaked around to see Faux-Heather backing out of the office, her gun still rattling off rounds as she waved to the two SUVs.

Ryman climbed to his feet and slid behind the counter, his gun already in his hand. He cursed in surprise. "Holy shit, Heather Graham has a gun."

Who thought I'd ever hear those words.

The gunfire went silent for a moment. Puzo looked over at me while Ryman called for back-up on his cell. "Good catch."

"Today I've seen a murderous Burt, a killer Mark and then my eyes fall on Heather Graham at the same motel that

Burt was at," I bragged. "After today I might never trust a single celebrity again."

"You're probably safer that way."

The sound of burst fire ripped through the office. Ryman peaked around to get a look. "Two men at the door, both have SMG and tact-vests. Heather Graham has back-up."

"She was talking to two SUV's," I explained. "Faux-Burt was supposed to meet up a Major Heins. This may be them."

"Two SUVs and possibly more on the way mean we could be dealing with eight armed people minimum. We got to coordinate this." He looked over at the motel attendant. "Is there a back way out of here?" He just shook his head no.

Puzo dug a Bluetooth headset from her pocket and slipped it into her ear. Ryman quickly followed suit. "Use it to call out positions."

Both agents popped up from behind the counter and opened fire, their 9mm rounds forcing the mysterious gunman back behind their cover. I wasn't going to sit around defenceless while the professional did all the gun fighting. My eyes fell on the brown wooden stock of a sawed-off shotgun, a lupara. I grabbed it and felt the usual shiver and twitch.

"Not now," I groaned as the vision took over. "Now's not the time."

There are three things in this world that as a psychic I hate putting my hands on. The first is a man's genitals; that one has less to do with being psychic and more to do with my own issues. The second is a wedding ring. Be it a happy marriage or a troubled one, the ring is the catalyst of every emotion the marriage holds. The third is a gun. Guns are built on emotion. When you fight to defend what you love or when you fight to kill what you hate, everything you do with a gun is emotionally driven. Fear, love, hate, and honour. A gun reeks with it all. It's why when my fingers grabbed the gun my head nearly exploded. A thousand screams of echoes past bounced off my skull until fate decided on the red-headed girl. The red-haired girl walked into the back of the office and gently pushed open a door. She gasped and covered her mouth with her hands. The grey haired hotel attendant stood over a dead body, a butcher cleaver in his hand. She screamed and bolted, running for the office door. The attendant cursed and chased after her. He grabbed the shotgun from under the counter, leveled it at her back and fired. The red-headed girl collapsed to the floor. The attendant fired another shot and the red headed girl was dead. The attendant walked over to the body and flipped it over.

"Nutting personal little girl," he muttered. "Wrong place; wrong time."

His eyes sparkled as he noticed the butterfly necklace. With a greedy grin and lick of his lips he knelt down and snatched it off her cold corpse. He immediately retreated to the back room and carefully deposited it into his safe. "Here you'll be nice and safe."

The nightmare ended and I returned to my bullet storm reality. Out of the fire and into the frying pan. I moaned in disgust and growled. Puzo looked over at me. "What's wrong?"

"God damn it." I sat up, cracked the sawed-off open and smiled at the two round already loaded. "Give me some handcuffs."

She gave me a weird look but tossed me a pair. The motel attendant had scurried into the back room, somewhat safe from the current firefight. "I'm heading into the backroom. Cover me."

Puzo nodded. The two agents popped back up and opened fire again. I left my cane on the floor and limped for the back room. I slammed to the door and spotted the attendant digging through his desk. "Hey, Norman Bates."

He looked up at me, scared and confused. I slammed the butt of the shotgun straight into his face. He crumpled to the ground, out cold like a beaten boxer. I cuffed him to the desk. How awesome was I? In the middle of a firefight I stopped a murder. Actually I think I stopped Dexter Morgan. I did what cancer could not.

I lumbered back to the counter. Puzo and Ryman, having dropped one of the mysterious gunmen, were by the office's door. I ducked behind the counter and grabbed the box of shells. I scooped handful after handful into my pocket. It's an army rule: never be caught without ammo. I limped to the front door with my stolen shotgun firmly held before me. I see two bodies on the ground, each with bullet wounds to their knees or chest. I count three more shooting at us from right side, across the lot.

"Going for the car." Puzo opened fire as Ryman bolted for the FBI vehicle.

"Behind you." Puzo didn't look back. She knew what I was doing. I was calling out my position so I didn't scare her.

"You're a civi, magic boy," Puzo yelled. "You're not supposed to fight."

"You're FBI," I tease. "You're not supposed to get out numbered."

I spotted another gunman coming from the left. I spun the sawed-off around and fire off a shot. The shell took off his leg and sent him falling to the ground. He winced away the pain, a trooper, and pulled his pistol on me. I fired a second shot before he could squeeze off a round. I ducked back into the office, cracked open the shotgun and quickly reloaded with the shells from my pocket. I stepped back out with my weapon ready.

Ryman opened the trunk and pulled out a rifle. He slapped in a full magazine, cocked the weapon and aimed it at the attackers. The rifle cracks off round after round in bursts of three, he moved from left to right, fired a burst then hopped to the next target and fired again.

Puzo dashed up the lot, her pistol banging rapidly as she downed another attacker. She ducked behind a concrete pillar as she reloaded, popping out with a fresh magazine to squeeze off another series of bullets. I clutched the shotgun tightly as I limped to the FBI car. Using the front end as cover, I peeked out at the battlefield. I didn't need my powers to see the past, my memories of missions long-ago flooded to mind; the horrors of Iraq. These men weren't the Elite Republic Guard but right now they felt like it. Being pinned down, outmanned and back-up hopefully on its way; you add in a leg injury or an IED or two and suddenly this motel become a dead ringer for my accident. My arms were shaking and I was sweating like a sprinter. Maybe it's good that I'm out. If I'd survived that injury I would have walked right back into battle. If I was anything like I am now I would have hindered my squad instead of helping them. I would have been less than useless.

But here I wasn't part of the plan. Puzo and Ryman chatted back and forth, planning their attack as a team of two, not a squad of three. I was there simply to keep myself alive. They'd worry about the menacing baddies shooting from across the parking lot. This gave me a chance to look and to watch. Heather Graham was still out there. I scanned the battlefield until I found her, trapped by gunfire behind a family mini-van, her pistol discarded for a dead man's Heckler & Koch MP5. Using the hood as a sturdy base for my weapon, I aimed at the blonde actress. The shotgun let loose a massive bang and the mini-vans' windshield shattered. I missed. A shotgun, more so with a sawed-off, is not a long range weapon. It's a close range firearm meant for those intimate occasions when everything you have to say can be done so face-to-face. Me missing my shot, at that range with that weapon, was not unexpected. The exploding glass caught Faux-Heather by surprise and for a moment her face changed. For half a second she was Burt Reynolds; then she changed back. She just pulled a Rebecca Romijn. She was a shape shifter.

It suddenly made sense. You don't need a cabal of celebrity look-alike assassins when you have one person who could shift their appearance. It must have been painful, the way her skin scrunched up and morphed. It was probably good that Rebecca Romijn had special effects for her onscreen. Although if rumours were to be believed, and they almost always are, it sounded less painful then marring John Stamos.

Heather scowled as she regained her composure and

aimed her SMG directly at me. A ratta-tat-tat latter and I was lying back on the ground. My shoulder sang out in pain. I clutched it with my arm only to have it sing out an encore. I looked at my finger, blood. Shit. I'd been shot. I started to panic. If I died who would save Robby? Who'd be there for him when his parents couldn't be? I was hit in the shoulder. TV always tried to tell me that a shoulder wound wasn't a big deal but Ranger school taught me differently, more times than not a shoulder wound proved fatal.

Ranger school. Okay, I had to relax. I had to block out the gun play that was going on behind me and I had to focus. I knew how to treat a gun wound; I knew how to treat an injury. Ranger school teaches its men two main things, how to fight and how to survive. I'll admit that my first aid certification has probably long since expired but when it comes to saving your life the basics never go out of style. I pulled off my jacket and started pushing my clothes away. I needed to find the wound and assess the damage before I went into shock. My clothes, aside from dirty and dotted with drops of red, were mostly intact. The shoulder was intact but the skin of the arm was torn. I breathed a small sigh of relief. The bullet only grazed me. I was going to live.

"Grenade!" I spoke to soon.

Two explosions ripped through the night, taking with it a car and the cover Puzo was using. I huddled behind the FBI car as debris littered the lot. I grabbed the sawed-off, quickly reloaded the barrels, and was on my feet. The two SUV's squealed out of the parking lot taking my mysterious attackers with them. The lot was bright with the flickering flames of burning cars and buildings. Ryman was safely behind the RBI car but Puzo was nowhere to be seen.

"Moving up." I limped forward and slowly scanned the parking lot for movement. I needed to see if any attackers were left behind, but more importantly I needed to find Puzo. Ryman followed behind, his rifle securely in his hands. He called out for her across the Bluetooth but got nothing in return. He pocketed the ear piece and started calling out for her.

NEVER BEEN TO MARS

"In here." Her laboured cry came from a motel room with a busted down door and little in the left in the way of windows. Ryman waved me over, his rifle's sights scanning the lot as I limped over. I entered the room, the bed and desk destroyed by the blast, and found sexy FBI lady sitting on the floor with her back to the wall. Chunks of stone and mortar littered the floor. Puzo sat there staring at the floor and breathed heavily.

"You okay?" I asked, leaning on the doorway to take the weight off my leg.

"Five by Five, magic boy," she said as the sounds of sirens approached. "Five by five."

I gave her my hand and help her to her feet, as ironic as that was, and raised an eyebrow as she winced. "I'm okay; just hit something on my way down." Upright by her own strength, she got the ten second run down from Ryman; the bad guys are gone, we were all clear and none of the good guys dead or damaged.

She nodded back and holstered her weapon. She looked at me to do the same. I couldn't holster the sawed-off, I didn't have a holster, what she wanted me to do was hand it to her but try as I might, I couldn't. It wasn't that I needed it, I wanted this murder weapon gone from my touch; instead it was like I physically couldn't. My right hand clutched the grip tightly, my index finger tightly pressed against the trigger guard. I couldn't let go. My adrenalin had begun to fade in the post-battle calm and I was starting to change. In a battle you think on your feet and react. Afterwards, when the rush is gone, you think about what you did and who you just killed.

I hadn't killed anybody in a while, ever since my accident and I was glad of that. I had become a cliché, the highly trained solider who gave up killing, but I was fine with that. Yet put me into a firefight and apparently I had no trouble popping a cap in someone's ass. My hands shake as my grip tightens. I can picture that man, lying on the ground and drawing his pistol on me. I just leveled my shotgun and a bang later he no longer existed.

"Benedict, you okay?" Puzo eyed my hands, shaking like hummingbird, and stepped forward. "Hey, what's wrong?"

I wanted to speak, to verbalize something, but I didn't know what to say. Somehow I didn't need to. Somehow she understood. Puzo stepped forward and took my hand into hers, the warm feel of her skin on her soothing my irritated nerves.

"You did good. You kept us alive and you're still standing." She said calmly, her voice calming my racing mind. "Now I need you to relax and let go. Everything's okay." And with that my grip loosened. She took the sawed-off and handed it to Ryman. She looked at me and smiled. "You okay there, magic-boy?"

"Five by five," I muttered. "Five by five."

I laid in the back of an ambulance fearing for my life. Two paramedics held me down while another approached me with a needle. I freaking hate needles. It's called trypanophobia, the extreme fear of medical procedures involving injections or hypodermic needles. I just call it oh my god you are not sticking me with that! My title isn't as catchy. I twisted and squirmed and tried to break free, but they won't let me. Those paramedics are surprisingly strong.

"Stop being a baby, magic boy." Puzo stood outside the ambulance with a band aid on her forehead. Her suit was tattered, torn, and was covered in dust and dirt but despite her sorry state she stood there laughing at me. "It's just anesthetic so they can give you stitches."

"It's a freaking needle!" I cried out, my voice trembling in fear and lingering with hate. The paramedic held the needle like a dagger and brutally stabbed it into my arm. "A freaking needle! Stop them, Puzo, stop them."

I looked away, hoping that out-of-sight-out-of-mind

would take effect, but it seemed to worsen it. "Okay, we're done." The paramedics released me. I scrambled to my feet and leapt out of the ambulance. My breathing was heavy, my heart was racing and sweat poured down my face.

"You're afraid of needles? A big bad ranger is afraid of needles." She was trying her best not to, but she's looked at my bare chest, at the scars that don my body. She was doing the whole staring without looking like your staring thing. The paramedic tossed me my shirt and I pulled it on and topped it off with my jacket.

"Hey, needles are sharp and they kill," I defended as Puzo handed me my hat and cane. I wasn't always afraid of needles but after my injury it developed. If you sit in a hospital getting half a dozen needles each day you are expected to get used to them. From time to time it has the opposite effect.

"Tell me again why we have a motel worker cuffed in the back of a cop car?" I listened to her as I stared out over the parking lot. Firemen had put out the flames and evacuated the tenants, police and FBI were combing the scene for clues while the safety inspectors were going room by room pointing out structural damage.

"He's a murderer. He killed one of his customers, a red-headed girl, when she stumbled on him killing another person. He has some of her trinkets in his safe. With a little more time I could find out where he buried the body." I removed my hat, resting it on the top of my cane, and rubbed my forehead. I had overused my powers today and I was starting to pay the price. My head throbbed in pain, a pounding beat across the center of my head like a slow drum roll.

"No, no more anything for him," the needle wielding paramedic ordered. "Take him home. He needs rest."

Puzo nodded. She looked at Ryman and frowned. He was yelling into his cell. She waved him down. He pulled his phone from his ear and covered the receiver. "I'm taking the psychic home." Ryman just snickered and went back to his call.

Puzo ushered me into her car and climbed in behind

the wheel. The engine roared to life and pulled out of the lot. I glanced at the clock on the dashboard. The digital numbers flashed 2:30am. "That was smart thinking diving into a motel room."

"Saw it in a movie." A woman after my own heart. "You were pretty trusty with that shotgun but I guess that comes from being a Ranger."

"Half and half," I explained. "I grew up on a farm. My dad taught me to shoot, taught my sister as well. He was hoping she'd live up to her name sake but I was the one who took to a rifle. The Rangers just taught me where to point it." Damn that was a good line. I should write that down or something.

"Damn that was a good line. You wrote that down months ago and just have been waiting for a chance to use it didn't you?" I laughed out loud like a sixteen year-old girl's text message. "Something like that, Puzo."

"You know you can call me Rachael right?"

"I have a hard time picturing you as anything but Special Agent Puzo," I admitted. "Using Rachael just kind of ruins your tough-ass image you have going."

"Senior Special Agent and don't you forget it."

She pulled up to white duplex build that acted as my home. I lived on the bottom floor, which was better for a gimp like me, and some random people lived above. I didn't know them, they didn't know me. It's life in the city. She killed the engine and exited the government issued car. I fished my keys from my pocket and let myself in.

"Are you going to invite me in?"

I shook my head in disbelief and nodded. "Duh, yeah come on in. Can I get you a drink? A coke? Juice? Water?"

"You got anything harder?"

"Do I ever," I delicately placed my hat atop the coat rack and hung my coat. "What do you want? I've got some beer in the fridge as well as some liquor. Help yourself."

My apartment only had four bedrooms, one is for Robby, and it came with a decent sized kitchen and living

# NEVER BEEN TO MARS

room. Puzo was already in my living room kneeling by my liquor cabinet. She pulled out a couple bottles and joined me in the kitchen. I don't cook much but I love my kitchen. It had two sinks, an island counter in the middle and nice window that looked out into my backyard. The sad part is my entire supply of kitchen appliances sucked. I had an old as sin stove, a broken radio-clock and crappy fridge to top it all off. I downed two Advil as Puzo placed the bottles on the counter and went for my glasses.

"Where's the vodka?" she asked as she pulled free two shot glasses and two lowball glasses. This girl was ready to drink. I pointed at the freezer.

"So I don't know what you Rangers do but in the FBI if you survive a shooting we have a shot." She placed two shot glasses on the counter, unscrewed the lid on the vodka and poured us each a drink. "To surviving the bad guys."

"To surviving." I raised my shot glass to meet hers and we downed the clear liquid.

"I saw you in the car," Puzo declared. "You touched my coat didn't you? I specifically asked you not to."

"Yeah I did. I didn't want to but I needed to." I grabbed a lowball glass and tossed a few ice cubes into it. I poured in some citrus vodka and mixed it with a coca cola. I handed her the drink and made another for myself. "You were keeping things from me and I needed to find Robby."

Puzo took a sip of the drink and nodded in approval. "Nice, what is this?"

"It's a drink I came up with. It's a Barbarosa but with some minor tweaks," I explained. "I use Absolut Citron Vodka instead of the standard stuff, I put in ice because I just like a drink with ice in it, and voila."

"You name it?"

"Not yet."

I had been working on this drink for a while. I'd always enjoyed a Barabrosa but wanted to make it better. I'd tested out different vodka's to see what helped improve the flavour. I'd decided on Citron vodka for its smooth and mellow taste, it also brought a fruity character of lemon and lime with a note of lemon peel. I sound like I know what I'm talking about but I really don't. I dove into booze websites and apps to get ideas. It was a project I gave myself after re-watching Casino Royale. I decided that if I was to be a detective, a decision that fate or Price had made for me, I was going to need a signature drink.

I might have too much time on my hands.

"What did you see?" I eyed her, not knowing how to answer. "I want to know what you saw when you touched my jacket."

"My abilities work in weird ways," I said between sips. "What I see is just a moment of time; a grain of sand on the beach that is Puzo. So anything I saw was like a photo, a snapshot of that exact moment."

"You're stalling."

"No, I'm trying to set disclaimer." I gently returned my drink to the counter. "I saw you in your office. I was there. You took me, slammed me against the wall and kissed me."

I can't describe her face. It was a cocktail drink of emotions; made from one part surprise, one part arousal, and two part cocky attitudes. Combine all ingredients, shake, strain into a senior FBI agent and garnish with a pear slice.

"You ripped open my shirt and teased my chest. I picked you up, carried you over to a bed and..."

"I get the idea." She starts to down her drink more swiftly now. "You saw my fantasy. Is that a common occurrence for your psychic powers?"

"Not even close. I saw something I'm not supposed to see. That's how my powers work. So I've gotten good at forgetting what I can see."

"That sounds like a bad habit." Puzo walked around the island and approached me. "It also sounds like bad detective work. You start forgetting what you see and you'll never be able to take advantage of your gift."

Then she kissed me.

Chapter 10
Checklist for Sex and Success

That first moment when your lips meet those of someone new is electrifying. The feel of a new set of lips pressed against yours, the heat, the taste, you notice it all. With Puzo it was wonderful; a firm kiss where my top lip covered her bottom one. I eased back, wanting to gauge her reaction after that kiss. She enjoyed it as much as I did. I moved backed in and kissed her back, harder this time, losing myself in the hunger.

It had been too long for me, the months without the sensual touch of a woman, without a kiss, without intimacy. But here, with my lips pressed against hers, I was like a fairy tale creature feeding on her energy, her lust. I felt her breath on my cheek, Puzo's arms circling my neck as she strained to reach up to my mouth, my own hands sliding inside her jacket and around her waist and pulled her closer. My hands started to move, through no thought of my own, as they peeled the suit jacket from her back, letting it fall to the floor, and tugged free her blouse from within her pants, pulling on the soft material with the urgency of a sailor pulling on a line. I wanted to lift her up onto the island counter and feed from her there but a flawed leg would never allow it. Puzo broke the kiss.

"Show me the bedroom, magic boy." It was all the invitation I needed. I grabbed my drink and finished in a single throw. I reached for her hand, to escort her to my bedroom, but she would have none of it. Puzo wasn't some damsel to be led; she was a lioness, strong and proud. She spun me around, slapped me on the ass, and told me to get going. With a laugh she finished her own drink, grabbed the bottle of vodka, and followed behind.

She shoved me to the bed, my back hitting the soft sheets, and like the hungry cat she pounced. She straddled me, my hips pinned between her legs, and took another swig of the bottle. Safely storing the booze on my nightstand, she grabbed my shirt and pulled it over my head. Once again she saw my bare chest, her fingers carefully tracing the scars. I tried to speak, to apologise for their existence, but she shushed me with a kiss. Her hands leapt to my belt, tugging the buckle free. Her fingers were like a surgeon's, tearing open my pants with precise movements, shoving themselves inside. She used her knees to keep balance, she couldn't grab the headboard or my shoulders for there were far more important thing to hold. My own hands were hard at work, eagerly tearing at her shirt. She released me, to both her reluctance and mine, as I pulled her shirt from her body and unclasped her bra. Puzo undid her pants as she rolled onto her back kicking them, and her panties, off her legs as I did the same.

I rolled on top of her, taking charge for the first time – a move Puzo loved – and leaned down to taste my prize. I had discovered a great beauty hidden beneath the layers of FBI and tailored suit, one I planned on enjoying. I kissed her body from head to toe, leaving her lips alone, and fed the hungry animal within me. This beast needed to feed and Puzo was the feast. After a few moments of devouring, moments where everything felt heightened, from the electric feeling that came from the bare skin of our toes touching to the feeling of her hands tearing at my back, the lioness in her revealed itself once again.

One can only feed for so long before they need to drink and the only thing nearby was the bottle of vodka but I didn't have any glasses. I'd have to make do. Straddling her for once I grabbed the bottle, opened it up, and teased her by running the chilled glass across her arm. The frightening cold glass just heightened the experience, putting each of her nerve ends at attention and making them more receptive to touch, to pleasure, hell to just about everything. I took a swig, the booze burning its way down my throat, before turning the bottle on her. The vodka poured out of the bottle's neck and splashed against her bare chest, each droplet bouncing further down her body.

"Ass," she laughed between squeals. "You're an asshole."

I didn't reply, I just leaned forward, teased her lips with my own – without kissing her – before moving down her body, drinking up each rogue droplet of booze. It was sin to let such good vodka go to waste. She grabbed me by face and kissed me, no longer allowing the teasing to continue, and regained control. The bottle, barely making it to the nightstand before slipping from my grasp, was all but forgotten. Puzo's hands slid down my waist, moving where I wanted them to be without words being spoken. We didn't need words, we didn't need badges, guns or psychic powers all we needed was this moment right here. It was the skin on skin that pushes us deeper into this harmonic instant. No worries about what happened earlier or what would happen tomorrow, we just focused on now. The sex, the pleasure and the physical gratification we both drew from each other.

I could see her, her body going from hot to cold, her senses in overload, her inner lioness roaring as she wanted more. I obeyed, I always did. I continued forward, unrelenting, never giving her a moment to rest or slowing down. I was a man possessed, a creature freed, and I wouldn't stop until I had my fill and couldn't take anymore.

Puzo could only take so much before she had to surrender to it, before she had to let it all come crashing down like the walls of Jericho, the blaring trumpets sending waves of pure pleasure through her body in a climactic conclusion. She rode it hard, draining the trumpets of bliss of every last note they could produce to an orgasmic end.

She collapsed beside me, her body while wet and

sticky from the vodka, fit nicely within mine. We cuddled for a while, her head resting on my good shoulder in lieu of the stitched up one. We fit nicely, her wrapped in my arms, like two puzzle pieces that drifted off to sleep. The trumpet sounds fading in the distance.

Our phones woke us up hours later, mine blaring the theme to Rocky while hers apologised, with musical tones, for party rocking. She dashed into the kitchen to retrieve both; I stared at her behind as she left. I couldn't help but smile.

My recent track record with women is not something to write home about. I don't have much luck with the fairer sex anymore. Unemployed, bum leg and borderline PTSD aren't normally on a girl's checklist for sex and success. The best I've done lately are army bunnies but an encounter with them ends with a hobble of shame. It's like the walk of shame just you've got a bum leg. This was different. I wasn't feeling indignity and she didn't seem to be suffering with any either. This may not be a *How I Met Your Mother* moment but it was something nice and new.

Puzo's already on her phone when she returned. She tosses me mine and I quickly answer it. "Hello?"

"You horn dog." It's Hotwire. I look up at the FBI woman. Somehow I find the idea of me chatting to a hacker while the FBI lady I just slept with is in the room humorous. It's like I'm tempting chance, and adversary I normally loose to. "When I said she was lonely and you should tap that I was mostly joking. So imagine my surprise when I look at her phone's GPS and find it at your place and it's been there since about 3am this morning. Tell me I'm wrong, tell me."

"Is this why you called me at...." I looked like the clock, "8:12 in the morning, to tease me?"

Puzo grabs her pants and darts into the kitchen. Again I can't help but stare as she leaves. It sounds trite but the old saying kind of fits here. I hate to see her go but love to watch her leave. Wow, could I be any more of a frat boy?

"First and foremost it should be congratulations; maybe I should send you balloons," my neighbourhood friendly hacker corrected me. "No I called because I have sorted through a lot of those medical files you brought me. This stuff is weird man."

Holding the cell between my ear and my shoulder I clumsily pull on pants. "Define weird. I just switched to Geico and didn't save a lot of money weird or turtles may actually be immortal weird?"

"Try Galactus and Silver Surfer fusing together in the MC2-verse weird."

If I didn't fear his lack of morals and the influence he could have on the kid I would totally introduce him to Robby. "None of that made sense to me."

"Geeks rule the world. Get on the train before you're left at the station."

Puzo stick her head in the room. "Can I use your shower?"

"Go ahead, towels in the closest." The word *towels* was pushing it. I had two and one was hanging on the back of my bedroom door.

"Okay, Hotwire, explain it to me."

"According to the files in the late 1970s a man by the name of Dr. Ashley Lycotta discovered the presence of a small gene. It was deemed inert by most medical science but Dr. Lycotta deduced that it was a genetic marker to guide human evolution. In his mind it's like a road sign telling you how to get from boring human like me and you, well maybe not you, to Superman. You know who Superman is right?"

"Yes, I know who Superman is." I mock his question with a high pitched voice. "I saw *Man of Steel*. Jerk. Keep going."

"His notes say the stronger the gene or the higher the gene count the more likely the subject is to develop powers. I had to compare journal notes, from both Caine and the archived ones for Dr. Lycotta, but the story goes he was approached by Visegar to develop his project."

"Any clue on what Visegar is?"

"Not a one," Hotwire continued. "Dr. Caine always talks about the times he compares his project to other ones Visegar was running. Some projects were having success, others were not. Apparently Visegar was shooting for the same result from different projects. You know, the saying about the egg and basket and all that."

"That probably makes the most sense in all of this. So what does this have to do with the Tenasine trial?"

"I'm getting to that. Dr. Lycotta goes and does super experiments. The notes get really shady here but there's talk of his tragic death, his revolutionary breakthroughs and his son. None of it is clear but I think he experimented on his kid, a lot.

"We fast forward to Dr. Caine and his team. Caine is working on the Project: Canaan. Now the Lycotta gene can activate on its own in rare cases like through puberty or undergoing traumatic events. They can be either physical or emotional. But most times the gene just stays dormant. Project: Canaan's mission was to stimulate the Lycotta gene. They did so by controlled breeding, surgery and environmental control."

The more I heard the less I knew how to react. I got Hotwire to pause for a moment, listened for the sound of running water, and once I was satisfied Puzo was still in the shower got him to continue.

"I don't know what happened to Visegar. If it was a company then it must have gone under or something because I cannot find hair nor hide of it. It hasn't had a footprint since the eighties, when the world went digital Visegar vanished. Whatever Caine was doing ten years ago, I think he was doing it for a rogue group, a private investor or something because there is no way a company just vanishes."

"Unless all of this is bigger than we think." My mind jumps to Price; the eye-beam shooting secret agent with a thousand names. If Will Smith, Tommy Lee Jones and the rest of the MIB were involved, Visegar could still be around.

"And the next thing I know Dr. Caine is working for this other company called Croxallé. They are relatively new. I think they found Visegar's files and picked up where they left off because the Tenasine trials have to do with the Lycotta gene. They are using the medical breakthrough from the last twenty years, coupled with Dr. Lycotta's work, to find super powers. They are giving Tenasine to expectant mothers to help stimulate the gene. They do this for one trimester. Then they give the women Ephemiphan to, and I quote, stabilize mothers while the fetus undergoes genetic experimentation."

"Don't kill the goose that lays the golden eggs. Yeah, I get it."

"Hey, we're on an egg theme!"

"No, no were not."

"This is the trial your sister is on. They are trying to make her baby have superpowers. They're trying to make the kid the new Hope – copyright Marvel."

First they thought Robby had superpowers, and then they try to force my sister's unborn child to produce them. I was getting tired of all of this. Whoever Visegar is, or was, they, and Croxallé, needed to leave my family alone. The sound of the showers stopped. I only had a couple minutes before Puzo was out. "Croxallé didn't kidnap Robby then who did; a remnant of Visegar?"

"I don't think so. Dr. Caine talks about other infringing companies. Things they had to build security measures around. I can't do much else with my access right now, so I am going to email you everything I've gotten then try and dig deeper. I'm going to see about hacking into Croxallé's systems."

I didn't know how safe of an idea that was. "Croxallé had armed security at their Clinic. They aren't afraid to fight back. Be careful man; make sure you have an exit, or security or something."

"Will do." I disconnected the line just as Puzo, wearing her dirty pants and blouse, stepped out of the washroom. She looked at me and smiled.

"I'm going to grab my bag from the car. It has a change of clothes." I smiled at her and nodded. "You mind if I use your laptop?"

"As long as you don't go snooping into my naughty folders then sure, go ahead." I laughed "I'm going to jump into the shower myself."

I stepped out of my pants and climbed into the tub, using the installed grab bars to stand. I always do my best thinking in the shower. I turned the dial and was hit with a blast of hot water. I like my showers hot, even in the summer. There is something about the hot water running down my chest and back that helps me think. It soothes my pain and lets me direct my attention on whatever it is I need to focus on.

Which for right now was the issue at hand: Robby.

As the hot water washed away the literal blood, sweat, booze and stuff I'll classify as *other*, my mind desperately tried to sort out the last eighteen hours. It didn't feel like eighteen hours, it felt like much longer. I had done more in the last eighteen hours than I'd done in the last month but for me that wasn't as hard as it sounded. Somehow in eighteen hours I'd gone from physiotherapy and annoying SRG cases that reluctantly pulled me away from my TV to superpowers, gun shootouts and FBI sex. While I wasn't complaining about the last one, which blue-blooded cowboy would? I was, however, frowning on the other two. All this information rattling around in my head, medical experiments to produce an army of supermen and shape shifter assassins, and I was still no closer to finding my nephew. I was in over my head. The FBI was great and all but I was quickly thinking that they were in over their head as well. I needed more help.

I needed Joseph Price.

Was this it? What this the moment? Six months ago I had my one and only vision set in the future. I was holding Price's card and calling him for help. I called in my favour and I was in deep shit. Sometimes when I get a vision of a person I have trouble deciphering their emotion but not with me. I know when I look scared, I know my tell for terrified, and someday soon I was going be terrified and overcome with a foreboding sense of dread. I hadn't hit terrified yet but dread was creeping up on me. Perhaps Price could wait. I wasn't in a rush to meet this future.

I shut off the water, dried myself off and climbed out of the shower. I hobbled back to my room and quickly got dressed. Dark blue jeans, a grey *Expendables 2* t-shirt and a sky blue denim shirt is all it takes for me to go from Lt. Dan to Rayland Givens. I reached the nightstand, still holding aloft the source of my hangover, and pulled open the top drawer. In a small dish sat two ball-chain necklaces. One holds two oval tags, my army dog tags, and the other held three keys. With the conveniently placed pencil I shove the first chain aside. I don't like to touch my dog tags anymore, which is the reason I keep the convenient pencil close by, psychic powers make reliving my military past more difficult than it has to be. I took the second chain and exited my bedroom (officially renamed the sex-nasium).

Rachael (still sounds weird to me) was sitting at the island counter in front of my laptop with her smartphone close by. She'd changed suits, the black one subbed for a three piece grey one, and the blue shirt replaced by a white one. Honestly I preferred her naked but I might be biased. Hanging onto her belt was her service pistol. She was back in a working mode.

"This is some *nasty stuff*." Puzo laughed at me. "Asian girls? Really? Could you be anymore stereotypically male? You really need to get out more."

None of what she is saying is true, I swear. Okay, almost none of it is true. I do need to get out more and I do have a video or two that may or may not have an Asian woman in it, I'm male – sue me, but I would never classify them as nasty. Truth time: more of that statement that was truth than I previously admitted. "Hey, no snooping."

I walked to the liquor cabinet and starting pulling out the bottles one by one and laying them on the floor. Puzo raised an eyebrow at me. "A little early to start drinking, going the hair of the dog routine?"

"No, I need something special." I pulled free a metal lockbox. The black box was roughly the same size as a case of pop. I placed it on the counter; fully aware that for the second time in five hours Puzo can't keep her eyes off of me.

I told Hotwire that if he was digging deeper into Croxallé and this Visegar mystery then he needed to take precautions. I needed to heed my own advice. I took the first key from the chain and unlock the box. Puzo peers with an eagerness of a historian while opening the arc of the covenant, a non face melting model. She tilts her head when she sees what's inside.

"You do have a permit for that right?" Always the cop.

Securely locked away is my Beretta M9 pistol. I keep my license to carry a hidden firearm, which came in my mysterious *you're-a-detective-now* folder, stored with the gun. I pulled it out and tossed it to her as I grabbed my gun. The second key unlocks the trigger lock, a bolt that prevents the trigger from firing. I started my gun routine, the same one I do every time I pick up this, or any other, weapon. I double-check to make sure the barrel is empty and there is no jam in the weapon, then I double check the magazines are full, fifteen round in each, and then load the weapon. I triple check the safety is on before returning it to its holster. My routine is the exact same, every time. Content that everything is set, I clipped the filled holster on my belt. I knew the gun was empty, I stored it that way, but the army had taught me never to take anything for granted with a gun. They drill that into you for weeks before they even give you a gun.

"This is in check." Puzo handed me back the license. "Why do you need a gun?"

"I stumbled across an assassin on my first lead and the second time I see them I get into an epic gun battle. I just want to be able to defend myself next time."

"When was the last time you used that?" she said,

NEVER BEEN TO MARS

nodding at the weapon. "How's your accuracy?"

"Not as great as when I had perfect footing." I wasn't just a good shot back in the day, I was amazing. "I'm still a pretty damn good shot."

Puzo shrugged. She obviously wasn't thrilled of the idea that a civilian was armed in her presence but I guessed that if it had to be someone wielding a gun that she'd rather it be an ex-Ranger. "About last night."

Oh crap. Whenever a woman says those words to me it never turns out to be pleasant.

"I had a lot of fun last night. I really did. I'm not really looking for a dating-relationship thing; I just got out of one very recently. My job doesn't leave me with enough time to have a relationship, which was a major reason for the break-up," she admitted, "but this, you and me having fun, I'd like to do it again. You're fun and good at what you do in there. You Rangers definitely know how to hit the bulls eye."

In the list of lines people say next morning I normally get tracks from the greatest hits, the i*t's not you it's me* or *I was really drunk last night* and my personal favorite l*ets just stay friends*. I rarely get the B-sides, the *let's do this again* stuff. It's new and I'll admit I could get used to it.

"I'm looking forward to it." I was smiling like a damn fool and I couldn't stop. To be honest I don't think I wanted to. "What you got there?"

"Kyle sent me the data on the shooting. Apparently CSI is just finishing up. He wants me to come down and check things out." She grabbed her suit jacket and closed down my laptop. "I'm going to head there now. I'd like my resident psychic there but..." Her voice trailed off as her face turned awkward.

"You'd like me to take my own transportation there?" I guessed. She was trying to save her professional image without being rude. I read somewhere, and by that I mean took it from cop shows on TV, that women in the law enforcement have it hard enough without getting a reputation of hopping into bed with every cute guy they see. It was a classic plot line. "I got it. No worries."

"Thanks." She opened her mouth to defend herself, to reassure me that she wasn't ashamed of being with me or something similar, but I waved it off.

The sudden rapping on my apartment door sent me spinning.

"'Tis some visitor,' I muttered. 'Tapping at my chamber door. Only this and nothing more." Puzo recited as her hand dropped to her gun. A mysterious knock and she starts reciting Poe. The worst part was whenever anyone recited that poem all I hear is James Earl Jones' voice. "You expecting anyone?"

"Nope."

"Do people often drop by unexpected?"

"Never." Like a synchronized swimming team we both drew our firearms and made for the front door.

Chapter 11
Switching Back to the Disney Channel

Puzo kept her gun aimed at the floor as I moved towards the door, only raising it when I stood beside it. She kept her iron sights firm, aimed at the door and never quivered - not even by an inch – and waited for my signal. My own gun rested firmly in my hand, hanging at my side just out of view. The Glock 22 was the firearm of choice for FBI agents but I'd never been a fan, I found it too light and small and it just didn't look threatening but seeing it in her hands I knew what type of damage this gun could really do.

There are literally thousands of guns to choose from if one is in the market but when I went on the search there was one weapon for me. The M9 was the army's sidearm of choice for decades. I had trained with a M9 and spent many nights in the field sleeping with one by my side. When I went into battle I had a M9 by my side and in Iraq when my rifle jammed and the Elite guard came over the wall I reached for my M9 to save my life. The closest thing I'd ever had to a long-term monogamous relationship was with a M9. A M9 had never failed me overseas and it certainly wasn't going to fail me at my own front door.

I carefully pulled the door open and peered outside. Elaine stood outside with a good looking man behind her. She looked okay but sadly, without her infectious smile, her body looked weak and her curly hair was lackluster. "Elaine? What are you doing here?"

"Hey, Ben. I needed to talk to you."

"Yeah, sure. Who is this guy?"

"Oh, right, this is Steve, my boyfriend." I tell her to give me a second and close the door. I gave Puzo the all clear, thumbed on the M9's safety, and returned it to my holster. Puzo lowered her weapon and returned to the kitchen to retrieve her stuff.

"Sorry about that." I opened the door and let them both in. Here I was letting the enemy into my apartment. Steve was a tall man with spiky black hair, strong arms and had a quarterback's stare. Elaine had talked about him quite a bit, commenting on her boyfriend like she felt guilty by the way she acted with me, so I knew a fair deal about him. He was in his mid twenties, was a male nurse, and played in three different sports leagues. This man was the enemy and I just let him in my house. I was pretty sure that your crush's boyfriends were like vampires; once you invited them in they could come and go as they pleased.

"Hi, I'm Ben Thompson." I offered the nurse my hand. Steve gave it a shake, a nice sturdy one. Damn, he even had a good hand shake. I was hoping for a limp wrist or a weak grasp. People often underestimate the power a handshake has. It is the strongest first impression a man can give.

"Steve Rapoza; it's a pleasure to meet you, Ben." The two moved down my long hallway into my living room.

"Hey, I've got to go," Puzo said, bag in hand, as she moved for the door. "Don't be too long, we need your help." With a kiss on the cheek she was gone.

"Wait..." Elaine's eyes went wide as she recognized Puzo.

"How're you doing, Elaine?" I asked. "You were in pretty bad shape yesterday."

"That's what we're here to talk about," Steve explained, putting his hand around her shoulder. "She needed to talk to you about what she saw. She blames you but I've been telling her it's not fair to. So we're here to talk this out."

NEVER BEEN TO MARS

I glanced at my watch. If this was anybody else other Elaine I would have said screw it and left. I really didn't want to talk about my emotions at that moment and especially not in front of a male nurse.

Elaine tried to speak, her mouth opening and closing several times before sound came out. "That was a dead body, Ben."

"I know."

"How can you act so calm around it?" She didn't bother starting with the easy questions did she? She went right for the big stuff.

"Experience," I grudgingly admitted. "I was in the army, Elaine, I fought overseas. It wasn't my first time."

"Why don't you tell us about your overseas deployment," Steve suggested. "She'll draw strength from learning how you found strength."

There is this unspoken rule about soldiers returning from overseas, you never ask about what happened. Everybody knows that fighting for your country isn't easy, no matter where you went you never came back the same. People change overseas, some see horrible things, some witness heinous acts and some suffer terrible tragedy. But no matter the case, no matter how different a soldier may be after they return, you never ask. You just wait until they open up to you. I'm not big on opening up, especially about Iraq.

I ignored Steve and took Elaine's hands into my own. It was an intimate gesture but not a romantic one. "My cases were always simple, stolen movies and cheating wives; very ABC – Disney," I explained. "But things changed. Either my show's jumped networks or I've been retooled because suddenly I'm looking very AMC. I didn't know there was going to be a body there; if I had I wouldn't have brought you. I'm sorry, I'm not psychic." That's a lie, I really was.

"One day soon I'll get over what happened overseas," I predicted. "And if we're still friends then I'll tell you all about it but until that day what happened to me needs to stay with me. As soon as I find Robby, as soon as all of this is over, I'm switching back to the Disney channel and I'm never touching the remote again."

With Elaine gone and the cab I ordered waiting impatiently, I finished getting ready. I pocketed my gun licence, as was the law, and grabbed my leather jacket. I stuck a finger through the bullet hole. This was my good jacket. With no other choice, the fall weather too cold to be without one and too warm for my winter coat, I spun it onto my shoulders. I dumped the extra magazines into my jacket pockets and grabbed my hat and cane on the way out. My leg was bad, this is a fact, but for simple movements around the house I didn't need it. I spent most of my time with my ass in my La-Z-Boy anyways. If you took me out of the house, on a case or for whatever reason thinkable, I took my cane. There are no La-Z-Boys in the real world.

I arrived at Traveler's Motel to see, for the first time in the daylight, the damage that had been caused the night before. The burning wreckage had long since been extinguished but the parking lot and motel still showed the damage of last night's skirmish. The lot, filled with debris and divots, was divided into sections by yellow rope. The CSI guys, who by the way look nothing like Dr. Grissom in real life, were still combing every inch. Every bullet and fragment was accounted for. Even in the motel building itself every bullet hole and piece of rubble was recorded and labelled with a little yellow card.

Puzo stood behind a FBI SUV, her laptop rested on the open tailgate as she rapidly tapped on the keys. She waved me over the moment she saw me. "I got the files from Croxallé."

"Really? All of them?" I was surprised. Croxallé was evil, Bond villain evil, and they just handed over their files.

"Yep but this seems like a waste of time. My CARD

team is going through the files, looking for anything, but so far everything seems legit. This is your standard medical company."

Oh, they were good. Whatever evil Croxallé had hidden underneath their skin they kept hidden with a shiny medical appearance. Croxallé was a generous company, donating monthly to medical charities like the fight against cancer, AIDS, and almost every other war medical science had against the maladies of mankind. But I had seen the truth; I took the red pill and saw just how deep the rabbit hole went. I just had to prove it to her.

"Well in my vision he was looking at the Tenasine trials."

"You and your visions, magic boy," Puzo teased but she eagerly tapped the keys to pull up the list. I didn't know what to expect when I saw Puzo here at the crime scene but if she was anything like the women of my past, the uniform-wearing-gun-toting ones, I figured the most likely reaction would have been professionalism. When you're on duty you acted like you're on duty, you do your job and let what happens in the off hours stay there. Puzo didn't disappoint. She was focused entirely on work. I, however, was acting like a pickpocket and stealing glances like they were wallets.

"Okay, here we go." A familiar file, filled with a list of names, flashed up on her screen. "This is the list of families participating in a trial for a new prenatal drug. Nothing seems out of the ordinary here, it's just....." Her voice trailed off as she scrolled down the list. The more she hit the down-arrow key the more her face scrunched up in confusion.

"Okay, this is weird." She pointed to the names. "Veronique Murray, Chuck Hairsine, and Patricia Ejsing. I know those names; I've worked on those cases. Murray's daughter went missing last year, the Hairsine child went missing four months ago and Ejsing was two years ago, maybe less." She brushed her forehead with her thumb as she tried to pull the facts from memory. "I'd have to check the files but each of those was a missing child. They were all found and returned safely."

"Were they kidnappings?"

"One was, a deadbeat father about to lose custody, but the others were simple childhood events. One kid tried to run away and the other was at their friend's house and just forgot to call home."

"What does this mean? Do we ignore and keep digging?"

"No chance in hell, magic boy. One is an event, two is a coincidence and three is a pattern. That's crime solving 101. Remember that." Her fingers dashed across the screen. "I'm going to pull up those case files and re-read them over; I don't want to rely on my memory."

"What should I do?"

"Go speak to Ryman. He has orders to allow you to touch any items that you need." I nodded and hobbled off. Ryman looked up as I approached, his face was less of a scowl and more of a grudging respect. He nodded at me and escorted me to the guns.

"I never thanked you." His words were unexpected. "You covered my ass in the firefight last night."

That must have been hard for the skeptic to say. He looked like he wanted to say more, like he was obliged to, but I really didn't want to force that on him. "No worries, man."

He understood. Neither of us said a word until we reached the guns. It was a full ten seconds of silence, highly awkward silence but silence none the less. Each weapon was laid out on a folding table the CSI dudes had set up. Each was protected by a plastic bag. There were nearly a dozen guns and I was not going to touch them all if I didn't have to. I hate visions that come from guns. I needed to narrow the search. "What did you guys find when you ran the numbers of the weapons?"

"Most were filed down, some were reported stolen from different companies like WhiteStar Securities, and others, I assume, were just guns picked up along the way from different places."

NEVER BEEN TO MARS

"What caliber of bullet killed Dr. Caine?" I asked. Ryman flipped through the police report on his phone. ".40."

"And the murders at the clinic, were they the same caliber?" Ryman just nodded.

I was certain that Burt Reynolds, Mark Wahlberg and Heather Graham were the same person. Well, 86.5% certain, so running by that logic the odds were decent that he/ he/ she used the same gun. Decent odds might be pushing it but it was all I had at the moment. During the Battle of Traveler's Motel Heather Graham ditched the pistol for an MP5. In my experience when you switch one weapon for another in the heat of battle you don't take the time to properly stow it. You drop it to the ground, grab your replacement and keep on firing.
I was hoping Faux-Heather did the same.

He/ he/ she had battle experience; I could see it in the way he/ he/ she moved and the way he/ he/ she shot. The dead giveaway was when Faux-Mark grabbed a blade and started fighting. Each branch of the military trains their boys a slightly different way. Everybody knows the basics, how to shoot, how to move, and how to work as a team, but when it comes to things like how to fight hand-to-hand and how to use a knife, Rangers are as different from SEALs as SEALs are from Delta Force.

Heather Graham was a SEAL, or at least that's where she started out.

"If both murders were done with a .40 caliber pistol then I'll start with them." Ryman pulled the pistols aside. I had just dropped from a dozen to four. God, I hoped it was one of these four, if it wasn't I was going to have to go one by one through them all. As I looked them over one pistol caught my attention. It was a SIG Sauer P226, the weapon of choice for the Navy SEALs. The more I inspected it the more I realized it was one of the variations. It was a P226 Tactical, a version of the weapon with an extended barrel and external threads to accept a suppressor. In my first vision of Faux-Burt he killed Dr. Caine with a silence pistol. I tried to steady my thought and emotions as I opened up the bag. I was going to be assaulted by a mind shattering amount of visions, each stronger and more heartbreaking then the last, and I didn't have time to view them all. I closed my eyes and repeated his name over and over.

Robby. Robby. Robby.

I needed anything related to him.

Robby. Robby. Robby.

Then I grabbed the gun.

A shiver and a twitch sent me flying back to Robby's school. It wasn't a clear vision like normal; instead it was like back in the days prior to digital TV when you had analogue signals and static-filled screens. It was like being young and trying to watch those naughty channels but the antenna wasn't pointed just right. You got most of it but every once in a while it would distort and suddenly you realize that what you're watching isn't porn, it's the shopping network's All Shoe Special.

I think that's how a foot fetish is born.

I was watching Robby in the playground talking about Spider-Man and his Uncle Ben, a vision I'd already seen, but this time I was focused on one of the teachers. It wasn't Ms. Briery, I could see her in the distance; it was another female teacher I didn't know.

The vision jumped to further in the future, bridged by the spliced image of a man on his knees and pistol to his head, and Robby is talking about how I almost died. I'm still focused on this mystery teacher.

It jumped a second time, this time I see a split second of a woman being pistol whipped, and Robby is being led to the chain link fence, away from the rest of the children, by the mystery teacher. She is kneeling before him, scolding him for climbing the links.

I jumped a third and final time, a woman is running for her life as she avoids gunfire, and Robby has just been shoved into a white van. The mystery teacher is speaking into a phone as she climbs into the driver seat.

"I've got him. I'll drop him off with Major Heins and

proceed to Proce Medical."

She hung up the phone, looked into the mirror and willed her skin to shift. I watch as the sex changed, the hair receded, and the eyes shift as the Ms. Teacher became Mr. Faux-Burt. The van pulled away from the curb and drove off. With a deep breath I returned to the land of the reality. Why is it always white vans? The international union of baddies really needed to grow away from the stereotype.

For the first time my visions start to make sense. Facts started to line up. I now knew why fate, or whatever deity that looked out for bum-legged psychics, gave me those visions, why they kept flashing the shape-shifter before my eyes. The shifter had nabbed my nephew. It was like a neon sign that I had missed. When I first touched the body I was worried about Robby, everything I'd done in the last eighteen or so hours had been about Robby so when the visions started flashing this shape-shifter I should have clued in. It was like Puzo said. One time, the doctors, is an event, twice, the clinic, is a coincidence and three times, the late-night shootout, is a pattern. That's crime solving 101.

I really needed to retake those classes.

I had a culprit, Lieutenant Chapman the shifter, but I didn't know what he looked like or where he was. I also had another name, Major Heins. "I need a way to search a couple names. Can I have access to your FBI database?"

Ryman just scoffed sarcastically. "Sure and while you're at it I'm going to give you my pin number, 5891, and tell you that because my sister and I have Daddy issues that if you wear Old Spice cologne and show interest in her art she'll basically sleep with you right there."

"Is your sister cute?" I shouldn't have said that. It was mean, a little dickish, and not the type of person I am. I'm Anthony Michael Hall with a pinch of cowboy

If Ryman could have shot me and get away with it I'm pretty sure he would have, right there. BANG! No more Benedict. That would have been a crappy ending. Instead his nostrils flared and his chin hardened. "You stay away from my sister."

He pulled me over to another computer and plunked be before a junior agent. "This is Probationary Agent Mitchell Lord-Alge. He'll search the DB for those names." Ryman stomped away, made it four paces, then turned back around. He pointed a death finger at me. "So help me God, if you even talk to my sister... They'll never find your body. I promise."

Agent Lord-Alge loudly coughed into his hands, the hacking being the best cover he had for laughter. "He's kind of protective of his sister."

Lord-Alge reminded me of Q. Not the old man Q from the classic movies but the new young guy from *Skyfall*. He had the hair wrought with chaotic curls, thick rimmed glasses that made his eyes seem bigger than they were and a slight shadow on his chin, the likes of facial hair that just didn't seem like it bothered to grow.

I fed the young agent my names and watched as he typed them into the database. Chapman came up with over two dozen possibilities but none were SEALs. Lord-Alge switched to Major Heins. As the database searched I looked back at Ryman. He was back on his cell phone angrily talking to whoever was on the other side.

"Okay, I have three Heins, each holding the rank of a Major. One is Major Samantha Heins of the Air Force, one is Major Terrance Heins of the US army and the third is Major Edward Heins, formally of the US Army's Special Forces. He's now registered as a member of WhiteStar Security."

That's twice. That's still just a coincidence.

I thank the agent and hobbled off. Despite my poor detective skills I seemed to have decent instincts. While they hadn't been good enough to keep me in one piece, they had proven more than adequate and keeping me alive. If my instincts told me to not trust somebody, I didn't. When they told me to make a move, I did. With Ryman I was getting something different. It wasn't a trust issue, it was a deception issue. I wasn't being lied to, I was being... withheld information.

Have I mentioned how much I hate that?

NEVER BEEN TO MARS

"Ryman," I called out as I approached the Special Agent. He was off his phone and dealing with the guns. "I need a favour."

He raised an eyebrow.

"I was kind of..." I coughed. "Busy last night. I didn't get a chance to charge my phone. Can I borrow yours?" He glares at me and hands it over. He realised his mistake almost instantly and tried to grab it back. I didn't have time to pull off my glove and touch the phone, not before Ryman reclaimed it, so I did the next best thing. I slapped it against my cheek.

I've learned my powers don't require my hands, they just require contact with my bare skin. This could be anything, my fingers, toes, butt cheeks, nipples, my nose, and yes, even my naughty bits. Please don't ask how I figured that one out. I'll give you a hint: it involves a late night encounter, a latex condom, and a vision of a factory on fire. It was mood killer to say the least.

My face stung as the usual shiver ran up my back and my eye twitched. I might have done it a little too hard. My vision doesn't move me, keeping in this very parking lot, but it does rewind time again. It's last night, pre-sex and post gunfight. Ryman grabbed his phone and dialed a number. The phone rang once before something picked up. No words were spoken; there is only another dial tone. Ryman punched in another seven numbers and waited. Thirteen seconds later the line beeped twice and disconnects. A girlish scream caught his attention; as it does for almost every cop, firefighter and paramedic there. Ryman snapped his head around to see a man getting stitches and freaking right the fuck out about it.

Oh wait, that's me. Damn.

It's always weird when I see myself in a vision. It's like looking at yourself in a mirror. Nothing looks just right. You expect yourself to be a certain way, your eyes, nose and hair, but in truth you don't look like you think you do. You don't look wrong or bad, just different.

Ryman shook his head at me and went back to his phone. After a couple minutes the phone rang and Ryman eagerly answered it.

"What the hell just happened?" Ryman screamed. "I was just shot at. Your men just opened fired on me. They shot at a FBI agent."

"What are you talking about?" The male voice is the polar opposite of Ryman, calm and collected to his rage and anger.

"I was just in a firefight," Ryman explained, "with your men. What the hell are they doing shooting at me? And where the fuck is the kid?"

"This would be the Belledin child?" Ryman screamed a determined yes into the phone. "We are aware of his disappearance. Why are you contacting us about this? The deal is we contact you."

Ryman paused as Puzo explained where she's off to. He nodded his partner away and went back to the phone.

"This is one of your children," Ryman said, a little quieter now. "The case was supposed to fall into the lap of another CARD team. We just came off a case but we got handed the file, not in the normal FBI way but in your fucked up way. This is just like every one of those children of yours you send me to recover. So where is this one?"

Silence. Ryman impatiently waited for an answer, each second an agonizing chore. "Robert Belledin is one of our children as you put it but we had nothing to do with his disappearance."

"You better find him or else shit will hit the fan for you and me."

"Let us not do anything hasty, Mr. Ryman. We all have much to lose, Bridgette Ryman for instance."

"Say her name again and watch what happens. I fucking dare you."

"Calm down, Mr Ryamn. We have a deal and we will not break it. We are searching for the Belledin boy as well. We have great interest in him. You'll know what to do when we do. And I assure you, Mr. Ryman, we did not shoot at you."

The vision ended, reality returned but all I saw was

NEVER BEEN TO MARS

red. Ryman pawed for his phone and finally pulled it from my grip. I didn't care; I was just filled with fury. You remember that girl you cheated on and how pissed off she was? (Don't judge me. I was an ass when I was a buff army boy with two working legs.) Her wrath was nothing compared to mine. I slammed the top of my cane into Ryman's neck and watched as his eyes bulged in surprise and gagging sounds escaped his lips.

"You son of a bitch!" My cane struck again, smashing the outside of his right knee. He leg buckled and he dropped a couple inches. "You fucking knew! You fucking let this happen." I struck a third time, a cross over strike across his face. He crumpled to the ground like the trash he was. "You fucking asshole!"

My arm arched upwards. I wanted to strike down at him as his lay on the ground, striking him time and time again until my rage died or he stopped moving, whichever came first. I didn't get the chance. Lord-Alge tackled me to the ground and pinned me to the asphalt as I tried to squirm free. I had to give the kid respect. He had a solid tackle for a toothpick.

I blinked and seven pistols were drawn and pointed directly at me. I wouldn't say I love guns, I can't honestly say I hate them either, but I do have a healthy respect for them. However what I do dislike is having numerous guns pointed at me. Is it wrong that my first reaction, now, is to count them?

"Everybody stand down," Puzo yelled across the lot. Her voice boomed. She didn't need a megaphone or a microphone, she just boomed. She was like my drill sergeant, except she was female and I've slept with her. My Ranger School Sergeant was male and had hair everywhere. I did not find him attractive. Puzo glared at me, red in the face, and watched me try my best to escape Lord-Alge's grasp. Seriously, how strong was this kid?

"You mind telling me what the hell is going on, Thompson?"

"Ryman is fucking working with the kidnappers," I

screamed. "They call him and tell him where to find the kids they kidnap."

If I ever want to be a great detective I should follow Puzo's example. Not only is she tough and a bit of a badass, she's smart. She has a wonderful mind for putting things together and she does it quickly. It took only two seconds before she spun, her Glock 22 in her hand, and lined up the iron sights on her partner. "If you move, Kyle, I will shoot you."

"You trust a con-artist psychic over me?" he coughed, air finally returning to his lungs. "I'm your fucking partner. He's lying."

"He has no reason to, Kyle. He wants his nephew back. You read his psych report; it's his only major human connection." The FBI has a psych report on me? That's got to be bad, very bad. I could be flattered but no, I'll stick with bad. "He has no reason to lie. It is Croxallé isn't it? That's how so many of the people on the Terrasine Trial go missing and how so many of them land in our lap."

Ryman didn't speak. He had the right to remain silent and it looked like he was taking it. Puzo started ordering her team to action. She had Ryman cuffed and brought into an empty hotel room with two uniformed cops as guards. She also had my M9 taken away, albeit temporary – I hoped – so that when temperatures flared, nobody got shot. I didn't like it but it made sense.

Ten minutes later I was in another hotel room cuffed to a chair. Puzo was standing before me with a scowl on her face. My rage has dissipated, slightly, but I was still fuming. I was royally pissed off but nowhere near as mad as Puzo.

"What the hell were you thinking?" She shook her head in disgust. "You grunts swing first and think second. I mean you just assaulted a federal agent."

When she uses facts and logic to support her arguments I look really bad.

I tried to stammer out an answer but she cut me off. "No, there is nothing you can say, Thompson. You lost your cool and beat a man. That's not the way I work and if you want my help it's not the way you work either."

Twice in two days I've found myself seated across a table from her. You think it would get easier. Spoiler Alert: It does not. TV has taught me that a good FBI agent can be nice and happy one day and turn on the angry intimidating bit for the next. If TV carries over to real life, and I'm in a lot of trouble if it doesn't, then by that basis of comparison Puzo is a terrific FBI agent.

"Okay, Ben, talk," Puzo ordered. "Tell me what you know."

In all my years as a Ranger I've had to perform an interrogation a couple times, most of which were on enemy combatants. The whole ordeal is like a play. You march in there with a game plan, a bit of a script and a role to play. TV has made popular the good-cop/ bad-cop routine but there are dozens of different interrogation styles. You could appeal to their logic, try and make a deal, you could turn one against the other or you could go straight ahead and scare them. That's not even counting the advanced interrogation methods. Those use some interesting math to obtain their solutions.

Water + Board = Answers.

Don't ask what happens when you forget to carry the one.

When Puzo stormed into Ryman's makeshift cell I was close behind. Puzo started with a silence technique. She entered the room, put a digital recorder on the table, turned it on and just stared at him while shaking her head in disgust. The silence was meant to keep the subject uneasy, make them worry about what you know or what you're going to do. The head shaking is used on someone who looked up to you. It forced shame and disappointment into their minds.

"How long?" Her first words cut through the silence like bullet to the brain. She wasn't beating around; she was going straight for the kill.

"It started three months after you and I were paired up."

"You've been working for them for four years," Puzo said calmly. "Four long years that I thought I could trust you and it turns out you're working against us the whole time."

"It wasn't like that," Ryman defended. "They call me and give me hints on how to find the kids. They always return uninjured and unharmed. They're well fed and looked after. And because of their help you and I have rapidly climbed up the ladder. Because of their help we're both being fast-tracked and nobody gets hurt."

"Why did you accept in the first place? What did they offer you?"

He didn't answer that question. It's a sore topic, you can see it on his face but Puzo won't accept his silence. Her questions continued peeling away layers after layer of his lies and half truth. It was like watching a surgeon at work, using words as scalpels.

"What does Croxallé have to do with your sister?" Puzo finally asked. "What are they doing with Bridgette?"

"She's sick. They're helping her," he finally admitted. "She's been sick for a long time, lung cancer, and in return for my help they put her into a new medical trial to treat her. It's a new development."

So far everything I've seen with Croxallé had ulterior motives. They were evil to the chocolate core with a candy shell of good around it. Croxallé was the M&Ms of evil.

Notice how nothing sounds as evil once you compare it to an M&M?

A medical trial to battle cancer, this could be legit but I wasn't counting on it. I was expecting a superpowered villain with abilities based around her magic C-word: Cancer. Not the other C-word that women hate: calories.

"Why did they kidnap them in the first place?" Puzo was asking everything I needed to know. It was part of our script, our plan of attack. Before the two of us had entered the room we'd figured out everything we wanted to ask him. We knew that he wouldn't respond to me, so I was going to keep absolutely silent, but for her, for the woman he respected above all else, he would pour his life and soul out.

"They wanted to examine them," he explained. "The way they told it to me was they had put a lot of money into dozens of children. It was a project from a previous company – KyroCorp – that Croxallé had picked up. They were able to get some of the people from the old trial to come in and be examined again but not all. Croxallé paid a lot for the Kyro-Corp files. They needed to get the data from these children to recoup their losses."

Trying to be as quiet as possible I grabbed my phone and texted Hotwire.

Me: Does KyroCorp pop up in our files?

"You just believed them?"

"Of course not. I did my research. KyoCorp existed. They went under in the late 90s. They were using the dot com bubble as funding and lost that when it burst. Everything they told me was true."

"How did they approach you?" Puzo asked. This was a tenuous time for the interrogation. We'd gotten him to speak, this was obviously the first step, but if we pushed too hard he'd fight back and clam up. If we didn't push hard enough then he wouldn't tell us everything. "Was it mysterious phone calls? Encrypted emails?"

"No, the first meeting was a straight up phone call. The voice introduced himself as Ivan Johns, an employee of Croxallé. He said he might have information on the missing child case he'd seen on the news and wanted to help. When I asked why he called me directly he told me he wanted to stay anonymous."

"How did it progress from there?"

"They called me again for another case, same style as the first, and helped me. After that they told me that we should talk. They wined and dined me and things just progressed."

Like a radio playing while you work their voices drift off into the background as I fell deep into thought. I wouldn't trust a single word that came from Croxallé, especially not after what I've learned in the past two days, but perhaps there was a grain of truth buried deep amongst their lies. Croxallé was making superpowered kids. Croxallé was kidnapping kids. They claimed it was follow-ups for medical trials the kids participated in, the polar opposite of house calls, but it was really follow-ups on their super-powers trial. These kidnappings were related to Project: Canaan; they were related to Robby.

"Where is Robert?" Puzo demanded, her tone starting to lose its tranquility.

"I don't know. They don't know. They said the boy wasn't kidnapped by them but by somebody else."

That was the limit. No longer was he being useful. I tapped Puzo on the shoulder, nodded towards the door and then hobbled out. She followed. We waited until we were clear of Ryman's hearing before we spoke. "I think we've learned pretty much everything we can from him."

Puzo nodded. She seemed distant, like she was implementing the final steps of a math problem. "What are you keeping from me, Thompson?"

I didn't know what to feel. My gut reaction was to be surprised. I hadn't thought I'd dropped any hints, but the truth of the matter was she is just plain smarter than me. "I have Croxallé files."

"From your mysterious phone call friend this morning?" I nodded. "Hush hush calls mean hidden sources or confidential information. Which one is it?"

"Both."

She shook her head. "What is it?"

"It's nothing but a couple journal entries, some random medical files, and a copy of the Tenasine trials," I explained. "Most of it is weird stuff; medical stuff beyond my comparison."

NEVER BEEN TO MARS

"You're not willing to give up your source are you?"

"Nope."

"I want those files." That wasn't a question. That was a hard-chinned and fist-clenched order. Rough and tough women: I fall for them every time.

"Why? You can't use them in court."

"I want them. I want to see what you saw. I need to know what Croxallé can offer to make an agent go rogue."

I nodded and hobbled to her computer. I plugged in my phone and started to transfer the files, the journals, the reports; anything important I had on my phone was sent to her. "Most of this won't make sense; it's nonsense at best." Sad part was less and less as the day progressed.

Puzo started to go through the files, browsing some and reading others in depth. Minutes passed before she spoke. "Your Tenasine trials file differs from the one they gave me."

"That's the file the assassin was after," I explained.

"So we compare them. See what's on this list and not on their official one. It'll show us what they are trying to hide."

One by one we went through the Tenasine trials file, comparing each name and each place to the version I had. An hour and a half later we were nearly done. The file was filled to the brim with names, almost two hundred children, each of them being fitted for powers. Most of the names had the words 'FAILED' beside them and others 'CANCELED'. This left merely two dozen active names.

"I got one." I leaned near the laptop and pointed at the screen. "It's an address of a medical storage facility."

Puzo switched screens and dove into the FBI database. "Our files show it's a registered storage area for medical supplies and pharmaceutical needs. It's owned by Croxallé after they bought it out from KyroCorp."

"Is that enough for a warrant?"

"It would if I told them about Kyle but I'm not ready to reveal his involvement; they would pull us off the case. Robby doesn't have time for us to be replaced," she stated.

"So why don't we go take a look instead. We might find reasonable cause."

"I'm game if you are."

"Good." She grabbed my M9, still in its leather holster, and placed it on the table before her. "Can I trust you not to lose your cool again?"

I nodded.

"Good." She slid across my M9. "Lock and load."

I raised an eyebrow and bit back a laugh as I stared at her.

"I just said that didn't I?" She asked sheepishly.

I nodded.

"Damn, I might be watching too many 80's action movies."

Damn, I might be in love.

Chapter 12
I Wonder What the Director's Cuts Are

Another short drive, with Puzo behind the wheel – apparently she didn't let anybody else drive -- and we approached the warehouse. We'd moved out of the commercial sector and into the industrial, a trip that would have taken the better part of an hour on a bus. Agent Lord-Alge sat in the passenger seat, he called shotgun first. The FBI has shotgun rules; who knew? Puzo wasn't allowed to go into a situation like this alone, FBI regulations, and the plain truth was she wouldn't want to. You always wanted somebody covering your back. Probationary Agent Mitchell Lord-Alge pointed to the building as we approached. Puzo slowed the car as she pulled in. I was expecting a dark shady place with thuggish looking men smoking in the shadows. The building was nothing like that. It was a giant white building with the top floor covered in glass acting as a greenhouse for rare plants. The exterior was decorated with symmetrical black lines that created the illusion that the building was built by putting hundreds of white cubes stacked atop of each other, like an adult version of Lego.

"He staying in the car?" Lord-Alge queried.

"No, he's coming in with us, Hitch." It's amazing how if you put a group of people together in a tight-knit unit, be they police, FBI or combat boot wearing grunts, it won't be long until they start nicknaming each other. It was comradeship at work.

"I'm useful," I boasted like a five-year-old child. A snort came from the front of the car. I wasn't sure from whom but I obviously made one of them laugh.

"Look: parking lot," the kid pointed. I could see nearly a dozen white delivery trucks, each with the image of two DNA strands criss-crossing to form a medical cross on the side. That was the logo of Croxallé.

I'll be honest. I saw the trucks but as to what relevance was, that was beyond me. Was there a secret to trucks that the FBI taught? Was it a class in Quantico: Trucks 101? "What of it?"

"Croxallé's trucks are all white," he explained. "Now look at the loading dock; blue truck with no logo."

"We might be here for a robbery," Puzo said. She looked at her watch. It was only 10:15 in the morning. "This place should be busy but it looks dead. Keep your weapon holstered but be ready. This isn't reasonable cause yet but we're getting close."

She parked the car and the agents climbed out. I looked at my cane and decided against it. I would be fine as long as things didn't get hectic, I'd be limping a lot but I would have to hold onto a cane if this turned into a firefight. I donned my hat as I climbed out. My right hand dropped to my M9, the steel-plastic combination feeling on my fingers was reassuring, not as reassuring as an a M4 carbine but aside from mom's home cooking, very few things in this world were.

I limped after the agents. Hitch held open the door and mocked a gentlemanly bow. I sneered at him. He was implying I was a woman. If he didn't look like a twelve-year old boy I'd slug him.

"We got a body." Four words and the agents had their Glock 22s drawn. Damn they were fast. I'd barely unsnapped the holster and theirs were already drawn. I limped over to see a body, just as she said. He wore a security outfit, ruffled and worn like he'd worn it every day for twenty years, and had a bullet hole in his forehead. I assumed the hole was new.

The agents were not messing around. Puzo's gun led

the way, guiding her into the backroom of the warehouse. Hitch followed, his weapon covering what hers couldn't. I limped after them. My M9 rested securely in my hand but sadly my hand couldn't stay still. It shook, only slightly but enough to warrant concern. It had been nearly two years since I'd been released from the Army and another six months before that since I'd seen battle but here I was, about to enter what I assumed was the second firefight in just as many days. I could feel how my body reacted; sweat pouring down my forehead, my heart racing and the unmistakeable feeling of sickness.

I didn't want to do this again but I couldn't just stop. I had to solider on.

With my gun pointed at the floor I limped into the main warehouse. Racks upon racks of cardboard boxes filled the room. It was like the end of *Raiders of the Lost Ark* or the beginning of *The Kingdom of the Crystal Skull*, just with red shelves, blue beams, dozens of forklifts and bad guys. To be honest the bad guys were in *Crystal Skull* as well. At least my movie doesn't have Shia LaBeouf. I don't know much about psychology but somehow I know that referring to real life as a movie can't be healthy but I do wonder what the director's cuts are.

There were a dozen men, some pulling wooden pallets of supplies off the shelves and bringing them down to the ground with the aid of forklifts, others were looking at a list and a map, to find the locations of their desired items and the rest just stood watch. If they were bad guys then we were out numbered. I heard the sound of heavy footsteps on a steel walkway above us. Hitch and I both glanced up.

I spoke with my fingers; using military hand signals to say I was going to check upstairs. Hitch nodded. Having me covering his back wasn't his first choice, I wasn't anybody's first choice – hadn't been in years – but without anybody else I was all he had. I limped towards the stairs, my M9 held before me as I climbed the metallic steps. I moved as silently as possible, a difficult task considering I needed the railing to climb the stairs, but somehow I made it up the stairs without tripping.

I saw him, a man patrolling the walkways with a Heckler & Koch MP5 in his hands. Obviously he didn't work here. This walkway was a makeshift second floor; it attached to several elevated offices and allowed the foreman to look over the work-floor at his employees. I pictured a man leaning over the rails and yelling at some poor sod named Jenkins. It's always a Jenkins, that guy who gets picked on and never stands up for himself. Man, I hate Jenkins; whoever he is I hate him.

I crept forward and leveled my gun. Using that scary Ranger voice that they teach each and every one of us I ordered him to freeze. He turned around and saw me, or more specifically my M9, glaring at him. I ordered him to drop his weapon and kick it across the railing. He grudgingly did. Another order from me forced him to turn around and put his hands on the railing. I crept closer, my M9 sights lined up with the back of his neck. One squeeze and I blow his vocal cords out through the other side. One squeeze and I'd alert every stock-footage looking bad guy to where I was. It was a win-lose.

I got closer and, after pulling off my glove with my teeth, I touched his jacket. I felt a shiver and a twitch and I dive head first into a vision. This bad guy, who had the super original henchmen name of Brooklyn, stood in an office, his boss standing before him and others.

"Okay, one more time for Jenkins over there," an exasperated team leader says. "I will go over the plan *one-more-time*."

Damnit. It's always a Jenkins. Man I love Jenkins; whoever he is I love him. My vision begin to turn, like a TV camera, as everybody turned to look at the whiteboard filled with files and writing. This is it! This is their plans. I start to read the writing.

    Step One: Kidnap Robert Belledin
    Step Two: Bring him to......

NEVER BEEN TO MARS

An elbow to the head knocked me out of my vision and back into the dull world that is reality. Before I realized what was happening my formally subdued bad-guy, Brooklyn, had stolen my M9, punched me in the face, grabbed my shoulders, kicked my bad leg out from beneath me and tossed my sorry-ass to the floor. I crashed into the steel walkway, my hat bouncing away, while Brooklyn stood a couple feet back with my M9 pointed at my head.

New rule: Psychometry is not a combat maneuver.

Brooklyn didn't gloat; he didn't talk or question me. He just lowered the weapon, slightly, and gave it a two-second check, cocking it and making sure the safety was off, before leveling it back at my forehead.

On TV this is where the bad guy would gloat for a second before cocking the weapon, pointing it at the hero and begin squeezing the trigger. Our damsel in distress would close her eyes and wait for death. The viewers would hear a single loud bang and hold their collective breaths. Was our main girl dead? Did they just kill off the love interest? Just then we see blood, not from the damsel but from the shooter. The bad guy falls to the ground dead only to see the hero standing behind him with a gun. It's an over-used cliché in TV and film, something that never happened in real life. The hero never showed up just in time and in a situation like this the damsel in distress always died. TV had lied to me again and considering I was the damsel in distress this time, I was pissed. If I survived this I was giving up TV for good.

Brooklyn suddenly convulsed as three tiny holes tore through his jacket and into his chest. He collapsed to the ground, unable to speak as blood quickly filled his lungs. I craned my neck to see behind me. Standing in that *I-just-shot-someone-at-the-right-time* pose, the one overused by TV, was the man with a thousand names: Agent Joseph Price. His silenced pistol stayed pointed at the body as he dashed over.

"What the hell are you doing here, Benedict?" he whispered in disbelief as he stepped over the body.

"I'm... investigating?"

Price knelt by the fallen baddie and checked him over. He shook his head and stood back up, leveled his pistol downwards at the fallen man's head, and squeezed off another round. He looked back at me. "He was suffering. I had to end that." He helped me up. "What the hell are you investigating?"

"In ten words or less," I explained. "Robby's been kidnapped and it led me here." I paused. I had two words remaining. I had to make them good. I had to make them Kool-Aid Man good. "Oh yeah!"

He frowned. "And that brought you to Croxallé's warehouse during a robbery? I'm going to need more detail than that. Grab your gun and follow me."

I retrieved my weapon, gave it a two-second check of my own, and limped after him. Price was everything you would expect from a super-spy. He dressed like the MIB, black pants, black jacket, black tie with a white shirt for contrast and a pair of black rimmed glasses. He moved like Jason Bourne, the product of a traceur-spider crossover, and he thinks like James Bond. I've seen him, through the power of visions, breach a room, kill a room full of terrorists, and even secure a bomb. This man was scary and that was before I saw his superpower.

FYI a traceur is a male person who does parkour. A female partcipant is called a traceuse. I didn't come up with that name, the French did. It's the rules of the universe. If you create something you get to name it. That's why my special casserole is called *What The Bloody Hell Surprise*.

"Where's the cane, Thompson?" This was the second time I'd ever met Price face-to-face.

"It's in the car," I admitted as I picked up my Stetson and returned it to where it properly belonged. "I didn't want it in a firefight."

"Who are you here with?"

"Two FBI agents, they're below trying to figure out how to approach this," I said with a nod to the baddies below. "Agents Puzo and Lord-Alge."

"Keep watch." Price dropped to one knee and started to dig through his pockets. He withdrew three different government ID wallets and started to look through each. He picked one, placed in his front pocket, and hid the others within his suit. "If your FBI people ask I am Agent Neil Green of the Secret Service. Don't mention eye-beams; don't mention spies; just go with the truth."

The man of a thousand names reveals another one.

Before I could answer he was back on his feet, his FN Five-seven pistol back in his hands. He squeezed off two rounds and both slammed into the body of another baddie emerging from the foreman's office. The man fell to ground, dead before he even knew that he had been fired upon.

"If you don't know about Robby then you're not here for me." Price, or Agent Green, just shook his head. "Then this is just a coincidence?"

"No such thing."

"Then what the hell are you doing here?"

Price stepped into the foreman's office and moved to the computer. "Watch the door. I'm investigating an organization we think is abusing powers." He seemed to be fishing for words, not knowing exactly what he was allowed to reveal to me. "But at this moment I am trying to stop a robbery."

"Why are they robbing a place during the day?"

"I messed up their plans for last night. I'm wicked that way."

"Who are they?"

He looked up at me and decided to take a risk. "They are soldiers of WhiteStar Security Consulting."

That was three.

"WhiteStar?" This was no longer a coincidence, this was a pattern. Puzo's lessons were paying off. "That name keeps popping up. I think WhiteStar kidnapped Robby."

Price looked up from the screen, his eyes narrowing. He was piecing things together, solving his own puzzle while leaving mine with massive holes, but before he could speak they were interrupted. Another baddie stormed the room, his

MP5 pointed at Price. "Don't mov..."

He never got a chance to finish his threat as twin tongues of blue flames shot from Price's eyes. The fire, which I had seen burn through a firearm like butter, had little resistance as it tore through skin and bone, making two little eye-sized holes in the chest of a screaming man.

"Shit. They know we're here." Price pushed his glasses back up the bridge of his nose. "Cover the door!"

I leaned on the doorway and stared out onto the walkway. Two more of these WhiteStar baddies were coming up the stairs. "Are all these guys bad?"

"Anyone on this mission is."

"Gotcha." I stuck out my M9 and squeezed the trigger. With two loud bangs I fired two rounds. They tore into the lead soldier and dropped him to the floor. I squeezed two more to drop the other. I switched to the left side and fired off another pair. One round went wide but the other slammed through the neck, forcing his Adam's apple out through the back. "Hurry up."

I looked down over the warehouse floor; a firefight had erupted between the FBI and the unsuspecting goons. Puzo and Hitch were separated and each was fighting for their lives. Hitch had downed one soldier and was coming up on another. The WhiteStar soldiers were well trained. One of them was laying down steady fire on Puzo's position, keeping her pinned down for fear of being shot, while another snuck up on her flank. Price grabbed his pistol, slid it into his shoulder holster, and moved to the door, he paused at the fallen body to grab the discarded MP5. He dashed to the rail and opened fire on the floor below. He wasn't aiming at anyone he was just spraying bullets like paint. None of them would find a meaningful mark, unless he was really lucky, they simple made a lot of noise and scared the living crap out of the people below; scare them enough so that their constant stream of gunfire paused. It wasn't a long pause, less than five seconds, but for a trained agent like Puzo that was all she needed. Like the world's deadliest jack-in-the-box she sprung up with a gun in her hand and started firing. Six shots were all it took for her to take out her attacker and drop the man sneaking up on her.

"Okay, let's go," Price ordered. "We're going down the stairs. I'm taking point; you follow."

I nodded and limped along behind him. The last time I saw Price with a gun he was a machine. He had single-handedly cleared a room of terrorists in mere seconds. It was an all or nothing moment and Price gave it his all. He had been injured at the time, and barely made it out alive, but Price was the type of guy that when shit was on the line he stepped up with a shovel. Being his back-up seemed a little out of my range but it was shovel time. I had to step up.

Price moved down the stairs, his stolen MP5 spraying bullets. He needed the stairs clear, like the landing zone in a military mission; you couldn't land if you were under fire. With fewer bullets in each magazine and a short effective range of fire, I couldn't follow suit. I had to pick my shots, aim carefully and squeeze off what I could.

Price's feet hit the floor and Puzo immediately turned on him. Her gun snapped to his chest, locking onto his black tie. "Stop, he's with me." It was like a scene from a romance movie, the girl crying out to her dad not to shoot the adorably cute drifter who she invited into her room.

Puzo turned back to the WhiteStar goons and kept firing. They were using covering fire as a means to escape. In the military world its called suppressive fire, which as NATO defined it is the application of fire, coordinated with the manoeuvre of forces, to destroy, neutralize or suppress the enemy. In short that means they fired at us with a shit ton of 9mm rounds using that, plus the visual and audible distraction, to degrade our performance in order to retreat into the back of the blue delivery truck. Suppression fire is a basic military tactic, every solider knows it from the grunts to the Rangers; even those pansy sailor boy marines know suppressive fire, and if the navy can understand it, it must be simple.

With the roar of an engine and the squeal of a tire the WhiteStar men sped away, leaving the injured and deceased behind.

"--- partial plate 257." Without the sound of gunfire Lord-Alge's voice could finally be heard. He was on a cell phone calling for backup.

Puzo ejected her magazine and replaced it with a fresh one. She gave Price a look of uncertainty, the type of gaze you only saw on the nature channel. It was the look a lion gave when a stranger in a suit carrying a machine gun showed up. "Any damage?"

"Five by five," I muttered.

"Who's my saviour?"

"This is Agent Green of the Secret Service," I introduced. "I met him six months ago."

My intro does little to ease the FBI woman but based on what she learned this morning I don't blame her. Once burned twice shy.

"Backup's on the way and cops are trying to track the delivery truck. Who's the suit?" Lord-Alge asks as he hangs up the phone,

"He's secret service. He's staying here with Ben while you and I clear the floor," Puzo ordered.

Hitch nodded. Both FBI agents moved together, going aisle by aisle with their guns drawn. The place was huge. There were dozens of places a single gunman could hide, and the two agents wanted to search them all. Nobody wanted another ambush. I looked down at my hand, it still held my M9. I wasn't ready to holster the weapon yet. My hand still shook, it was little more than a twitch but it was one that wouldn't go away. I thumbed on the safety and tried to take deep breaths.

"You okay?" the agent formally known as Price asked.

"Yeah, I'm fine." I did little to reassure him. "I've just been... different since I returned home."

Price lowered his weapon and looked at me. He pointed to the gun. "First put that thing away. Now take off your glove." I listened, first holstering my weapon and then pulling off my left glove. "I need you to take a deep breath. I want you to focus on what you're feeling now, the fear, the anxiety and the nausea and let it overwhelm you. It's like being trapped in a room and water is rising up. Let the water rise. There's no way to escape it, you are going to drown."

I could visualize it, the water climbing up my body, passing my waist and heading north. My heart beat faster, it was like a xenomorphic creature buried within my chest slamming against the ribs in an effort to get out. My stomach was no help; it churned as my nausea grew. The room started to spin like a tilt-a-whirl and I couldn't think straight. My thumb squeezed as hard as it could and I tried to fire off a round; the safety kept the round chambered.

"It's getting higher. It's risen past your chest and shows no sign of stopping," Price whispered. "Now it's at your neck."

Like a thermometer for fear, the water kept rising. The water was at my neck, I could feel it, the freezing cold and the torrential dampness. Every nightmare I had, time and time again, and every flashback just flooded my mind.

"You feel it on your lips, the water just about to pour down your throat," he illustrated. "But before it gets there, before that last moment when the water washes you away you need to touch the floor. Do it. Touch the floor. Now!"

I didn't argue and I didn't think. I just dropped to the floor and slapped my hand down on the hard concrete. Since my accident I have seen literally thousands of visions and I could gauge the method of which I was escorted into the past but this was unlike anything I had ever seen. Every inch of my body shivered and every muscle and nerve twitched. I looked like I was having a seizure. My consciousness slammed against the past like a high speed crash. The engine and hood crumpled on impact, the windshield shattered into thousands of deadly shards, and the rear end of the car lifted off the road flipping the entire vehicle. The only difference was my consciousness didn't come with airbags.

My vision was like a water slide and the waves were forcing me along. I could see the enclosed slide all around me except the sides weren't made out of the same ugly orange material as the rest; they were made from fractured moments of the past. I saw Puzo and Hitch, mere seconds ago, clearing another hallway. The further down I slid the further into the past I could see. I could see the firefight I was just in, I could see the robbery in progress last night and in the distance I could even see glimpses of the building being built.

I don't know what the hell this tunnel was, some sort of Clarity Channel, Psychic Passageway or Super Subway, and I was a little too engrossed into the situation to choose a name but whatever this vision-based slide was, name to be determined, it was giving me access to everything, every point in time for this object.

I tilted my head, if I had one – I seemed more of an essence instead of a body in Tunnel-TBA - and looked to my right. I saw a room with three WhiteStar grunts and Price stuck in the middle. I reached out with my hand and gave it a touch. Suddenly I was there, not as an omnipotent presence like normal but as Price himself. I was seeing what he saw and doing what he did.

Our left arm wrapped around that of a WhiteStar soldier as our right hand slammed against his face. I could feel the bones in our hand, toughened by years of fighting, connecting with the soldier's jaw. We punched him three times in total, a little excessive but we deemed it necessary, then we grabbed his trapped arm with both hands and jerked it upwards. With a loud crack the bone snapped.

Now that was excessive.

We turned to see two remaining soldiers ready to lunge. One had a combat blade out while the other searched the floor for a pistol. Our memory reminded us that there were three pistols lying out there, we had disarmed them when we ambushed them. The blade-man slashed at our face but we leaned back. We could see the blade passing by, mere inches from our glasses-covered eyes. We fought with a style I couldn't recognize, using swift kicks to the knees and open-palm strikes, slaps really, instead of punches. We dodge the knife as much as we could, our arm feeling the full effect of a slice we were too slow to dodge. We kept at it, avoiding the blade as we moved closer. A kick to his knee finally forced his leg to buckle and gave us the moment we need. We grabbed his knife arm and wrist and folded it like a detention slip from a teacher. His wrist cracked and we grabbed the blade and stabbed it deep into his shoulder. With one remaining we spun and lunged. The last WhiteStar employee, now holding a gun, moved to fire. He didn't know what he was doing. He was good with a weapon but not in close quarters combat. We were. We stored the knife in his gun arm and kicked the firearm across the room as it dropped from his hand. The metalplastic mix skips across the concrete. We moved faster than a stabbed soldier, pretty much everything does, and our arms wrapped across his neck and put him in a sleeper-hold. Our arms compressed one or both carotid arteries and the jugular veins without compressing the airway. The result is his body went limp in a matter of seconds. Damn, we're good.

    Reality returned with another car crash, one that sent me flying backwards and put me on my ass, hard. I was gasping for air and screaming out in pain. My head screamed for release, using a migraine as its voice. My stomach flips like a pancake and the rest of my body was being just as helpful. Every ray of light and ping of sound made my head want to explode like a Michael Bay movie and moving to cover my eyes or ears just caused more pain.

    Then it came.

    I rolled over, despite the pain-filled cries of protest, and vomited. What little I had to eat that morning, combined with the excessive amount of drink I had had the night before, flew out in a painful experience. I hadn't felt this bad since the Ranger School graduation party.

    Stop the world. I need to get off.

    What the hell just happened?

    "You took everything you were feeling," Price explained. "The fear, the anxiety, everything; you took it all and used it to fuel your powers. First time I did that I blew a hole in the side of a jeep and couldn't see for a week."

Price stood over me and picked up my fallen hat. If I was a sorority girl he would have rubbed my back and held my hair. "It's dangerous; to throw everything you are back into your powers, if you don't know what you're doing."

"Then why?" I asked between groans and fits of vomit. "Why make me do it?"

"You have so much potential, Ben," he explained. "You just have to learn what you can do. I wish there was an easier way but when it comes to abilities like yours and mine and the dozens of others it's a sink or swim mentality. Each power is not without its own risk."

"We're clear," Puzo's voice called out as she approached. She looked at me on the floor, raised an eyebrow to the vomit, then looked back up at Price. "What happened to him?"

Price just feigned ignorance, something we was deviously good at. "Psychic backlash." I groaned. What a comic book answer. It was something I'd heard Robby used to describe the *X-Men*. It was probably somewhat true, it made sense, but it was such a theatrical choice of words.

"You're going to be okay?"

I groaned a positive reply.

"Good. The floor is clear. We're calling local police and our guys in. In the meantime, Agent Green, I'd like to see some identification please."

I noticed how neither Puzo nor Hitch had holstered their Glocks. They hung by their legs, still secure in their hands but pointing downwards at the ground. Green/Price reached into his suit jacket and withdrew his leather badge holder. He handed it off. Puzo looked it over, content in its authenticity she returned it and holstered her weapon. Hitch followed suit.

"Not that we're not grateful for your assistance," she explained. "But what the hell is the Secret Service doing here?"

"We've been investigating a faction threatening

the President. My investigation led here." There are apparently signs that a person isn't speaking the truth, signs that they're being deceptive. They could range from avoiding eye contacts, change in voice and body language, or changing subjects. Price exhibited none of these. He was a perfect liar. "How does a pharmaceutical company link to a missing child?"

"That's what we're trying to find out."

The jurisdiction stare; a common device use in cop TV. Who had access to the case? Who was allowed to know the case details? Whose boss had the bigger pull? It was like a governmental dick-size contest. On second thought scratch that last one. I'd rather not link the woman I just slept with to a penis metaphor. Call me old fashioned that way.

"Here, Ben," Price/Green helped me up. "Back on your feet."

"I am never drinking again," I promised, "and this time I mean it."

"You weren't drinking in the first place," Puzo reminded me.

"Then who's up for a drink?" I suggested. "Green's paying."

Chapter 13
Better than an Elephant

Do you believe in déjà vu? As I looked out over the warehouse floor and watched the CSI circus examining the makeshift battlefield I got the strongest sense that I had seen this before. In two days I had seen the FBI's resident CSI team four times. Between two murders and two separate gun fights these guys had been working their asses off. I hoped they were getting overtime. Puzo and Hitch were overseeing the project, pointing out every shot they could recall. I was sitting on the sidelines, watching.

"Hey, touch this." Am I the only one who thinks that sounded dirty?

I looked up at Puzo. She handed me a plastic bag with a spent round in it. I took the bag from her and poured it out into my hand.

Nothing happened.

No shiver, no twitch, and no vision. There was nothing. I rolled it around in my palm and tried to concentrate; nothing. Thousands of items no longer trigger visions; normally they are the same items I touch daily, like forks, knives or my hat, but never a bullet. Just like a gun everything a bullet done is based in emotion. There's no way around it. In the hierarchy of vision-based items a bullet ranked high.

I shook my head. She shrugged and walked away.

What the hell had happened? I was scared and relived

at the same time. This could have been the end of my psychometry curse, the end of my problems, the end of the constant troubles and SRG interruptions, yet I couldn't help but be scared. I had come to expect my powers. They were there when I woke up, they were there when I slept, and they were there for everything in between. They had become a security blanket, my voyeuristic peephole into the world since past. My powers elevated me above the rest of the injured war-vets. My visions made me special. Without them what was I but a sad stereotype?

Price, still using his Agent Green pseudonym, eyed Puzo's departure as he approached me. "Your visions will come back."

"Are you sure?"

He nodded at me. "When you throw everything that you are back into yourself it tears you up inside. It won't take long to heal. You should be seeing things again within the hour."

Somehow this was reassuring.

"Okay Green/Cook/Wind/Price," my voice suddenly took an unexpected confident tone. "We need to talk."

"Figured as much; outside."

I followed him out of the warehouse and onto the loading dock. "It was you, wasn't it?"

"You're going to have to be a little more specific than that, Thompson," Price smirked. "I've done quite a lot."

"My mysterious brown package," I explained, "the one that made me a detective overnight. That was you?"

He just ignored me. "What brought you to this warehouse? How does all of this link up to your nephew's kidnapping?"

So I elucidated. I told Joseph Price everything, the man I had met only one other time before this, the man I accused of treason and of being a terrorist. I told him it all. It started with the kidnapping, I explained how I got to Dr. Caine, how I learned of Project: Canaan and the Lycotta gene and how that gradually led me to WhiteStar.

Price just listened. He never said a word as I spoke; he just took it all in. He reminded me of Puzo. They both shared a similar look, one they reserved for when pieces of the puzzle were falling into place and the picture finally started to make sense. All that white was a windmill and those yellow slivers were ducks.

"Superpowers and evil medical companies, conspiracies and men in black, I don't know what the hell I've dived into, Price, but I'm in way over my head." I was close to pleading. Saying everything out loud had just made me realize how ridiculous it all sounded. A world full of hidden superheroes and medical conspiracies, I'd seen this show and, from the second season onward, Zachary Quinto ruined it.

"You've learned a hell of a lot in a short amount of time," Price explained with a surprised tone laced with respect. "You've learned stuff I didn't know yet. Croxallé isn't the only company developing – super powers— it's just the first one you've run into." Price adjusted his glasses, pushing them back up his nose via the bridge. "There are literally dozens of companies spread out across the world searching for the exact same thing, the secret to human advancement."

He looked around; making sure none of the CSI or Puzo's team had snuck up on them. "There used to only be one company, big enough to experiment untouched. They got a little too big for their britches and stepped out of line. They got spanked."

"Visegar?"

Price shook his head. "No. There was older company that used to exist but it's gone now. A couple decades later and two new organizations show up. One is the Visegar Company and the other is Polaris Industries." I had heard of Polaris Industries, everybody had. They were a massive mega-cooperation like GE or Disney. They existed in the public eye. Visegar, on the other hand, was the shadow of a mystery.

"Visegar doesn't exist though," I said. "I can't find anything about it."

"In the eye of the public, Visegar went under in the

eighties," Price said. "But they're still around. They are hidden in hundreds of smaller businesses, originations, NGOs and even non-profits, all spread out across the globe. It was easier when they had a face. Now they're like splinter cells, hidden and waiting orders."

"So who are you guys? The MIB? The Secret Service? I mean you have an army right?"

Price thought carefully before he answered. "We are Oversight. We are small, we always have been; we just have reach. We can stick our fingers into almost any cookie jar and pull out something sweet."

My head spun. "So what does this have to do with you and Robby?"

"I've been investigating WhiteStar for a while now. They popped up overseas with a couple energized humans. There was an earth manipulator who could control sand with his mind and a guy who could spit acid. We've been seeing this more and more with WhiteStar.

Their meta numbers are beyond what they and their parent company can produce. We're trying to find out where they keep getting them from. A certain percentage is from recruiting but the rest of the math doesn't make sense, until now. You just solved the riddle: they're kidnapping Croxallé's children and making child soldiers."

Oh Jesus. I need to find my nephew before they put a gun in his hand and made him kill. I'd taken a life; it's not an easy thing to do or an easy thing to live with. Never in a thousand years would I ever wish that upon him.

"I take it Robby hasn't shown any superpowers?"

I shook my head. "Robby is just your average everyday kid. He's okay at sports, he hates school. He's about two years away from noticing girls but in the meantime he likes comic books, science fiction and fantasy."

"No flying then?"

"None."

"He hasn't hit puberty yet so his powers wouldn't have fully manifested," Price instructed. "But he should still be showing some signs. How's he at school?"

I shrugged. "He hates it. The kid's bright. He knows a lot, he may not understand it all, but he knows a lot of school facts. If he'd try harder he'd be amazing."

"Sci-fi and fantasy," Price said as he brought the conversation back around.

"The kid loves it. He'll see a movie and become obsessed. He'll learn everything he can about the world and series. He can name just about every battle that took place in *Star Wars* movies, books, comics and games. He can tell you who won, how it played out, and what was the turning event," I bragged. "If he could take one fraction of that attention and put it to actual wars or actual history, we could have an amazing professor."

"He remembers it all?"

"Every last piece," I confirmed. "I've watched him speak for two hours about Spider-Man. He talked about powers, enemies, deaths, clones, movies, comics, and something called the Ultimate version of Spider-Man. It was overwhelming and impressive all at the same time."

Price cracked a smile. "I think your nephew's powers have started to develop. I think Robby has perfect recall ability; he will remember everything."

"He'll have an eidetic memory?"

Price shook his head. "Let's use the popular metaphor: photographic memory. Even the best memory still has some gaps in it, your photo has a thumb in the way or the light was too bright to see every detail on the picture. Robby's memory will take a perfect picture, in mere seconds, every time without fail. Nothing can ever stop him from remembering something. He will literally never forget. He'll be better than an elephant."

"He remembers everything now?" I was worried about him even more now.

"No. His powers aren't fully developed yet, puberty does that, his are subconsciously triggered right now. If he's excited and wants to learn, like with comic books or *Star*

Wars, his powers will kick in otherwise they just stay dormant." Price nodded his head, as if he was answering his own question, "Yeah, I could see why a private military would want him. He'd be an invaluable resource."

"This is my nephew here, not some resource." Suddenly it hit me. "He'll remember everything?"

Price nodded. Shit. High school was going to be hell for Robby. Every bad moment, every shitty day, every heart break and soul crushing moment, he'd remember them all with perfect clarity for the rest of his life. It was soul crushing at best. He'd never fail a test and he'd never forget a birthday or holiday, he'd never forget anything. It sounded beneficial but was it worth it? God help him if he underwent something like I did. If he suffered so much that he broke. Most people could get over anything, they did it by forgetting or letting the memory fade away, but his never would. Perfect recall was going to be like psychometry, a curse.

"Alright, tell me about WhiteStar," I asked. Rangers lead the way, it was our motto, but we didn't do it idiotically. We always knew where were going and what to expect when we got there, it didn't always go according to plan but nothing ever did. So if I planned to go after WhiteStar, and I was, I needed to know everything I could about them.

"WhiteStar Security Consulting: they are a private military. They're a subsidiary of Polaris Industries. They rose to power during the early days of the Iraq war. On the surface they are exactly what you'd expect them to be, modern day mercenaries with government contracts. They mostly work within US contracts but have branched out across the world. They now do missions for almost every major country.

"Everything says they're legitimate. It's only when you dive deep do you see the dirt," Price explained. "They have a reputation of completing the most difficult tasks. Nobody ever really knew why their men were so good. Oversight eventually learned what they were doing; WhiteStar was recruiting super powered humans. They're Blackwater with capes."

"So what do they want with all the supers anyways? Is it just for money?" A private army armed with super heroes and super villains, deep down I prayed all they wanted was money; the other possibilities were too frightening.

"We have company." I looked up. Three cars were pulling into the warehouse's parking lot. The door opened and, like a clown car, suit after suit poured out. My simile turned out to be more astute then I had originally anticipated. The suits were mostly lawyers; clowns indeed.

"Oh, what fresh hell is this?" I muttered.

"This is Croxallé," he scoffed. "They have lawyer after lawyer backed by the company's top notch security specialists."

From the last car a tall man exited. He had brown hair, cut short, blue eyes and a solid chin. He wore a blue suit, a white shirt and a multi-coloured tie. It took one look from me to recognize the man.

"That's Jason Daggett," Price explained as he noticed my stare. "He's Croxallé's chief of security."

I just stood there stunned. "No he's not," I muttered. "He's Greg Hazeltine. He's Robby's father."

I stared in anger, my gloveless hand clutching my cane so tightly that my knuckles went white. Then I felt the familiar feelings; the shivers up my spine and the twitch in my eye. My visions were back.

Chapter 14
You Screwed My Sister... Figuratively and Literally

I sat in a bar; dark, dank, and something straight out of a movie. It was a hole in the wall gin joint, the type of place normally reserved for cops, gangsters, or writers. This place had a solid oak bar, a mirrored wall laced with drinks and a grizzled old bartender who'd been working there since before he was legally allowed to. He was the type of man who spoke with grunts over words. I never learned his name but I always called him Matt. Every Matt I knew was a quiet guy, never loud or outgoing, always quiet and humble.

I loved this bar. There was no pop music and no university students. There was just hard working men and women, a handful of cops, both current and retired, a couple off duty sergeants and even an old grizzled writer, a Hemingway wanna-be, drinking in the corner as he typed on his laptop. I loved this place but for the life of me I could never remember its name. It was a block from my apartment, had the best burger I have ever eaten and gave drink discounts to those who serve and those who had.

It was wonderful.

Truth was I didn't do this bar justice. A place like this deserved the dedication that only an alcoholic could provide. The endless nights of drinking, the sacrifice of your hard earned money and time, a level of devotion that only an addict provided. I wasn't an alcoholic but I was getting there. Only two weeks had passed since I'd made it back from Iraq and I had spent nearly every evening here, looking in the bottom of every bottle for an escape.

An injured war vet turned alcoholic. I was in the early stages of becoming a cliché.

I sat there watching the TV; a grudge match of a baseball game was on – Yankees versus the Red Sox – and I barely paid attention. I didn't care about the game, I didn't care about the family I had been avoiding the past two weeks, I didn't care about what I was going to do with my future, with my life, I didn't care about anything.

At the moment all I cared about was my guardian angel. It's not a religious thing; it's just the proper name for when you mix Crown Royale and Coca Cola. Most people call it a crown and coke, and I don't blame them, but right now, when there was little else looking out for me but my drink, the name guardian angel seemed to fit.

Matt was a grey haired man in a white shirt, blue jeans and an apron. He looked like something right out of a television sitcom but then again how would I know? Aside from the odd western movie I hadn't seriously watched TV in years. It never was my thing; no time. He handed me my food, a pub burger with fries literally pouring off the side. The burger was a thing of art, a patty nearly an inch thick filled, topped with ale-braised onions and mushrooms, creamy peppercorn-ranch, melted cheddar and Swiss cheese, and fresh tomatoes on a toasted onion bun.

The first bite is always an endeavour. How do you take a bite from a burger bigger than your mouth? You do it with a great deal of practice. My taste buds happily sang out as the burger hit my mouth. The onions and mushrooms danced a jig in the cheese and peppercorn while the meat, with just a hint of red, joined in. You don't often find places that will cook a burger rare for you but this place would. Maybe it's a good thing I don't know this place's name. I'd hate for it to become too popular. I liked my hole in the wall. Then again, who the hell do I talk to?

"I'll take a red-headed slut."

"Wouldn't we all?" I muttered between bites. I looked over at the guy. He was six foot nothing with short brown hair, blue eyes and a solid grin atop a solid chin. I coughed and stuttered, my food bunching up in my throat. I grabbed my drink to help wash it down, my guardian angel once again coming to my rescue. With my airwaves finally free I gasped. "Greg? Greg Hazeltine?"

"Hey, Ben."

I took a swing at him.

I tried to at least but my leg gave way and I crumbled like a house of cards. Greg caught me, a noble move considering I had just tried to knock his ass out, and helped me back to my stool. I eyed the black medical cane beside me, leaning up against the bar. I still wasn't used to it. I never thought about it. I needed it to do everything, I couldn't even get up to take a piss without it, but there I was, still thinking like I was whole, like I could walk upright on my own. I was thinking like I didn't need anything or anyone to help me. None of that was true anymore.

"Take it easy, big guy," he pleaded. "I just want to talk."

"Talk about what?" I muttered. "How you broke my sister's heart? How you knocked her up? How you pulled a ghost and vanished? Pick a topic – we'll talk about that."
Matt reappeared with Greg's drink and gave the both of us a look. Greg smiled and thanked him. He tossed back the drink and returned the empty shot glass to the counter. The drink, – the red headed slut - was a shot that had half an ounce of Peach Schnapps, half an ounce of Jagermeister and half an ounce of cranberry juice. "Get Ben another of whatever he's drinking and I'll take a Jack dashed with grenadine please." He looked over at me. "It's called a Spanked Piece of Ass."

Greg Hazeltine: classy as ever.

"Fair warning, buying me a drink will not win me over." It would help but I didn't tell him that. "You screwed my sister... figuratively and literally. I'm more worried about the first one."

Greg just stood there, quiet, and didn't say anything for the longest time. "I know."

"If you want to me to help you get in good with my sister I'm going to let you buy me a couple more drinks before I say it's not going to happen."

Greg chuckled. The bartender showed up with our drinks. Greg thanked him and slipped him a couple bills. "I came here to talk to you, Ben," he admitted. "I don't have any family and my friends wouldn't understand what I'm going through, but you would."

I just listened. I remember Greg being a bit like me, cocky, arrogant and believing that I was God's gift to women (in all fairness up until recently I hadn't come across any evidence proving that I wasn't) but this side of him was different.

"You know I didn't want to meet your sister," he began. "She was a rural girl raised on a post-Daisy Duke attitude. What the hell was I going to have in common with her? Our love of jean shorts? Work made me meet her."

I racked my brain to remember what Greg did. I wanted to say he was carpenter but that didn't sound right. That was the guy Annie dated after him. The more I thought of it the more I realized that I never knew what he did.

"I was the good boy employee. I did as I was told and met her, and I liked her." He laughed. "Your sister is quite amazing. She can handle a gun; she's tough as nails and hell, she looks amazing in Daisy Duke cut-offs."

"That's my sister's ass you're mentally ogling there. Please stop putting that image in my mind."

"Sorry," Greg laughed. "So I meet your sister and I fall in love with her. For the first time in years I'm happy. My employer isn't though. They were livid that I was with her. They said I shouldn't be involved with a..." He paused as he searched for the proper word. "With a client; they ordered me to end the relationship."

He drank from his glass, using the sting that alcohol provided to build up his courage. "You're a Ranger. You know what it's like when you're ordered to do something that you'd rather not. When an order goes against everything that you are as a person but you still do it."

Every soldier knew that feeling. Every man or woman, from any country, that went overseas for a posting knew that feeling. Even thinking about it in that bar, thousands of miles away from Iraq, caused my hands to shake and my drink to rattle.

"My co-workers don't get it. To them there is the company and nothing else. The company comes first, it comes before family, it comes before friends, and it comes before sex and money. It's a cut-throat world at the company; each of us is trying to climb that corporate ladder before somebody else kicks us back down. So for all of us when the company says jump we say how high.

"I'm just like the rest of them but then I met your sister. I realized there was more than the company. I was starting to change, to grow as a person. But when work told me to end it I fell on old habits and I ended it," Greg admitted. For the first time since he vanished I wanted to feel sorry. I shouldn't have, he bailed on my sister, but now it didn't seem so cut and dry. The more he talked the more I understood him. Most people would say he could have said no but in truth he couldn't. He was able to say no as much as any soldier was able to say no to their sergeant. Was I being too hard on him? He wasn't father of the year, that option was out the window, but he wasn't the monster we once thought he was.

"Did you know she was pregnant?" I asked.

"Yes."

And any sorrow I'd felt for him vanished with that answer, honest as it was. I could never say no to the army, they raised me, sculpted me into the man I was, but even the army couldn't permanently separate me and my hypothetical child. "So what do you want now? Do you want to meet Robby?"

"More than you'll ever know," he admitted. "But that's just selfish of me. I haven't been there for a single moment of his life. I don't deserve to meet him. Dave's his father.

He put the time in; he's been there for the kid. He's earned the right to call himself Robby's father; I haven't."

Today's just been a big day of surprises. I never expected to see Greg stroll into my favourite bar, order naughtily named drinks, and then spill his guts. I also didn't expect him to have such an honest and level headed view on this fatherhood thing. Most of the men in the army cling to being a father, even when they aren't there for most of their lives. I also heard the words baby-momma a lot. It was discouraging.

"So how is the kid?" he sheepishly asked. "I've tried to keep an eye on him but you spend the real time with him. What's he like?"

I loved my nephew, I really did, but the topic ripped me in two. A foolish promise I made to the kid when he was born, without a father, pulled me through when shit hit the fan in Iraq but here I was, back in the land of air conditioning, back in the land of freedom and shitty healthcare and I hadn't bothered to see him yet. Robby looked up to me, a lot of my family did, I was the guy that enlisted and went to fight a war. I was like a beacon of strength and health. Now I was a cripple forced to an ugly cane.

I didn't want any of them to see me like this.

I didn't want anybody to see me like this.

Yet there I was, sitting beside the man I spent years loathing, telling him about his own kid. I showed him a picture of eight year old Robby, a mop of blonde curls on his head and a smile three miles wide. I told him about his son, how he loved comics, adored science fiction and fantasy in all of its forms and was just a source of endless energy and happiness.

"If we could harness the kid they're be no more energy crisis," I joked. Greg laughed.

"So the kid's not weird or anything?" he asked. I just shook my head.

"He's as normal as any other eight year old. He thinks girls are icky; he loves any cartoon that has lasers and explosions, and loves trying to imitate a kung-fu punch in the air."

NEVER BEEN TO MARS

"Good." Greg smiled. He seemed lost for words again, his tongue running over his teeth, beneath his lips, as he carefully selected his verbal ammunition. "My family has a habit of being... off. Small little health hiccups. There hasn't been anything... different about him, physically, has there?"

Again I shook my head. "Nothing. He's in perfect health. I mean the kid's broken a bone or two, the occasional sickness, but all that's normal."

"Good, good." Greg reached beside him and pulled out a long zip-up black carrying case. It almost looked like a rifle case but was too flimsy to firmly hold a heavy stock. He obviously brought it with him and had it resting along the bar, like I kept mine, for the entire conversation. How I didn't notice it I don't know. I guess I wasn't that observant. It was probably a good thing I wasn't a detective or anything, because I'd be horrible at it. "When I heard about the accident and how bad it was I decided to get this for you."

He handed me the bag. I unzipped it and withdrew a wooden walking stick with derby handle made from a blend of silver plate and faux ivory. The handle had a mustang horse carved in basso-rilievo. It was beautiful.

"You shouldn't be using that black-plastic medical cane," he said with a smile. "You should be using something with class."

Before I had a chance to thank him he stood up and declared he had to leave. He slapped four bills on the bar and affirmed that my meal and next couple drink were on him. Then he left. As quickly as he had appeared he was gone again. I had learned so much about him today but one thing seemed to stay the same. Greg was always good at vanishing.

Chapter 15
He Always Replied with a 'Will Do' or a 'You Betcha.'

"Are you sure?" Price's words were the first I heard as reality returned. "Jason Daggett is Robby's father? That can't be possible."

"That's him," I said. "I'll never forget his face. That's Greg Hazeltine. That's the guy who knocked up my sister. That's the guy who met me in a bar two years ago, and that's the guy who gave me my cane," I declared. "That's him."

"That's Jason Daggett," Price explained. "He's the chief of security for Croxallé, not just the division in this city but all of Croxallé, all across the world. He's a skilled fighter, a hell of a shot, and a... special person like you and I."

I looked over at Price. I wanted to be surprised but the truth was it was getting harder and harder to be so, especially if this shocking revelation followed the one where Greg Hazeltine showed up under another name.

Puzo, with Lord-Alge following close behind, strutted right up to the suits and started to talk. Greg never seemed intimidating to me but be it the suit, the job or the company, now as Jason he did. He never faltered, he never twitched, and he didn't even shift his weight from foot to foot. He just stood there like a rock withstanding the river's current.

Price and I walked over. Daggett saw Price first and a smirk grew on his face. Then he saw me. His smirk faded and his eyes narrowed. I doubted that the odds of seeing me

NEVER BEEN TO MARS

weren't completely impossible but coming face to face with me here must have had been unexpected at best.

"Jason Daggett, this is Agent Neil Green of the Secret Service and Benedict Thompson, a local private investigator." With the FBI introduction coming to an end we were left in staring match. Greg/Jason, Cook/Wind/Price/Green and I, Ben/Just-Ben; we were a triangle of men just staring at the other, wondering who would break first.

"May I ask what the Secret Service is doing here?" Jason spoke first, a potential sign of weakness, but he cut through the bullshit with ten small words; an interesting opening gambit.

"My own investigation has seemed to coincide with the FBI," Price explained.

Jason looked at my cane and let loose a small smile. "Nice cane."

I shrugged.

"Enough with the pleasantries, you need to vacate the property. We cannot allow our corporate secrets to be viewed by *this* many people."

"This is an active crime scene. We are not going anywhere," Puzo said.

"It didn't become a crime scene until you unlawfully entered the premise," one of the lawyers piped up. "We will be filing a junction to have you removed."

"I don't know how long you've been out of law school," Puzo asked. "But a dead body in your lobby counts as probable cause. Now you need to leave. I cannot have you contaminating the crime scene. Hitch: get them out of here."

Puzo walked away, she didn't even give them a second glance. Hitch shoed the lawyers back. Price asked for Daggett to stay behind.

"Agent Green," he mocked Price with his Agent Smith tone once the FBI was out of earshot. "So that's the name you're going by today; last time you and I crossed paths you were Jacob Paige of the US Marshals."

Another name for the list, with each one I added on I

was getting closer to one apparent truth. Chances were Price was not his real name.

"I'm sure you have me mistaken for somebody else," Price replied calmly.

"I'm sure I do, just as Ben there has me mistaken for Greg Hazeltine." He eyed me with a smile. "What are you doing here, Ben? I didn't know you were a PI. I mean you show up at two separate murders, both at medical centers belonging to Croxallé, and now you're here. Frankly, I'm a little surprised. What in the world are you investigating?"

"They didn't tell you, did they?" And just like that I suddenly felt smart. I wanted to sing and brag like an eight year-old child would.

I knew something they didn't know.
I knew something they didn't know.
I knew something they didn't know.
I knew something they didn't know.

I could really learn to enjoy that feeling. "You were activated after a call from Dr. Caine ended. What did they tell you? Two attacks? Missing child? Stolen files? Murdered employees?"

His eyes narrowed. He was trying to figure out how I knew what I knew. "I got a file on all of that. I assigned a team to find the missing child, one to examine the stolen files, while I looked into the attacks and the murders."

"You know the stolen files were why the doctors were murdered?" He nodded.

"You know that WhiteStar was behind the killing and espionage?" He nodded again.

"Then you must know that the missing child is Robby." His eyes went wide. He hadn't been told. The missing child case must have been handed to him simply as a subject number, an alpha-numeric code.

"Robby is missing?" His fist clenched and I heard the unmistakeable sound of steel being crushed. Price and I looked to the left, to the parking lot, and saw that one of the Croxallé delivery trucks suddenly had a massive dent, the size of a large fist, in the side of its cabin. "Stay out of this, Ben, I'll get my men and we'll storm WhiteStar until we find him."

"You're not starting a war with a private military company," Price commanded.

"The hell I'm not." He glared at Price. "I know who you are. I know what you and your rag-tag band of spooks do. Don't think you can pull this government agent crap on me. You're not strong enough to stop me."

"You're willing to risk that, Jason?" It was a straight up super-hero taunting match. All we needed now was that iconic American hero to interrupt us and order us to stand down in order to deal with Loki. I saw that movie with Robby. It was a pretty kick-ass film. I liked the red-head – for her acting talent, I swear. "Are you willing to step up to the big boy leagues... Specter?"

Specter? Specter? Was that a super-hero name? O-M-G! That was a super-hero name. I had been waiting for those; super-hero names. Outstanding! I wondered what mine was going to be.

"Do you know what my guys call you Agent Green?" Jason taunted in a mocking tone. "You've been called Whisper, Delta, Griffen..."

"From *The Invisible Man*," Price interrupted. "I like that one."

"Murmur, Phantom," Daggett continued. "Ghoul and even Claude Rains."

"Like in *Heroes*." They both stared at me. "What? It was a good show back then."

"I'm a man of many names." That was putting it mildly. "So you should think twice before trying to go up against me. I will smack you back down. I don't care how powerful you think you are."

"Focus on Robby," I blurted, interrupting this meta-human pissing match. "He's been taken and we need to get him back. We need to figure out where WhiteStar took him and what their plan is. Right now we're operating under the assumption that they've kidnapped him and want to make him into a child solider because of his powers." Greg/Jason's ears perked at the word powers. "What would they do with him? How would they train him?"

"Assuming he isn't the only child they are training," Price began. "They couldn't do it on US soil. They'd never get away with it. They'd have to do it in either Uganda, Haiti --"

"Columbia, Sri Lanka, Burma... the possibilities are endless," Jason finished.

"What about Iraq? They have a base there." I knew nearly nothing about WhiteStar's bases but obviously these guys did. All I knew was WhiteStar fought in Iraq.

Price shook his head. "Iraq is too visible. They'd need to use a smaller base."

"Or call in a favour from one of their illegal allies and clients."

Watching these two go back and forth was like watching Jack Bauer chat with Chloe O'Brian. It was fast paced, used the names of a lot of foreign places and even though I knew little to nothing about any of those places, a grunt never asks he just goes there and shoots, I still knew to be afraid.

"We have to catch them before they leave the country."

"There's no way they're getting on a commercial plane with kidnapped children," I began. "Maybe a military plane?"

"Those are subject to US military inspection. They won't risk it," Dagget explained. "They'll be going by boat."

I grabbed my phone a quickly typed Hotwire a text.

Me: I need you to find any boats owned by WhiteStar Security

Then I waited. The other two seemed to have phones of their own in their hands, frantically typing away. I looked down at mine. I hadn't heard from Hotwire in a while. He had yet to answer my text about KyroCorp and now this one seemed to be going unanswered. Hotwire never gave me a report right away, he wasn't that good, but he always replied with a will do or a you betcha. I'd gotten nothing. The last thing he said was he was trying to dig deeper into this Visegar thing. I hoped it wasn't turning out to be a bad thing.

"Okay, I have three ships that I know of," Price spoke first. In the digital race for information the secret agent man came in first.

"I've got two more." The tragic chief of security came in second. "I'm calling in my men. We'll have all five of these ships cleared out."

Price eyed him. It wasn't a trusting look, far from it, it was a look that said do yourself a favour and don't cross me. "You look after your two boats, Ben and I will go for the other three."

"We will?"

Price nodded. "I assume you have Ben's number? Then call him when you clear a place. We'll need updates."

"Fine." Daggett walked away, his phone already to his ear.

I looked at Price. "Where we going?"

"That's a good question, boys." It was Puzo. Damn that woman was clingy. She approached us with a stern look on her face. "Where are you two going?"

Price looked at me. I nodded. I wasn't going to keep things from her about the case. She knew almost everything already. She was the reason that I had the leads I had. "We're going to investigate means of transportation that WhiteStar has available to them. We think they're getting the children out of the county."

"Children? You are expecting more than one?"

The man in black just nodded. "I expect you'll get a rash of missing children cases in the next couple hours. Anywhere from four to seven children, from this city alone, will vanish or have vanished in a twenty-four hour period. For whatever reason these children have been chosen, they're being shipped overseas today."

Puzo waved over Hitch. "I want all transportation out of the city shut down. No boats leave, no planes take off and shoot a bus driver or two to show that we're serious. Our children are being pulled out of the country today." He nodded and dashed off. "That should buy us some more time. Now where are you heading off to?" Puzo asked again. This, despite her cyclical cries last night, was not a woman who enjoyed repeating herself.

"We have a couple boats we're going to check out."

"You're not sure which one is the right one?" I just shook my head. "I might be able to help."

Puzo led us to the back of a police paddy wagon. She pointed to two men sitting in the back. "These two survived your little McClane acts," she explained. "They were smart enough to wear a vest."

"Do you have a name on them yet?" I listened as Price and Puzo chatted but my eyes never left the two rent-a-soldiers cuffed in the back. They looked like most soldiers I'd seen, the hardened stare that only comes from battle, the nerves long since dead, and the calculating mind always working. I could have been like those men if my leg had learned how to take a hit or two from high-speed shrapnel.

"Their names are Jesper Bierek and Mike Ejsing. Both are ex-navy marines. Both have seen overseas action and both were recruited days before they were due to resign." Puzo read off her phone. "We're going to transport them to the nearest FBI building and put them into interrogation."

Price shook his head. "We don't have time. Cuff one to a chair in the office upstairs. We can interrogate him there."

Puzo just shook her head. "I've already done one illegal interrogation today; I'm not going to do a second."

"Look this is a Secret Service matter," Price lied. "That means my jurisdiction supersedes yours. You take one of those marines and bring him up into that office."

"You really want to get into a jurisdictional pissing match with me?"

"Not really, Special Agent. What I want is ten minutes alone with this suspect," Price explained. "But you're not going to give that to me are you?"

Puzo stared and then shook her head with a sigh. "Put him in the upstairs room."

Watching an interrogation is nothing like on TV. You don't get the witty banter, you don't get the sudden realization, and you don't even get the tricky wording that catches the bad guy up in a lie. What you normally get is a bad guy sitting in a chair refusing to talk while the cops yammer on at them. That's what I watched as I stared through the glass window as Puzo drilled Mike Ejsing with every question she had.

"He's not going to break." Price was losing his patience. He had stood by me for the past thirty minutes while Puzo hammered her questions into the marine. "He's an experienced navy marine; they're trained not to break. It would take a hell of a lot more time and effort then we have available."

"What do you suggest?" Rangers were trained to resist interrogation. In my prime I was pretty good at it. Sadly my prime and I had parted ways, irreconcilable differences.

"Something a little more drastic." He knocked on the office glass with his thumb and waved Puzo out. The FBI agent grudgingly exited the room.

"He's not breaking."

"I noticed. I have plan B," Price suggested. "I'll need Ben though."

"Have at it."

Price escorted me to the door. "If he attacks either me or you, shoot him."

Price opened the door and ushered me in. He locked it behind me. I have only ever seen Price as the calm collected person he is. Even when I was ankle deep in vision and he was shooting his way through ridiculously uneven odds he had kept his cool. That was the Price I knew.

God, was I wrong.

"I tire of this," he explained calmly as he removed his glasses. He carefully folded them and slipped them into his inner suit pocket. "I've been playing nice with you guys. It's been all tea parties and lollipops. That stops now. I am going to ask you some questions. If you do not answer them with the upmost honesty I will hurt you."

The marine just scoffed.

"We know the kids are being transported by boats." Price looked for a reaction. There was none. "You cannot train the kids here so that means you have to go overseas." Still there was no reaction.

"So where is the boat?" Price's asked in an ice cold tone. "Where is the boat that the kids are being transferred to?"

The marine scoffed yet again.

"Last chance," Price offered. "You have five seconds to answer before I have to hurt you."

He slowly counted down from five, each number ticking away as I impatiently waited. Yet with each number the marine seemed less interested. As the final second passed without an answer Price was left with no other choice but to act.

He sighed loudly. "I warned you."

He moved faster than I could see, his hand darting out to grab Mike's. He slammed it down on the table. "Did you see the new Superman movie, *Man of Steel*? What about any of the *X-Men* films? Of course you have. Everybody has. Now Superman and Cyclops have a lot in common. They are both team leaders, Superman for the Justice League and Cyclops for the X-Men, they both have incorruptible ethics and both of them have father issues. Both of them also share the ability to fire beams from their eyes and the morality to only use it for good. I also share many of their traits, leadership and eyebeams, but we get to the morality and that's where Supes,

Cyke and I start to differ."

His eyes began to glow, the coloured iris flaring brightly as twin tongues of flames shot down at the marine's hand. Mike screamed in pain as the tongues of blue flame burned the back of his hand.

"You are doing WhiteStar's wet work. So you've obviously heard of me," he yelled over the Mike's screams. "I'm the government worker who can kill you with his eyes. I could burn a hole right through your chest or cut off your arm with a stray glance."

Price slowly moved his gaze up the marine's arm, the blue flames searing a path in the skin. "What I am doing to your arm is barely an eighth of my power. It took me years to get this level of control over my heat vision. If I'd tried this when I was younger, I would have burned right through your bone. Hell, back in the day a small snicker would have been enough to send my beams tearing up your chest."

Price closed his eyes and extinguished the azure flames. The Marine sobbed in pain. "Now I need to ask you again, where are the children? Where is the boat?"

I could hear the handle rapidly turn as Puzo tried to get into the room. Price remained unwavering in his advanced interrogation. "Still no answer? That's a shame, for you mainly. You are aware that of all the places I can burn with my eyes that your hand is just the bottom of the list."

Price's face once more became flush with anger as his eyes flared with flame. With his gaze redirected to Mike's chest he reignited the blue flames. His gaze burned into his chest, two small burn marks appearing just below the sailor's right nipple.

The screaming continued.

"The first time I ever used my eye beams on a human being I tore a hole right through their chest. I burned through their heart and clear through the other side. It was like something from a cartoon; a hole straight through the middle and out the back."

Price moved his eyes across the man's chest, burning a line from beneath one nipple to just under the other. He moved slowly, savouring every inch of pain and the smell of searing flesh.

Price closed his eyes for a second time, his eyelids putting out the flame. His calm facade returned. "There was a story about Superman, when he died fighting Doomsday, it was in all the papers. Superman Dies! It's funny what makes the papers. Needless to say the papers failed to mention how Doomsday died. It wasn't pretty. In one version Superman takes his eye beams and fires them directly into Doomsday's skull. He burns a hole into the alien's brain and lobotomizes him. I can do that to you. I could burn your mind away and leave you little more than a sniffling mess. It wouldn't be fast either. I would put my beams onto your forehead, I'd make you see it coming, and start with the mildest setting that I can manage. It would only itch at first, maybe even just sting, but the stronger I make it the more pain you'll feel. It'll be like trying to cut a coconut with a butter knife."

Price's rage returned as he grabbed Mike's head with both hands. "Where are the children?"

His eyes glowed and fire returned. Just as promised he put the beams on Mike's forehead and started things off low. I couldn't do anything but stare. Price was a government suit; he was the epitome of the legendary Men in Black. Torture never seemed out of the realm of possibility but this was beyond anything I'd ever seen. I'd witnessed water boarding, stress positions, sleep deprivation and even seen an artist play on a victim's fear but burning a subject with eye beam... I didn't know how to react to that.

The worst part was I didn't know if I wanted him to stop.

Puzo did. When the doorknob failed to give her access she was determined to find her own. She kicked the door over and over. Price just continued.

"At the rate I'm increasing my intensity you have twenty seconds before my flames start to cook your brain. What will go first? Your cognitive functions? Your memories?

Will you forget math or will your mother be the first thing to fade away?"

He sang.

Mike Ejsing, former member of the United States Marine Corps, cried out with every piece of information that Price asked for. He told us what ship they were on, when they were leaving and the SOP for security and staff. He told us everything and I mean everything. I now know who his first crush was (babysitter – classic), who his first kiss was (his cousin – weird) and who his first was (same babysitter – props).

The door burst open and Puzo stormed in, her Glock 22 drawn. "Get the hell away from him!"

Price closed his eyes and brought the flames to a halt. He reached into his pocket and withdrew his glasses and returned them to his face. "What the hell are you doing?"

Price held a closed fist in the air and slowly opened it, one finger at a time, until a silver device dangled from his middle finger. It looked like a very expensive version of those cheap laser pointer key chains.

"Relax, Agent Puzo." The calmness returned to his voice. "We have what we need. There is no need to overreact."

"What the hell is that thing?"

"It's an interrogation device," he lied. "It makes a blue light that can..." He paused for dramatic effect. "Encourage a man to speak."

Puzo wasn't a dumb woman. There is nothing that Price said that could've possibly been true but she seemed to accept it, at least for now. I read somewhere (saw it on TV) that the human mind is willing to accept a blatant lie instead of accepting an obvious impossibility. It could also be that Puzo was great at prioritizing and figured that trying to decipher how Price just tortured a man was not the most important thing at the moment.

"I have the information we need. Call your team and prepare a strike force. We need to move quickly."

"You just tortured a man," Puzo reiterated. "I can't just let that go."

"I did what was needed, Agent. Fault me if you will but I know where those children are. We can save them."

"I get it," Puzo explained. "You're Jack Bauer and I'm Renee Walker..."

"What does that make me?" I asked without thinking.

A smile crept up Price's face. "You're the mentalist."

I could deal with that.

Despite his joke, Puzo's Glock never wavered. The iron sights trained on the bridge of Price's glasses. "Red alert, Boss, we have a holy hell!" Lord-Alge entered the room with a file in his hand. He spotted Puzo's gun and instinctively drew his own, mimicking his boss. "What's going on? Why am I pointing a gun at a secret service agent?"

I just stared. I didn't know what to do but somehow I felt left out. I wanted to draw my M9 and point it at somebody but I just didn't know who. Also it was obviously a bad idea.

"What do you want, Hitch?"

"Message came down the pipeline. We just had three missing children reports show up and two kidnappings. This is big."

"You're running out of time, Special Agent," Price articulated. "What are we going to do?"

"We're not done here." Puzo lowered her Glock back into her holster. She looked at Lord-Alge. "Mobilize a FBI SWAT team."

With a final glare Puzo grabbed her phone and marched out of the room. Lord-Alge quickly followed leaving me in the room with Price and a sobbing Marine. I snapped my head towards my resident MIB.

"You can't torture people, you're the good guy."

Price slipped the key chain into his pocket. "You need to remember something, Ben. Just because I fight on the side of angels doesn't mean that I am one."

Chapter 16
I Should Totally Watch Expendables 2 When I Get Home

There is something miraculous about the way a SWAT team operates. They show up out of nowhere, with a van full of guns and equipment, save the day and then drive off into the sunset. They're like a myth. Everybody wants to see a SWAT team in action but that requires a horrific event and nobody wants that.

I expected SWAT to roll up in an armoured black vehicle and for Steve Forrest to jump out the back all while the classic SWAT theme music blared from unknown speakers. It's always a shame when real life doesn't live up to TV. This, however, was the rare time that real life was cooler.

In the world of Special Weapon and Advance Tactics teams there are none better then the FBI's Enhanced SWAT team. They are a specially trained squad able to assist the FBI's Hostage Rescue Team. Enhanced FBI SWAT teams are comprised of squads made up of larger numbers and have access to more extensive range tactical equipment. The Enhanced SWAT has the unique distinction of being available for a worldwide deployment.

When Puzo put in the call for SWAT and mentioned the key words KIDS, KIDNAP, and HOSTILE FORCE, the FBI sent their best. They sent Herron Unit. Those of us in the army were trained to be living breathing bad-asses. The Navy trains nancy boys, and the air force trains seats warmers. Yet all three branches, and those marine punks, have one thing in common. We name our biggest and meanest units after the animals that match. We don't name ourselves after birds. I'll never understand the FBI.

Yet despite their lame-ass name Heron Unit rolled up ready to do some damage. They were led by Agent Zachery Childs, a bald headed mean looking son-of-a-bitch. Take two parts Thomas Highway and one part Sam Jackson and you get the unit's leader.

Watching Childs work was impressive. His team moved almost without his orders and seemed to respond with almost a psychic link to his desires. The man took one look at our intel and set up a staging area three blocks away from the dock. From his team of twelve he sent three snipers, each on different points, to look down at the cargo carrier and prepped a team to board the ship. The team would initially be made up of nine people but once they got boots on the deck they'd split into three squads of three.

I wasn't going to be part of this rescue and I was fine with that. I was done with guns and shoot-outs. As of right now I was going to limit my action scenes to action films – no more real life recreations. I was no Stallone and my life wasn't the *Expendables* and I was fine with that.

I should totally re-watch *Expendables 2* when I get home.

Watching a SWAT unit work is nothing like TV. There are no wise cracks; there is no banter or inter-unit romance. There is just business. The snipers sit perched on a roof with their eyes on the boat. The units stand by the van waiting for the go call, each of them nervously gripping their firearms. Each of them had the look every soldier did before going on a mission or walking into battle. No matter how many times you'd seen action or battle, you were always nervous before the next one.

I stood with Puzo and Price, safely secured in the staging area watching the feed from a hacked close circuit camera overlooking what was to be my third battlefield in two

NEVER BEEN TO MARS

days. I hoped to god I could avoid this one, not to be involved, but even looking out over it brought a twitch to my hand and a rapidness to my pulse. All I needed was a flashback to complete my broken solider trifecta.

"All points: check in." Childs listened in as the groups called in over the radio, the three units by the van and the three snipers on the roof. When roll call ended Childs barked out his commands. "All units prepare to move. Overwatch: clear the deck."

The radio roared to life as the snipers coordinated their targets. High above the street snipers stood on their perches, aiming down at the lookouts patrolling the ship's deck. With a near unified crack the first three fell, it took less than a second for the next two to drop. They didn't even have a chance to reach for their radio or scream out loud. One of the lookouts didn't even notice that the other had fallen before a .308 round passed through his skull.

Damn these snipers were good. Hell they were better than good, they were amazing.

"Van: Go." With Childs' command the van sped out from the staging area and down the two blocks. SWAT members waited in the back, some sat in the van and a couple hung from the side, their MP5 hanging from around their necks. With a squeal the van came to a halt and the men poured out. Their guns secured in the grip and aimed up the ramp.

"Overwatch: climbing the ramp now. Watch our backs."

That's when the plan went to shit.

Murphy's Law says that no plan survives contact with the enemy; Heron's plan to board the ship wasn't an exception. Heron unit boarded the cargo ship to find a small army of armed men waiting for them. They were obviously hiding but damn if anybody knew where. They just seemed to shimmer into existence. It was like that scene in *The Rock* where Sean Connery and the marines breach Alcatraz and find themselves surrounded by Ed Harris and his evil men except here there was no Sean Connery, no Ed Harris and no idealistic talking.

There was only gunfire.

Heron unit shot first. If the two sides were muscle cars waiting to race, then the first crack of gunfire from a MP5 was the traffic light turning green – and all I could do was watch, short of breath and my heart racing.

WhiteStar had the advantage, they had surprise on their side and they had position but Heron had skill, they had the training and they had the gear. WhiteStar was a private military, they had no shortage of guns or armor but when you were trying to hide and to appear covert, you couldn't carry big rifles or wear bullet proof vests, instead you stood around with small rifles, automatic pistols, and shotguns while wearing whatever clichéd bad-guy jacket you could find. These guys seemed to favour denim. SWAT didn't have that problem. They could carry big M4 carbines, MP5 submachine guns and they could wear the biggest body armor allowed. Best of all, SWAT could easily carry grenades.

Heron unit pitched smoke grenades onto the deck and moved for cover, using cargo containers and lifeboats for protection as they took aim. Both sides traded weapon fire like baseball cards, passing it back and forward all the while hunting for that rare Roger Clemens rookie card. They were looking for that opening that would allow them to overtake the other. I prayed it would be Heron unit, it should have been, but WhiteStar wasn't playing fair.

The radio waves danced across the sky as the teams called out the positions and as the team leaders barked orders. Even the snipers, Overwatch, couldn't get a shot off. Their angry cries broadcasted across the radios. They couldn't see. Someone was shinning a light in their direction and it was leaving them blind a useless.

"Damnit, Child. Pull your men back," Puzo snapped. "They ran into a trap! They're going to get slaughtered out there."

"My men are fine. We're getting false transmission," he snapped. "Look at the cameras. There aren't any lights pointed at our sniper. My men will be fine."

NEVER BEEN TO MARS

"WhiteStar's cheating." Price grabbed a headset. "Flash Bang the deck – now! Everybody!!"

In the military technical terms a flash bang, or a stun grenade, is a non-lethal explosive device used to temporarily disorient an enemy's senses. In regular-people talk it surprises the living crap out of you. Movies and TV (god bless their soul) have always focused on the blinding light that a flash bang makes. In truth the stun grenades make a flash of blinding light and a loud noise, neither of which cause permanent injury. The flash produced momentarily activates all photoreceptor cells in the eye, making vision impossible for approximately five seconds, until the eye restores itself to its normal, un-stimulated state. The loud blast causes temporary loss of hearing, and also disturbs the fluid in the ear, causing loss of balance.

In short you're in a dark room and somebody just cranked on the lights and the radio all the way up to eleven at once – just stronger.

The ship should have lit up with a dozen flashes but instead all we got was a massive beam of light shooting upwards. It was like somebody shut down the containment grid in the firehouse. The beam was big and it was visible. We had a clear-as-day view of it shooting upwards at the staging area, three blocks back. I looked at Price with a confused look on my face.

Before he had a chance to answer, or Childs had a chance to rip off his head and crap down his neck, the radio came alive with gleeful voice of the snipers. "The lights are gone. We have clear shots. Support fire is a go."

Childs looked back to his screens. I looked at Price and whispered. "The hell was that?"

"That was a levikentic, a light bender," Price explained. "He was moving the light from around his guy and throwing it up to blind the snipers." Bending light around a person to make them invisible; I hated to admit it but that was cool. It was clearly cheating but that didn't rob it of its potential coolness.

"Then that beam of light was all the flashbangs?"

Price nodded. "Yep but the sound dropped him. Sensory powers often have a give and take; if you're good with sight then you're bad with sound."

Superpowers acted as a giant game of rock-paper-scissors; that was bad for me. I always lost that game. Now I will admit that ninety percent of that came from me always choosing rock. Good old rock, nothing beats rock. That being said it was reassuring that nothing was unbeatable.

I listened for a while as the gunfire echoed towards us, the sound getting lower and lower as the team moved further into the ship. I huddled by the radio like a child of the forties, listening to radio wondering if the Green Hornet and Kato were going to survive. Each transmission they sent, each update, felt like a cliff hanger at the end of an episode and the gap in between feeling like the week between shows.

"Room clear. Moving down."

"Children spotted: moving in."

"One more step and I'll shoot the kids."

"Hostile spotted. He has a hostage. It's one of the kids."

"Drop the weapon or the kid's brain will decorate the floor."

My eyes went wide and my heart raced. I bolted for the boat but didn't get very far. Puzo's hands grabbed mine and slammed me against the side of the second SWAT van. Her usual stern eyes were replaced by a sympathetic look. "Let SWAT do their job."

"He has the kids. He has Robby," I pleaded. I had lost dozens of friends overseas and I barely survived that. I didn't know what I'd do if I lost family. I didn't think I could survive that.

"I know, Ben, I know," she said softly. "But they know what they're doing. They're trained for this. Let them do their job and Robby will be safe."

Let them do their job.

I repeated those words over and over in my mind and

NEVER BEEN TO MARS

tried my hardest to not freak out any further.

"Drop the gun or we'll fire."

"Fuck that. Bullet in the mother fucking kid's head. Now back the fuck off."

"This is your last chance."

"Are you not listening? Fine I'll fucking make you listen."

Bang. The sound of gunfire fills the radio.

My lungs seem to reject air and my legs choose that moment to ignore every minute of physiotherapy I've had over the last two years and just gave way. I collapsed to the ground gasping for air and dry heaving at the same time. Reality seemed to fade away as all I was left with were visions of Robby. A sports center highlights reel of the kids life, the best moments, his birth, his days hanging out with me and him meeting his step-dad for the first time, the bad moments, broken bones, crushed memories, seeing me injured, and everything in between. Fate had given me this vision for one reason: It had chosen that moment to reclaim one of its chosen individuals.

Robby was dead.

Chapter 17
OMG! Wait Until I Text Becky

I sat on the ground, oblivious to everything. I didn't notice the sounds on the radio, the movement of the SWAT or even how cold the ground beneath me had gotten. All I could think of was that mind-numbing thought running through my head over and over.

Robby was dead.

It was my fault.

How was I going to explain this to Annie? How do I look in my sister's eyes and tell her that her only son is dead? How do I tell her that I tried my best to save him but failed?

"Ben," Puzo whispered. "Ben. He's okay."

I blinked. What did she just say? I looked up at her with a quizzical look.

Puzo grabbed the radio. "Hotel 4: Say again."

"Hostile down; no innocent casualties," the voice explained. "The kids are okay."

The kids were okay.

Robby was alive.

I don't know if I'll ever be able to explain how I felt at that moment. I had lost friends before, war has a habit of doing that, but that feeling of relief I felt there, the feeling when things looked terrible but at the last minute they go right, I'm not used to that. You put me in a life or death situation and things tend never to work out for me.

"Team 2: Secure the kids. Team 1 and 3: clear out the rest of the ship," Childs ordered over the comms. "I'm not bringing them out or anybody else in until we know that ship is clear."

I sat there, anxious and eager, waiting for them to clear out the ship. It took them nearly thirty minutes to check each deck, room by room, to make sure that all of WhiteStar's men were either subdued or taken out. It was the longest thirty minutes of my life. Every second was an agonizing wait before I could board the ship, before I could see the kids, and before I could see Robby.

Ever watch a bad episode of a TV show, like *The Office* or *The Big Bang Theory*? It's like that. You stare at the screen, hating every moment, cringing at every joke and wondering why they kept going post-Carell or even decided to make the show in the first place. For whatever reason you cannot look away but you regret every moment of it. It was like that but instead of a laugh track and poor writers you got a life and death situation where at any moment a guy could pop up and put a bullet in your head.

That'd still be funnier than *The Office*.

"Ship is cleared." The voice was like a Seraph singing down from the heavens – just manlier. "We're bringing the kids out."

Puzo was already on her phone, calling in her team, a couple ambulances to check out the children and somebody to deal with the dead bodies. Price put his hand on my shoulder and smiled. "Let's go get your kid."

I climbed into the passenger seat of Price's car and with a roar his government-issued black sedan roared to life. He drove me the three blocks so I could be there when the kids came out. We pulled up just as the kids stepped foot onto the dock. I could see them as I climbed out of the car; each is dressed in a grey jumpsuit with a number etched on the front. Each had a belt around their waist and an empty brown holster hanging at their side.

I saw him immediately, a mop of blonde curls on his

head and a look on his face that is scared and worried. He saw me and his face exploded with a smile three miles wide. I hobbled over to him as he ran towards me. We meet somewhere in the middle, he dove into my chest and I wrapped my arms around him.

"Uncle Ben!" He was happy to see me, relived, but the pain on his face is clear; he'd just gone through hell.

"I gotcha, Spider-Man!" I whispered to him. "I gotcha!"

He nuzzled deeper into my chest, if that was humanly possible, and I pulled him closer still. My face brushed the grey material and I felt it. The familiar shiver shot up my back and my eyes began to twitch. The world dissolved and I fell head-first into a vision. I saw Robby, standing before two WhiteStar grunts and their boss. The man-in-charge wasn't the suit wearing type of boss-man; he was wearing jeans and a sweater with a pistol hanging from his waist. He was holding a clipboard and carefully reading it over. He cleared his throat as he looked up.

"From this moment the life you used to know is over," he explained. He didn't yell, he didn't scream, he just spoke in a chilling calm voice. "I want you to think long and hard about the last time you saw your mommy or daddy because that was the last time you'll ever see them. If any of you try to leave here and go back to your family we will put a bullet in their heads."

He let that thought linger. He could hear the sharp intake of breath from the older children and the sobbing from the younger. "From now on your family is right beside you. These will be the boys and girls you'll grow up with. You will see them every day of your life. These will be your brothers and sisters. Look after them and they'll look after you."

The boss-man, First Sergeant Ryan Delgado (name courtesy of VH1's Pop-Up Vision), moved down the line giving each kid a new name. "Remember these names. These are your new names. Never again will you be referred to as your old name." He stopped in front of Robby. "Never."

He looked at his list again. "Solider # 56789: Your new name is Will Graham."

Robby was smart. He didn't say a word, the girl beside him wasn't. "No. I'm not Janet O'Grady. My name is Cassie Pym."

Delgado didn't yell and he didn't scream, in fact he did nothing. He left that to his grunts. Sergeant Lang stepped forward and struck her; a solid backhanded slap that sent her crashing to the ground. She sobbed on the ground. Delgado cleared his throat again. "I apologise, I missed that. What was your name again?"

"J... J... Janet O'Grady," she said between sobs of tears.

"Very good."

The vision faded away and reality returned. WhiteStar was threatening their families, giving each of them numbers and forcing them to change names to disassociate them with their past lives. WhiteStar was making child soldiers. I felt my face swell with tears and anger. I wanted to lash out and rain hell down upon them but instead I just pulled Robby closer. "I gotcha, webslinger. I gotcha."

For the next hour I sat with Robby as he, and every other child, was looked over by the paramedics. Each child was checked for injuries. I leaned on Puzo's car watching quietly during Robby's turn. The young paramedic gave him a once over, looking for broken bones, concussions or any other serious injuries. All he found on my nephew were cuts, scrapes and bruises, most likely from the abduction. My Robby's a scrapper; he fought back when they grabbed him. What the paramedic wouldn't find would be the mental anguish. The past two days were going to leave a permanent mental mark on my nephew. Kids are resilient, they can get over nearly anything and while I didn't doubt that Robby would bounce back having the abilities that Price said he did was going to make it all that much harder.

How do you forget the bad times when you can't forget anything?

I grabbed my phone and fired off a message to Hotwire.

Me: I found Robby. The FBI and I tracked him down! He's safe with me. Thanks for the help

I'd sent him that text shortly after the convoy of ambulances and FBI cars showed up. It was a little convoy but it was a beautiful sight. Yet since then I had gotten nothing from my resident hacker. The truth was I hadn't gotten a response in a while. Not since Ryman's interrogation, hell not since before that. I started to get worried.

Puzo escorted Robby to me. "Paramedic says he's good to go. So we're going to drive him home. I'm sending Robby home to his mother with Lord-Alge and two members of Heron Unit."

"Thanks." Three FBI members meant that even if they came after Robby again he'd be protected. I felt better knowing that since I couldn't go home with him, at least not yet.

"Local police just got an anonymous tip of gunfire at two other cargo ships across the city. Officers arrive on scene to find nearly a dozen children on board. Sound familiar?"

Shit. WhiteStar had more kids? How far spread was this operation of theirs? We saved Robby and the other kids aboard the ship but how many more were WhiteStar going to get away with?

"This wouldn't have anything to do with your friend Mr. Dagget would it?"

Hell, Jason/Greg did say he was going to check out the other ships. The scary part was this ship took a highly trained SWAT team to take them down. What the hell did Greg bring with him?

NEVER BEEN TO MARS

"I have no clue," I replied honestly. "But whatever happened it seemed like you caught a break."

Puzo gave me a smirk, the kind of disbelieving smirk that two brothers give each other when they think they've gotten away with a lie to their parents. "Lucky, right. I'm heading out to the ship and taking a couple people with me. Any chance you want to come?"

I looked over at Price. "Thanks but I have to take care of something before I can go home."

Puzo shook my hand and smiled. "Be careful. Despite what you think of Agent Green there, he's dangerous. Don't forget that."

I glanced over at Price. The things I had seen this man do, both within the visions and out in the real world. There was no way I was ever going to forget how dangerous Price really was. "I'll keep that in mind."

She started to walk away but turned back after a couple steps, an unusual smile on her face. "I'll call you."

She's going to call me? She's going to call me! OMG! Wait until I text Becky and all of the rest of cheerleader squad about this.

Sarcastic humour: it's a defense mechanism. Whenever I'm flustered or confused, which is a lot more often than I am comfortable with, I resort to sarcastic humour but if you're just learning this now you really haven't been paying attention. So a cute girl had me flustered. That hadn't happened since – wait had that ever happened?

After a quick explanation to Robby and a promise I'd see him in just a little bit, I put him in the car with Lord-Alge, and two other SWAT, and sent him home. It'd been a long couple of days for me, for him and for Annie. All parties just wanted to go home. I on the other hand still had to find Hotwire and Price would know how to do just that.

Price was standing within the crowd of suits, moving from person to person, reading some files, ordering others around and most importantly he seemed to be talking to the children. I walked over and joined him. He was kneeling before a little girl with a black eye, one I recognized as Cassie Pym. The two were talking. I tapped him on his shoulder. "We need to find Hotwire."

"Who?" Price asked as he rose to his feet. The man was too good of a liar. He didn't even show the slightest hint of recognition.

"The hacker. He's one of your guys. He was a contact you sent me in my brown package." Price just blinked as he escorted me away from Cassie. "Look I know that package was from you, which means Hotwire is your responsibility."

"I cannot confirm or deny anything," Price began. "But if somebody or some organization sent you that package covertly then they wouldn't send you a link to their own men, they'd outsource just in case things didn't work out. That being said if this Hotwire is in danger he will probably be looked after."

Damn spies.

"Why send it to me in the first place?" I asked. "Why the hell would you give me a PI license anyways?"

"Perhaps somebody wants to recruit you but you're not ready yet," Price hypothesized. "You are an ex-Ranger. You know how to think quickly but you were out of practice. You had no motivation to even get up in the morning. I think whoever sent you that package wanted to whip you into shape."

"You mean Oversight?"

Price just shrugged. "I don't know but my suggestion is just keep doing what you've been doing for the last couple months and you'll get there."

"My recruitment aside I need to make sure Hotwire is safe."

I couldn't even plan what happened next.

In the biggest case of cosmic irony the moment I was

done my question the phones went off. Not just my phone, not just Price's, but seemingly everybody's phone in the area. My phone played a jaunty little tune to signal a new text, Price's made the sound the phones did in *24* but the rest were stunning. Dozens of ringtones from simple beeps, to dogs barking and cats meowing filled the air. One phone even sang the words *I want my MTV* over and over. Damn Dire Straits. Everybody had gotten a text at the same time. I pulled out my phone and looked down at the newly arrived message.

Unknown: WhiteStar is moving to plan B. They're going after Robby's mother.

Seconds later every phone rang again.

Unknown: PS it's Hotwire. I'm fine. Go save your sister.

Speak of the devil and he comes forth. I'd hate to see what happens if I look into a mirror and say his name three times.
Hotwire. Hotwire. Hotwire.
I just gave myself the shivers.
"They're going for Annie! We have to do something!" I yelled. I'd just gotten Robby back and now they wanted to take away Annie.
"Childs!" Price called out. He dashed for SWAT commander with me hobbling behind.
Childs was standing at a makeshift table with a dozen or so different papers lying on top beside a pair of SWAT helmets, a radio and a laptop. The team leader looked up at Price. "What the hell is this message? Who is Annie?"
"She's my sister. Her son, my nephew, was one of the kids rescued today; Robby Belledin." Childs typed the name into his laptop.
"I just sent him home with Lord-Alge, Quinn and Markus." He grabbed his radio. "I'll warn them to hold posi-

tion."

Childs called for them over the radio but nobody answered. He drummed his fingers on his helmet as he waited. With a grunt he dropped his radio onto the table and pulled out his phone. A couple clicks later and the phone was ringing. Once again the SWAT leader drummed his fingers on the top of his helmet, each finger making a hollow tap.

"I'm not getting an answer."

Something wasn't sitting right with me. I started looking around the dock. Each of the children was being sent home with FBI agent and SWAT members, which left roughly six remaining here. As I looked over each one I began to notice a pattern. Each SWAT member had on them a main firearm, a pistol, a knife, what few grenades remained from the firefight, a tactical vest and a helmet. Each SWAT member had every piece of their gear accounted for. Even their pouches were filled with spent magazines. I glanced at Childs. He didn't have his helmet on but there it was beside him, always within arm's reach. Instinct even forced him to touch it while on the radio or phone. In short the SWAT was like the army. We never left our gear behind. So whose helmet was sitting on the table?

The table had two helmets. The first -- Childs' -- but the second one had no owner. Which SWAT member had left his gear unattended?

I pulled off my glove and reached for the extra SWAT helmet.

The moment my fingers touched the protective headgear my body reacted. The shiver ran up my spine and my eyes started to twitch. Reality rewound showing me the world that was not an hour earlier. Heron unit was coming off the ship with a dozen children in tow, and moving for the ambulances and FBI vehicles. As the last SWAT member stepped off Child's voice came across the radio.

"Team 1: On me. Team 2 and 3: I want a sweep of a couple blocks. Eyes open. I don't want an ambush. Snipers maintain position."

NEVER BEEN TO MARS

Agent Miles Markus rolled his eyes. Childs was a pain, constantly double-checking the area and re-securing their position. He always seemed paranoid but often he was right. Markus kept his MP5 raised as he moved outward, watching the docks and scanning the rooftops.

Three docks down, as his attention slowly began to diminish and his adrenalin had reached its limits, a pair of hands grabbed him from behind and spun him into the side of a wall. He smashed into the steel structure with a loud clang. The mysterious hands grabbed his helmet and yanked it off his head and tossed it aside. Markus fought back, whoever this attacker was he wasn't going to let them get the better of him. He struck with his elbow, kicked back with his foot, and spun clockwise striking with the butt of his weapon. The butt slams into the side of his attacker's skull, dazing him for the briefest moments. Markus levels his weapon at his attacker and slides his finger around the trigger.

Markus was a highly trained and highly decorated FBI SWAT agent. He had seen numerous firefights, survived them all on his skill and just a touch of luck. Agent Markus was not a man to freeze with a hostile in his sight. Yet as he stared at his mysterious attacker he found it impossible to pull the trigger.

The mysterious attacker that stood before Markus was – Markus.

It was genius to say the least. The last thing that any well adjusted man wanted to do was to pull the trigger on their doppelganger. That brief hesitation gave the attacker two seconds to strike and that was plenty. Faux-Markus struck, grabbed the SMG and with the help of the weapon's sling, spun the real Markus around and forced him to his knees. The doppelganger drew a .45 pistol and pressed it against the original's back. Faux-Markus put two rounds into his back and a third in his skull.

"Two in the heart and one in the head, it's the only way to make sure they're dead."

Reality snapped back with a string of curses spewing

from my mouth. Markus was dead and the Heather- Graham- Mark- Wahlberg- Burt- Reynolds doppelganger was here and s/he had infiltrated the SWAT team.

I looked at Price. "Burt Reynolds is here. Markus is dead." He nodded.

"What the hell are you talking about?" Childs demanded. "I just saw him no more than fifteen minutes ago.

"Markus was killed on route to the Belledin residence. Chances are Quinn is dead as well." Price explained, weaving lies in with truth. "That text was a coded message from Secret Service intelligence. They have been monitoring this investigation as it is crossing over with ours."

It was amazing watching a man like him lie so easily. It just rolled off his tongue. He didn't freeze, he didn't look away, he kept eye contact and he never stammered. This man was a perfect liar.

"You need to coordinate checks on all other cars," Price continued. "I need you to check to see who else had been attacked."

Childs turned to what men he had left and barked the order. I suspected he started recalling what cars he could and demanded check-ins from those that were too far out. Truth was all I could do was guess at what the SWAT commander did because I wasn't there. By the time Child began barking orders Price and I were in his car speeding towards Annie's house. Spies are good at a lot of things, lying, killing, but what they really excelled at was vanishing when things got busy. Price sped through the street. He moved at speeds reserved for action films and the bat-mobile but with a skill normally reserved for stunt drivers. We were driving so fast I felt like humming. It's from a Stalone film; look it up.

"Who the hell is this guy?" I screamed as I slapped the dashboard in anger. "He's a shapeshifting ninja who's freaking everywhere."

"Shapeshifter named Chapman?" I nodded. "Lt. Hugo Chapman was a SEAL. After you mention the shapeshifter I reread his file. He was an excellent sailor, even won a Silver Star, but in 1993 he was sent to Mogadishu for the hunt for Mohammed Farrah Aidid. He suffered minor injuries but lost several friends and allies. He left the US Navy and was scooped up by the CIA after they learned of his abilities. Tracking him became difficult as the CIA sent him on literally hundreds of missions in the next decade. After that reports say his mind snapped under the weight of all the lies and personas he'd taken. Basically he lost himself in all the faces he took. WhiteStar scooped him up and uses him now. He's a fraction of what he was mentally but physically he is still deadly."

The hunt for Mohammed Farrah Aidid was a joint operation between SEALs, Delta Force and Rangers. It was called Task Force Ranger but historians knew it as the Battle of Mogadishu and regular folk knew it as *Black Hawk Down*.

"We're going in and chances are we're going in hot," Price explained as he drove, taking a corner with a skid, his sirens blaring. "I need you behind me. Is that going to be a problem?"

The moment he mentioned it I felt those same symptoms start to swell up. The increased heart rate, the shake in my hands and the sweat from my forehead; I felt them all. "I need you to take whatever you feeling right now and stow it. Right now I need you at fighting form. Your family needs you."

I reached down and drew my M9, my hands shaking as I ejected the mag and did an ammo check.

"You can't be blamed for what happened in Iraq." People had been telling me that since the accident. I didn't believe a single one of them. How could they know? They weren't there. They weren't fighting for their lives. They weren't the ones lying in the sand bleeding out as their friends starting dying. That was me, not them. "I know you blame yourself, everybody in that same situation would, but it wasn't your fault. You couldn't save them but right here, right now, you can save your family. You can do here, at home, what you couldn't overseas."

My hand shook as I counted my rounds. I had two

full clips remaining. Thirty shots to storm my sister's house, kill the bad guys, and save my family. I was scared. Whenever I'm scared I fall back on humour. It's my shield but right now I had nothing. No jokes, no quips, nothing. (I was working on a mother-in-law bit but I felt wrong doing those while being single.) All I could do was ponder what would happen if I failed again.

We pulled up to the grey townhouse that acted as my sister's house and home. Price parked across the street along the curb. I gave Price a final look and slid the full clip into my M9. "Let's do this." I murmured with a heavy dose of false bravado. "Let's go be heroes."

I reached into the backseat for my cane but Price stopped me. "Leave the cane. You don't need it. I've seen you fight without it. You got into a gunfight at the warehouse without it," Price explained.

I pushed him away and grabbed the walking aid. "That cane is a crutch." I'm pretty sure that's the medical definition if not the dictionary's. "It's holding you back from the soldier you once were. It's just going to get in your way."

I looked down at my cane and with a disbelieving shake I released it and let it fall back into the rear seat. "I'm coming back for it," I muttered as I opened the door and climbed out."

"I'm moving around back," Price explained as he climbed out the driver's side. "Watch your fire, your family may still be in the house."

I just nodded as I moved to the front door, holding the pistol behind my back as I limped. I didn't want to scare neighbours if I turned out to be wrong. I eyed the FBI car as I passed, dragging my fingerless gloves across the black metal exterior. The usual shiver and a twitch fill my body and reality is replaced by that which was not but twenty minutes ago. Lord-Alge and his two SWAT escorts park alongside the curb in front of Annie's house. Robby exited the car and ran for the house. The front door opened before he got there and Annie rushed out, tears in her eyes, and wrapped her arms around the kid. She hugged him tightly and didn't let go.

"We need to take this inside," Faux-Markus said. "So we can secure the area."

Reality returned and I'm no better off then I was a few seconds ago. I knew Faux-Markus had my family and I knew he doesn't falter when he had to kill. Lt. Chapman was a true warrior, an unwavering, unhesitating solider – just like I used to be. The only difference was he had both his legs and I still had my soul. I wasn't sure if that was a fair trade.

I grabbed the doorknob and gave it a twist, then slowly pushed the door open with my left as the fingers on my right danced over the grip panel. As the door opened I stared down the hallway and first time since the Traveler's Motel I came face to face with my reoccurring attacker, face to face with Faux-Markus, face to face with the shifter known as Lt. Chapman.

It was that moment where our eyes meet, when time slowed down and we were left just staring at each other. It was like a chick-flick-romantic-movie moment, where the guy and the girl see each other across the field as the rain pours down except in those in movies neither side is equipped with semi-automatic weaponry.

How cool would chick flicks be with guns?

Then Chapman opened fire. What a mood killer.

Chapter 18
Jackie Chan v. Jet Li

I've always found that an MP5 sounds like someone smashing a sheet of aluminum plating with a hammer, just much faster. I've also found that I really dislike being shot at. Who knew? I duck behind the doorway as bullets zoom by, some crashing into the drywall, others into the door. One even zoomed by my face and missed me by mere inches, but there I stood, behind the cover of a townhouse wall, my M9 in my hand, cursing my horrifying luck once again. I popped my hand around the corner and returned fire, popping three rounds into the house.

Crap! Crap! Crap!

Damn it, I hated this guy. He was everywhere, he was everyone and he always seemed to be shooting at me. I ducked my head into the house and gave it a quick scan. Annie's house was a split townhouse; two houses built into one building. A house on the left and a house on the right; Annie lives on the left. So from the front door I could see down the hallway and directly into the kitchen. To my left was the living room, which moved into a dining room which connected to the kitchen, and to my right the stairs going up, and under them stairs going down. Somewhere between here and the kitchen was the bathroom which was good because all I wanted to do was throw up and shit myself.

I ducked back behind cover as the next volley of gunfire ripped into the wall. Any other gun and I'd be worried that the bullets would tear through the wall but not with a 9mm. As a century old cartridge the 9mm round is a highly tested reliable round but it's still one of the babies of the bullet world. It's smaller and weaker than most other sizes. That being said the 9mm can still be vicious with the right pistol, the right ammo and the right person behind the trigger. Chapman was, in every definition of the word, the right person.

I popped back out and fired another three rounds. Chapmen's backed into the kitchen, using the fridge as cover. As my own 9mm rounds, fired from my M9, slammed into the brand new stainless steel fridge I couldn't help but think of how pissed off Annie was going to be.

I heard the sound of glass shattering and caught a glimpse of Chapman ducking for cover. Price was opening fire from outside. Chapman spun around and returned fire, tossing 9mm rounds at Price like they were candy.

I limped into the house, snapped off another two rounds, and ducked into the dining room. I saw two dead bodies on the floor, the pooling blood staining the carpet – something else Annie was going to hate. One was in a suit and tie and the other in full SWAT gear: the other two FBI agents. The bodies lay beside their discarded firearms, a Glock 22 and a SWAT issued MP5. I slid my pistol into my holster and limped over to the submachine gun. I didn't care about the vision or the ensuing migraine, all I cared about was my family. I grabbed the gun and felt my body react. A shiver, a twitch, and a vision; they all felt amplified in the heat of battle.

I was in the room with Annie, David, and Robby, Lord-Alge, Quinn and Chapman disguised as Faux-Markus. Annie and David were all hugs and kisses, tears of happiness at the return of their son. Lord-Alge stood before them, his face beaming a small smirk of *we did good* to the world, as Quinn and Chapman stood by the door. A phone rang and Chapman answered it.

"The child is at home with the parents." Quinn looked over at his partner, a quizzical look on his face. "Yeah it's just me, the suit and the other SWAT."

A pause.

"Twenty minutes: confirm." Chapman hung up and returned his phone to his pocket.

"What's happening in twenty?" Quinn asks. Chapman's hand quietly drops to the silenced .45 that hung from his waist. "Hey, when did you get a new phone?"

Chapman moved fast, faster than most people I'd seen, and drew his .45. He pressed it into Quinn's chest and fired twice. He slammed Quinn into the wall and turned his gun on Lord-Alge. Two shots put the agent on the floor, bleeding from the chest.

"Don't move." Chapman eyed David as he spoke; his gun pointed the Annie's stomach. "Do as I say and the baby will live."

Annie pulled Robby in close, shielding his eyes as Faux-Markus pressed the .45 under Quinn's chin and pulled the trigger. The back of Quinn's skull exploded sending grey matter across the wall. Chapman released the body and let it fall to the ground. He approached the family, putting a final round into Lord-Alge's skull as he passed, and frowned. "Two in the heart and one in the head, it's the only way to make sure they're dead."

Annie shook in fear while David just stood there. Nobody wanted to move, nobody wanted to play hero. "Upstairs now!"

The vision faded and my firefight based reality returned. I cocked my newly acquired firearm, pocketed some extra clips I grabbed from Quinn's corpse and limped for the stairs. I cleared the stairs faster than I ever thought possible, my body ignoring the searing pain my legs were producing. I hit the top floor and paused for a listen. The gunfire from downstairs seemed to have stopped only to be replaced by random smashing and two men grunting.

That would sound dirty out of context.

I headed for the master bedroom, the one that overlooked the front yard, and threw open the front door. I was rewarded with a vase smashing over my head. Say what you will about the Thompsons but we do clichés well. I crumpled to floor in a string of curses and pain. I'm ashamed to admit but there might have been a slur in there as well. It's the army – it does things to you.

"Ben? Oh hell, man. I'm sorry."

"A vase?" I muttered as David helped me up. "What are you? Sean Connery?"

"Would it make you feel better if I told you it was a fake?" And people wonder why David and I are friends. "What the hell is going on?"

"It's hard to explain we just need to get you out of here," I grumble. "The safest place is outside."

Like the set-up to a bad cut away gag the squeal of tires fills the air. I limped to the double windows and stared down at the street below. Three black SUVs were parked on the street between us and our car. Like a clown car of death the doors opened up and WhiteStar goons poured out, each with a M4 rifle or a P90. For the first time since this fiasco started I didn't hesitate, I just acted. I aim down at one of the baddies below, lining him up with my iron sights, and squeeze the trigger. The first burst shatters the windows while the next rips into the man's leg. I switched to a second merc and fired again.

"Ben! What are you doi..."

"Get down!" My Schwarzenegger scream interrupted Annie as I dove for the floor. Bullets ripped into the house as the goons open fire from the street. "You three get into the bathroom. Hide in the tub."

I climbed to my feet and awkwardly moved to the door. I watched as Annie and Robby did as I asked, David, however, didn't. "I can help."

I just nodded at him.

We didn't need to speak, training had taught us to do without; we just acted as the army had instructed. I moved down the stairs first and David followed. My MP5 caught sight of a WhiteStar goon coming in through the front door and I opened fire. A burst of three rounds sent the nameless soldier falling back outside. David spotted a discarded firearm, an MP5 like mine (Chapman's I assumed), and leapt over the banister to grab it. David hit the ground, rolled, and scooped up the SMG all in one seamless motion. He was up on his feet before I could blink, his newly acquired firearm aimed at the front door.

Back in my prime, the pre-IED days, I was good. Hell, I was better than good but David was smooth. Even with the entirety of my Ranger training I could never pull off a move like that. I'd end up flat on my ass. David was like a cat. He was smooth and always landed on his feet.

The jerk was a total show off.

We both headed for the front door and opened fire. Our flurry of 9mm rounds fired across the street and into the SUV's they used as cover. We ducked back as they responded in kind, six rifles pumping an ungodly amount of lead into the house. I watched as groups of the goons used the covering fire to run out from behind cover and move around back. They were trying to flank us, just like Price and I did to Chapman; those dirty plan stealing bastards.

David moved before I could say a word, his infantry eyes seeing their movements before I did, and goes to cover the rear entrance. He was two steps away when he paused, looked back, and spoke. "Not a single person gets through those doors."

It's wasn't an order nor a question. It was a statement, one neither of us were going to allow to be proven false. I tossed him an extra clip, one of two I held, and he caught it easily. "Make it count. David."

I looked back to the front door and clutched my SMG tightly. I snapped off another burst, my bullets doing little else but ventilating an innocent vehicle, and tried to formulate a plan. I couldn't hit any of them while they hid behind their SUVs and I didn't have the ammunition needed to hold out for long. They would overwhelm us and quickly if I didn't act.

That's when Chapman's skull crashed into the living

room.

It happens in every action movie, we see a high octane action fight and then the camera cuts away to a boring office where two boring people are chatting about their boring business lives. You sit there for a fraction of a second watching this boring scene until the fight smashes through a wall or a window and suddenly this scene is no longer boring.

Price dashed into the living room, used the couch to vault him into the air, and slammed his knee into Chapman's face. The shifter stumbled back but quickly recovered, striking the agent twice with his fist and once with his foot.

The Man with a Thousand Names versus The Man with a Thousand Faces: Fight Night!

Here I was, defending a house from a platoon of invading private military mercenaries, and compared to those two fighting each other I was still the boring guy talking about his boring life.

They both were fighting unarmed, their firearms long since disarmed or kicked across the room, but they still went at it. Karate smack and Kung Fu slaps, they used them all. I'd witnessed Price fight first hand but that was him taking on nameless nobodies. This was different. When you see two people fighting, two people who know what they're doing, it's a whole different show. This was Rock v. Diesel in *Fast Five*. This was Jackie Chan v. Jet Li in *The Forbidden Kingdom*. This was Stalone v. Momoa in *Bullet to the Head*. This was Schwarzenegger v. Noriega in *The Last Stand*. This was Stalone v. Van Damme in *Expendables 2*.

This. Was. Epic.

And I had better things to do than watch this.

Chapter 19
I Had My Own Keanu Reeves

I could hear gunfire from behind me, David's weapon snapping to life at those invading from rear, but as much as I wanted to rush to his aid I couldn't. I had to trust in David, in his skill. The man would sooner die than let anybody get close to his wife and son.

I snapped off another burst, catching one unlucky solider in the face, but mostly achieving little else. I needed an opening, I needed a clever move. I had to MacGyver my way out of this situation. I needed to make a bomb from paperclips, an elastic and two coconuts, rig a car to run on rockets or something just as weird but I was shit out of paperclips. Damn my luck.

Luck has a funny way of showing up when you least expect it. Often for me it's bad luck, but occasionally something unexpected happens and I benefit from it. This time the SUVs moved.

Nobody was driving them, the engines were off and they were in park. But, as if by some unseen force, the three SUVs all rolled forward, screeching as if they were pushed leaving a squad of stunned WhiteStar goons without cover. I didn't question it I just lined up my sights and fired. I wasn't going to look this gift horse in the mouth. My aim was faster than theirs, being shocked played in my favour, and I fired burst after burst, my 9mm rounds ripping through their legs and chests before they could even react. I caught three before they started to move and another two as they tried to scramble behind cover.

That's when I saw him.

A man dressed in a suit walking down the middle of the street. No trepidation in his face and no worry in his step. This man was pissed off and he wanted everybody to know it. His suit jacket flowed with every step, like a superhero cape, and his tie fluttered behind him like a scarf. I recognized the man from the start, I just never expected him to show up here.

I never expected Greg Hazeltine.

What the hell was he thinking? He was just walking into a firefight with no weapon or no cover. He was being idiotic. I opened fire, more recklessly then before, trying to give him covering fire but with the mercs hidden again behind the SUVs I had no shot.

Turned out I didn't need it.

Greg held his hand upwards, twisting his wrist like he was screwing in a light bulb or waving like the Queen. From the corner of my vision, and I nearly missed it, I saw the head of some nameless goon snap to the left with a loud crack. It was like an invisible ninja grabbed him from behind and snapped his neck. Two goons turned their M4s on Greg and opened fire. Greg didn't dive out of the way, he didn't panic, and he didn't even change his stride. All he did was thrust his palm forward. The bullets just stopped midair before they reached him, dropping to the ground harmlessly.

Greg Hazeltine was Neo.

Holy hell, I had my own Keanu Reeves on my side. Whoa! (Somehow saying *excellent* and doing air guitar seemed out of date.)

Greg swiped his hand to the left, like he was using the world's biggest touch screen tablet, and sent the two gunmen flying. It was like using Tinder but with consequences. When Greg said no, he meant it.

I watched in awe as I switched out an empty mag for my last fresh one. I snapped off another burst, catching one more unlucky merc in the leg. I watched as Greg ripped through the few mercs that remained out front, telekinetically tossing them across the street or slamming them into their own SUVs. The tides were turning in the Shootout at Annie's House, turning in our favour.

Of course that was when David cried for help.

"Ben, I'm out!" It was the cry that no soldier wanted to here. The one that followed that cursed click. It's when you're staring down the charging enemy and have nothing left to shoot them with.

"Along the floor!" Ejecting the nearly full mag I passed it to David, sliding it along the hallway floor. David dove into a roll, ejecting his mag, grabbing the replacement and slapping it in all by the time he was back on his feet. Show off. David spun for the back door, ready to fire at the goon brave enough to breach the back door, but paused as twin tongues of blue flames ripped through the goon's chest. The man didn't scream, you needed air and lungs for that, he just gurgled as and fell.

I spun towards the living room, my pistol back in my hand, and stared at Price. He stood with his head tilted, staring over his glasses, as he held Chapman in an arm lock. Even in the middle of his epic brawl with the evil shifter Price had taken time to save us both. That was sweet of him.

Chapman was not one to let a momentary hesitation like that go to waste. He kicked up and caught Price in his crotch. The man with a thousand name winced as he doubled over, his grip on the shifter's arm weakening. Chapman squirmed free, grabbed the closest thing he could get his hands on, an Xbox 360, and smashed it over Price's head.

Robby was going to be pissed at that.

Chapman spotted Lord-Alge's dropped Glock and moved to pick it up but the crack from my gun sent him crashing to the floor. The 9mm round fired from my gun shattered the kneecap. I limped over; my M9 locked onto the fallen kidnapper like a kitten's eyes on a ball of yarn, the barrel glaring down at him menacingly.

NEVER BEEN TO MARS

Then he did the unexpected, he shifted again.
His face bubbled like boiling soup, until it was unrecognizable, and then settled, his face took on a new form. Gone was the visage of Markus and replacing it was that of a weary solider, broken and bruised and lost to the world. Lt. Chapman wore my face.

It was a brilliant strategy. The last thing that any well adjusted man wanted to do was to pull the trigger on their doppelganger but I was the farthest thing from sane, I was a Thompson. Staring down at the Faux-Ben all I saw was the last two years of my life; the pain I'd endured in Iraq, the misery I had suffered at home and the torment I put myself through day after day since. I saw how I'd shut myself off from the world, excluded myself from the lives of my friends and my family. I couldn't even name a friend I still had anymore and it had even been a couple months since I'd seen Robby. As I stared down at my doppelganger all I felt was disgust. That form before me represented everything that I had become and I'd hated it. I had hated what I had become.

I pulled the trigger.

My pistol snapped off a bang, the bullet finding a home deep into Chapman's chest. Before he could react I squeezed the trigger again, pumping a second round right beside the first.

"Two in the heart and one in the head," I found myself saying, my words sounding dark and menacing. Chapman's eyes, my eyes, grew wide with fear. He knew what was coming. There was no stopping it. "It's the only way to make sure you're dead."

I leveled the gun at faux-me's skull and squeezed off a third shot. The bang drowned out my doppelganger's scream, his head snapping back as the bullet passed through its brain. I stood over my dead body thinking about how I just killed myself and how messed up I truly must be. I don't know why I said what I said, it didn't even make sense, but I found myself whispering a final goodbye to my fallen self. "Farewell, Broken Ben. You will not be missed."

It's amazing how quickly a battle can end when the bad guys lose their man on the inside. Add with that the difficultly of being flanked by a pissed-off telekinetic and an eye-beam shooting super spy and things quickly turn against you. The icing on the cake was when Puzo and Childs showed up with SWAT. Out gunned, out matched and out supered, the WhiteStar cronies tried to escape. COPS taught me that when the bad guys try to run from the police they end up topless in a trailer park. I guess the rules didn't apply for private military merc because when the FBI scooped up the few they could find they each came back fully clothed.

Watching police arrest rednecks is a lot more fun.

The moment SWAT showed up, and WhiteStar surrendered/ran, David dropped his gun and bolted up the stairs. I wanted to follow but Puzo called me over. She had a look on her face, a shake of her head mixed with a look of amazement. "You can't stay out of trouble can you?"

I slid my pistol into my holster and but try as I might I couldn't let go. Just like at the motel my hands were locked around the pistol grip, my index finger pressed tightly against the trigger guard. Puzo saw my hands and took them into her own. Just like before my grip eased up and I pulled my fingers away.

"Hey you did good, Ben," she whispered. "Your family's safe and you're all okay."

I point at Chapman's body. The corpse no longer looked like me; it shifted to the form of an older grizzled solider, one I could only assume was his prime form, shortly after he died. She just nodded.

"You did what you had to, Ben, and you did it well."

I just nodded.

"This is all over now," she whispered. "It's all over and you can go back to being good old Ben."

No, I thought. *Never again.*

"Ben!" David's voice ripped through the house. "Ben! Call an ambulance! Annie's going into labour!"

Chapter 20
Be Seeing You

So there I was in a hospital, stressed out because I hate hospitals and worried for my sister and niece. A preemie baby was never a good thing. It wasn't healthy, it was unsafe for the mother and it was dangerous for the baby. So I sat, waiting and stressed out, twiddling a black jewellery box in my fingers.

Robby was sitting beside me, a living wreck, but still kicking. The kid's tougher then I am. If I had to go through everything he did today only to end up here in the waiting room, I'd be the gooiest goo from goo town. He hasn't said much since the Shootout at Annie's House. He's just sitting there, quiet and worried.

"Wanna see something?" Robby nodded at me. I hand him the black jewelry box. The kid opened it and looked inside. Sitting on the protective felt was a horse head pendent inside of a heart all made from white gold. "I got that a couple months ago for your sister. Back when your Mom and Dad found out that the baby was going to be a girl I ran out and bought this. It'll be years before she's old enough to wear it."

"Like the cowboy hat above my bed?" I nodded. Robby looked at my cowboy hat and frowned. "Is being a brother hard?"

I couldn't help but chuckle as I put my arm around him. "Yes. A younger sister means you have to watch out for her, you'll have to babysit some days and you'll have to keep the creepy guys away from her.

"She will annoy you like nobody else can, she'll bug you to the moon and back and some days she'll make your life a living hell." Robby giggle at my cursing, he always did, just like I did with Annie when I was his age (Oh who am I kidding, it's still funny. Hell, he he he.) I thought back to before the accident, how things were when Annie's life sucked and I was there for her. How time and time again, despite being the younger brother, she looked up to me. "But in the end it's all worth it. Having a sister, younger or older, that can count on you, that looks up to you with pride. There is nothing like it, little man. It's the best feeling in the world."

"Does this mean we have to hang out even less now?"

"No, Robby, it's going to be like it used to be. You and I hanging out all the time," I said, promising myself as much as the kid, "It just means that from time to time it's going to be you, me and your sister." I held out my fist and he bumped it, then our fingers blew up with a loud explosion sound that may or may not have come from our lips. Spoiler Alert: It did.

David stuck his head into the waiting room and called Robby. The kid handed me back the jewelry box and bolted toward his Dad. I smiled.

"Ben." Price took a seat beside me, plopping down with and exhausted thud. His face was bruised, his right eye swollen; his lip was broken and his arm bandaged as he rolled down his dress shirt. "Any news yet?"

"Holy hell, Matt Damon, ever think of giving action films a rest?" He smirked. "No news yet. What about you?"

"Made some calls and surprise, surprise WhiteStar says that the masterminds of the kidnappings today were all ex-members of their organization. They all either quit, retired or were fired anywhere from six months ago to last week."

"Convenient." I've seen enough TV to know what a bad cover-up looked like.

"Don't worry. They'll get theirs," Price reassured.

"Somebody is always watching. Also, tell you sister to expect a cheque from WhiteStar; a big one."

"They are not guilty but they don't want their name tarnished."

"Exactly. See, Ben, you're learning how the game is played."

I could hate the company but at least someone was going to pay for all the stuff that was smashed, broken, and shot full of holes. I thought back to the broken Xbox 360 and all I could think of was how Robby was going to weasel his way into an upgrade, how he was going to get an Xbox One. "So what now?"

"I'm going to be heading out." I raised my eyebrow at him as he climbed to his feet. "We found Robby, I have dozens of names of future *blessed individuals* to put on our watch list, and for the first time since I started my investigation into WhiteStar I have some massive leads; all in all not bad for a day's work. I have to say, Ben, you're good for business."

Price tipped an imaginary hat and started to back away. "Be seeing you, Cowboy."

And with that he was gone. He didn't tell Puzo or the Heron Unit guys standing guard, he just slinked away vanishing into the crowds. Hell, I think I was the only one to notice him leave. The only way his exit could have been more spy-movie like would have been if a bus suddenly passed between us, blocking my view of him, only to reveal that after the bus passed by he was gone. That being said a bus suddenly appearing in a hospital would probably be out of place.

Damn spies are annoying.

I shook my head as I looked around the room. I saw the two SWAT standing guard, just in case, and the dozens of patients, doctors and nurses running around but in the far corner stood the one man who didn't fit in; Greg Hazeltine. I replaced my hat on my head, grabbed my cane, and hobbled over to him. I hadn't seen Greg since he whipped people around as easily as one would toss a furious fowl. By the time SWAT showed up at Annie's house, Greg had vanished.

Like a true spy.

"What is this, the moment each of you says your teary covert goodbye?" I asked. "If this ending is going to last as long as that third *Lord of the Rings* movie let me know now so I can go to the bathroom now instead of trying to hold it."

Greg just smirked. "I watched as super spy said his piece. Be careful around him, Ben."

"He's dangerous," I finished. "So people keep telling me but then you're no timid sheep either."

Greg looked past me, ignoring my statement, and glanced toward the delivery room. A quick glance of my own told me what he was staring at. From our semi-hidden position in the waiting room I could see Annie, David and Robby. "You can go see them if you want, not saying it won't be weird but you did just save their lives."

Greg was tempted, anyone could see it in his eyes, but he just shook his head. "I've made my bed so now I sleep in it. I broke a lot of rules coming to save their lives, and I'll do it again if it comes to it, but I cannot be a part of it."
Spoken like a true spy.

Have I mention how much I hate spies?

"The investigation is going to show that this is connected to me." He explained slowly. "It's all part of the cover up the super spy is throwing down." I had always figured it was Price's job to keep superpowers a secret. "So don't be freaked out when they say Robby was nabbed because of who his father is."

"They'll be looking for Greg Hazeltine," he nodded. "What about Jason Daggett?"

"He'll be in the clear. He's always in the clear."

"So it's Jason then," I carefully asked, "That's your real name?"

He nodded. I grabbed his hand and we shook. "It's nice to finally meet you, Jason."

Robby bolted out of the delivery room screaming my name. The kid's face had a smile so bright it could dwarf the sun. "Uncle Ben! Uncle Ben!"

I looked over and smiled at him. "What's the good word?"

"I'm a brother!" he said with a beaming smile. "I'm a big brother!!"

"Way to go, webslinger!" We bump fists again, complete with the explosion sounds that we may or may not have provided ourselves. Spoiler Alert: we did.

"Who's this guy?" Robby asked. I looked over at Greg.

"Well, Mr. Parker," Greg said with a smile as he offered his hand. "Just call me Gabriel Summers."

"Nice to meet you, Mr. Vulcan."

I stood in the intensive care section of the maternity ward looking down at the small newborn child that lay sleeping within the medical incubator. The name on the chart read Alice Juliet Belledin – my niece.

The technical term is a Neonatal Intensive Care Unit but it looks like something from a bad made-for-TV movie starring John Travolta. The nurse explained it to me using simple terms, which was probably the only way I was going to understand it. As a result of Alice being born a month early her lungs weren't ready to work on their own. This machine was breathing for her – or something like that. Apparently it was also pumping her full of baby steroids. There was a small testicle joke there but it seemed inappropriate at the moment, so I let it pass. The nurse assured me that the baby would be fine. They were keeping a close eye on Alice.

Alice.

The naming tradition continued. She was named after Alice Ivers, a Colorado cowgirl best known as Poker Alice. I know I'll keep the naming tradition going, I'm a sucker for a good western, but I don't know what to call him. Hell, maybe I won't name him; leave him as the Kid With No Name.

"Hey, pretty thing," I whispered to the child. "I'm your Uncle Ben. Your parents don't know this yet but you are going to have a hard life." This scene felt familiar, like I'd done this before. In truth I had. I'd stood over a newborn child before, spilling my figurative guts while making lifetime promises. "You were born different than most people; you're going to have super powers. If things stay the way they are now that means events like today will happen to you. So I promise you this, right here and right now, no matter what happens to you, your family or me, I will always be there for you."

I flipped open the black jewellery case and looked down at the horse pendant. I repeated my promise over and over as I traced my thumb along the gold heart. My body reacted but not in the usual way. Instead of my shiver up my back and a twitch in eye the shiver ran up my left leg and my right hand began to twitch. This vision was not of the past but of the future.

The hospital melted away only to be replaced by a teenage girl's bedroom. Annie was there, older but still retaining her Thompson good looks, sitting on the bed beside her daughter Alice. Sitting at the desk was a young man named Clint.

I couldn't help but smile at the sight of Alice, she was a sixteen years old girl; tall, long black hair she got from her mother and strong eyes she got from her dad. She was an athletic girl and very attractive. Say what you will about Thompson genes but throw some Belledin in the mix and you made a good looking kid, one that's still my niece; hands off! The best part was that seeing her here, in this vision, meant she made it. She fought to live and did.

Then there was Clint, the fifteen year old boy who looked a hell of a lot like me. He had the same scraggly hair, the same cowboy chin and the same --- holy crap; Clint was my son. Clint. Nice name. I stared at my boy with awe and pride but found myself drawn to his eyes. They were unmistakable eyes that reminded me of someone that was dead.

They were impossible eyes.

Zoey.

Annie looked like she was fighting back tears as she handed Alice a familiar black jewellery box. The teenage girl opened it, her own eyes swelling up with tears. The horse pendant rested comfortably inside, virtually untouched in all the years since its purchase.

"Your uncle gave you this on the day of your birth," Annie explained; her battle against the tears becoming more and more futile with each word she spoke. "This family loves its cowboys and they love their westerns. It's kind of a family tradition, one he wanted to pass down to you."

Annie turns to Clint and hands him a black ring with a dark green inner circle. I didn't recognize the ring. I'd never seen it before in my life. "This was your father's lucky ring. It meant a lot to him. There were days I would just see him staring at it, deep in thought."

Clint took the ring in his hands and rolled around his fingers. It was a hardwood ring with a jade inlay in polished black zirconium. Clint seemed to fear it, not so much the ring but everything it meant, and nervously slid it onto his right hand. "I miss you, Dad," he whispered.

"It's been ten years since we lost your father," Annie recounted, tears finally pouring down her face. "Ten years since he gave up his life to save all of us. I miss him every single day but he wanted us to go on, to live for ourselves and to look out for each other. He wanted us to be safe..."

"He wanted us to be family." A new voice interrupted. I didn't recognize it or the person it came from. There was a man standing at the doorway; blonde hair, half smile and a look of hope. Then it hit me.

It was Robby all grown up.

"Uncle Ben was there for us all," he added. "No matter the case, no matter what happened, he was always there and we can never forget that."

Never forget that. They all nodded at those words, no eye left dry. The future faded and reality returned leaving me standing in the IC unit of the maternity ward standing over my newborn niece. I stared down thinking about what I'd just seen; about what the power of psychometry had just shown me; about the future and my ill-fated destiny.

......
......
......
Well – crap.

Epilogue

Hotwire's fingers danced across the keyboard as he typed. His eyes darted up from his laptop's screen at every person who walked by. He wasn't supposed to be here, hidden in the upper offices of a well known bank – their security was a joke - but when his nightclub proved not to be as secure as he'd hoped he needed an alternative form of internet connection.

He had been riding around in a car, bouncing his signal off of any and all wireless networks in reach, the deeper he dug the more he needed to stay moving, but he come across a firewall he needed to punch through and for that he was going to need more than a weak wireless and a 4G signal. He needed some hardcore T lines.

The banks proved helpful.

A quick wave of his phone got him past the security locks and a few taps gave him access to the system. All that was left was convincing everybody else that he was meant to be in that office. That was by far the easiest. Act like you belong and nobody stops you, not even in a bank.

Warning: results may vary.

Hotwire didn't look like most other hackers; he looked like a successful business man, slicked hair, a goatee and Italian suit and tie help cement the image. There he sat, hidden amongst the dozens of other bankers and techies,

NEVER BEEN TO MARS

breaking international laws in a secure building.

His phone vibrated again, it had been buzzing all day, but the hacker just ignored it. He knew Ben was looking for him; the problem was that Ben wasn't the only one. Someone else was looking for him, someone with more punches than psychic-boy. He had to stay off his phone. His scrambler kept them from triangulating the signal but the moment he sent data or made a call they'd lock onto him instantly. Whoever these people were, the group formally known as Visegar, they had power; real power; bad power.

His viruses and worms slammed against the firewall like an egg onto a brick wall and with much of the same effect. Everything he tried seemed to have the same outcome; splattered albumin on the metaphorical wall. The hacker had grabbed dozens of gigs of data from his digital dig but there was so much more to learn, so much left to discover if he could only get past this wall.

It wasn't just the firewall, it was the system on the other end that seemed to adapt to whatever he threw at it and the system learned faster than most. It even had the nerve to throw viruses of his own making back at him, taunting Hotwire with his own material.

A corner of his screen blinked. Another stolen file safely secured on his laptop, a regular occurrence when stealing gig after gig of data, except this file opened on its own. Hotwire quickly scanned it, curious as to what he had found. It was an intercepted message from WhiteStar command to their field agents.

Exportation failed. Apprehend primary target's birth mother.

The file continued on with page after page of data about Robby and his mother Annie. They were planning on taking Ben's sister. The hacker scowled quietly at the screen. He wanted to keep swinging at the firewall, a China sized wall in digital form, but he had to warn Ben. He knew he didn't just stumble across this file, the one file he needed to save Annie's life; it was thrown in front of him as a distraction. It was a genius ploy, Hotwire had to respect that. Not only would they get him to stop his assault, even for a few moments, but they would tempt him to use his phone for direct contact, allowing them to trace him, all while weakening their other foe – WhiteStar.

They were good.

Too good.

Hotwire ceased his assault and started up another program on his laptop. He was going to hack into the nearest cell tower, find Ben's phone on the network, and send him a direct message. It wouldn't come from Hotwire's phone or this computer; it would just be a sms text from the ghost in the machine. It took thirty seconds to get into the tower and two minutes to find out where Ben was. The problem came after that. It would take almost fifteen minutes to narrow down the message so only Ben got it, the cell companies were getting better at securing their lines. Fifteen minutes was way too long.

"Screw it," he muttered. "I'll send it to everybody."

He fired off his message, painting every phone in the tower's two-mile radius with the identical message. Hotwire blinked. They'd be after him now, the FBI and homeland security, but he could hide from them. They were weak-sauce at best. The blowback would fall on this bank but truth was they probably deserved it. Besides what was the worst that could happen to the bank? They get more government money? A bank is too big to fail.

Suddenly his screen blinked with a message. It had no sender, no return IP address; no nothing. It was just a message from the ghost in the machine. Those jerks had used his own trick against him - again - and had done it faster than he had.

They were good.

Hotwire shook his head and read the message.

You had existed beneath my radar before now, like the insects below my feet that toil away, but like the ant who invades a peaceful picnic I am now aware of your existence. Do yourself a favour, *HOTWIRE*, and hide. – Thaddeus Clay

THE END

Benedict Thompson will return
in
To Money and a TV

AUTHOR NOTES

Once upon a time there was a man in a bar. He was a man with an idea for a story and an awfully large bar tab. Unfortunately he had no way to share that story or rid himself of that bar tab. Five years later and a lot has changed for that man. He's become an uncle a couple times over, he found a way to tell his story and he's found to share it with the world. He still has no clue how to deal with his bar tab though. That thing just got five times bigger.

A lot has changed for me since the original launch of Never Been to Mars. I published my book, was nominated for an award by my fans and have even begun to tour Canada to promote my work and do speaking engagements on writing. In the past five years I have been blessed enough to not only have fans but to be able to meet them face to face and engage with them.

Time has a way of taking from us. There were people in my life five years ago that are no longer around. Some have passed on and others have chosen to move on. However, time also has a habit of giving. I have new people in my life that I would not have met if it were not for Never Been to Mars. People that now mean the world to me.

No man writes a book alone. Every story is product of the people around them. This book is as much theirs as it is mine. If that is true then I have a lot of people to thank (and hope none ask for their cut).

There are the female fans dubbed as the Gentle Girls (How did that name catch on?). Your legion is many and each is helpful and supportive. Thanks go to MM, KC CL,

KF, SC, and AVV

Through it all, there have been the pillars of my creation. These are the friends that have always been there and have never wavered. Cliff, Lenny, Jordan, Shannon, John, Adrienne, Kayla, Jay, Heidi, Sara and Ken – Thanks.

To My family: You were the ones who fed me books, kept me reading and encouraged me to create.

Bowser and the Princess: A powerful duo that both help me, teaches me, stops me from going bankrupts and, most importantly, saves me from myself.

Megan: You're a friend, an editor, a sounding board and my biggest challenger. You force me to grow as a writer.

Mom: Everything I do here is because of you. EVERYBODY HEAR THAT? BLAME HER!! But seriously, I read books to be like you. My humour is because of you and the reason I am the adult-ish I am today is because of you. I can never stop thanking you.

Val: I don't know where I'd be without you in my life. I'd probably be some guy who spends too much time on his Xbox while eating an endless supply of peanut butter and jam sandwiches. You are the reason I became an author. You were the one who encouraged me to make that leap. I love you and always will!!

Elder Kami Zid: All Hail!!

Thank you to everybody who helped me get here today. You made this grizzled old man cry tears of meat at the joy he has found.

But seriously, does anybody know how to get rid of a bar tab?

Larry Gent
March 2018

My name is Benedict Thompson and I am a superhero. With a single Touch, I can read an item's past. I can tell who used that pen before you, I can describe how that shoe was made and I can describe everything that has been done on that motel room bed.

The problem with having superpowers is that people want you to actually use them.

I just want to watch TV but here I am dealing with a movie-quoting assassin, murderous celebrities, kidnapped children and secret government conspiracies.

My family's in danger, my life is in ruins and worst of all, my TV is being ignored.

I miss my TV.

NOT EVERY SUPERPOWER IS A BLESSING

THE BENEDICT FORECASTS

Book 0.5:   Be All That You Envy (2018)
Book   1:   Never Been To Mars
Book   2:   To Money And A TV
Book   3:   Bedroom Walls That Save Us (2018)

Author **Larry Gent** transports you into a world spies, espionage and superpowers. Each book is an action-packed thriller that'll keep you on the edge of your seat.

Winner of the silver medal in the *Best in Halifax* award, the Benedict Forecasts deleve deeper into the ever growing Lycotta mystery

WHAT'S WORSE THEN BEING STUCK IN A VIDEO GAME AND NOT BEING ABLE TO LOG OUT?

My name is Rake and I'm stuck in a MMO. It wouldn't be so bad if I was in my max level main but I'm not. I'm stuck as my level 1 Rogue. I'm stuck in my bank alt.

Now I'm running for my life, I'm fighting to stay alive and I'm trying to figure out how the hell to get out of here.

Where's a GM when you need one?

HELP!

BEING STUCK IN YOUR BANK ALT!

Vörissa's Catalyst
—ONLINE—

Patch 1.01: New Game+
Patch 1.02: Escort Mission
Patch 1.03: Corpse Run
Patch 1.04: In Another Castle
Patch 1.05: Silent Protagonist

In this new series by Award Winning author Larry Gent, we dive in the action and mystery of the *Stuck Online* genre.

Follow Rake and company as they fight in a harsh digital world. If they're smart, they'll keep their lives. If they're lucky, they'll keep their sanity and if they're both, they just may find a way to log out.

TO ARMS, SOLDIER

LIGHTYEARS TO GO
BEFORE I SLEEP
ON SALE NOW

Allana Guiver was the Legendary Soldier that all of history knew. She won the great war but lost everything she knew and loved doing so.

400 years later, Major Guiver wakes up from cryo-sleep to find a world she doesn't reconize.

Earth is gone, humanity floats through space on a massive ship, searching for a new home and a new alien threat wants to rid the universe of every human.

Humanity needs their Legendary Soldier but how do you ask a woman who gave up everything to give up more?

YOU'RE NOT DONE YET

Photo by Lisa Liteplo

ABOUT THE AUTHOR

Larry Gent is a is a bottomless well of knowlegde on historical wars in worlds that are, sadly, fictional.

Larry is a enthusatic gamer whose dreams as a child was to be either a detective or a TARDIS Repair Man (it's like a VCR repair man except you just see the ending of the movie first). He got into writing to give back to the worlds he's enjoyed so much from.

A Perth, Ontario native, he lives in both Ottawa and Halifax where he works as a freelance writer and full-time dreamer. He lives with his wife Valérie and his owner Zid the cat.

Website: Larrygent.com
Twitter: @42webs
Instagram: @xan_in_the_hat

CPSIA information can be obtained
at www.ICGtesting.com
Printed in the USA
LVOW03s0528270318
571262LV00005B/10/P